I0614637

The Duke's Defense

by

Carolina Prescott

Dukes in Danger:
A Haversham House Romance

This is a work of fiction. Names, characters, places, and incidents are either the product of the author's imagination or are used fictitiously, and any resemblance to actual persons living or dead, business establishments, events, or locales, is entirely coincidental.

The Duke's Defense

COPYRIGHT © 2023 by Carolina Prescott

All rights reserved. No part of this book may be used or reproduced in any manner whatsoever without written permission of the author or The Wild Rose Press, Inc. except in the case of brief quotations embodied in critical articles or reviews.
Contact Information: info@thewildrosepress.com

Cover Art by *Debbie Taylor*

The Wild Rose Press, Inc.
PO Box 708
Adams Basin, NY 14410-0708
Visit us at www.thewildrosepress.com

Publishing History
First Edition, 2023
Trade Paperback ISBN 978-1-5092-5057-8
Digital ISBN 978-1-5092-5058-5

Dukes in Danger: A Haversham House Romance
Published in the United States of America

Edgewood turned and sucked in his breath at the vision before him. His mind went blank and his mouth went dry.

"Will I do, then?" Henrianna executed a graceful turn in front of him. "Maybe I'll set a new style. It's not high fashion, and I'd have to tuck it up a bit to waltz, but the velvet is so soft and lovely, and it is my favorite color."

Without a doubt, Henrianna Barbour was the most beautiful woman he had ever seen. She stood there waiting for his approval, her cheeks pink from the heat of the bath and her hair still styled for the evening, with curling tendrils kissing the nape of her neck. She was completely covered by his emerald-green velvet dressing gown—the same verdant green as the McDaniels tartan—but she'd wrapped it almost twice around herself and secured it with a satin tie in the back, creating a short train and showing the tips of her toes warmly ensconced in his best woolen socks.

Wrapping the velvet so tightly around her had created a high neckline that completely covered her décolletage, but it also outlined her figure and the graceful lines of her legs, which, without the usual layers of petticoats, were clearly visible beneath the soft, green fabric.

Edgewood swallowed hard as he tried to remember his own name. "I think…" He took a deep breath and started again. "I think you look beautiful."

Dedication

To all the authors whose stories
helped me through some pretty tough times.
Thank you.

Chapter 1

Haversham House, New Year's Eve 1815

"*Why* am I here, your grace?"

"I take it you mean in addition to celebrating Christmas, my brother's wedding, and the new year?"

The Duke of Whitley—known by most of London's polite society as the Ice Duke and to only a select few as His Majesty's brilliant spymaster—frowned at the implied criticism from his best friend, the Earl of Edgewood. It felt good to frown. Indeed, Edgewood's poorly concealed annoyance and blunt questions were a welcome respite from the effusive fawning and unceasing felicitations he'd been forced to endure over the past few days.

As host for the recent familial nuptials—held at the country home of London's famed hostess, Lady Haversham—Whit and his duchess were also honored guests at the sumptuous New Year's Eve festivities. As such, the formidable Ice Duke had been forced to be more charming and more agreeable than he had in decades, contributing significantly to his irritable state.

"Do I need a reason to issue an invitation to my best friend?"

"It's not an invitation unless I can refuse it. It was a summons. I *had* other plans, you know. I *do* have a life."

"Don't sulk, Edgewood. It's unseemly for a man of

your rank. If I can smile and nod at these legions of celebrating fools without snapping their heads off, then I expect nothing less from you. And besides, I know about your life. You would have spent the holidays alone. Or worse, with ghosts from Christmases past."

Edgewood was in no mood to be lectured—certainly not by Whit. Only recently married himself, the Duke of Whitley had acquired an insufferable air of contentment. The coldly condescending duke was now a domesticated beast and it was only the slightest bit amusing to see him direct his legendary icy stare—a look that, in the past, had brought all manner of friends and enemies to their collective knees—at anyone who might inconvenience his duchess, who, in the spirit of the Christmas season, was great with child.

There was little use in telling Whit that he was not the first man to be apprehensive as he waited for the birth of his offspring, just as there was no use telling him that other men, too, had wives who glowed and appeared even more beautiful in the graces of pregnancy. Edgewood found it all rather tiresome.

"I wasn't alone."

"Scotch whiskey—no matter how old—does not count as companionship," said the duke in a patronizing tone, as if admonishing a petulant child.

"I wasn't referring to the whiskey, although now that you mention it, that might be the better option. I was referring to—oh, never mind. I have no need of reprimands from you, so I ask again. *Why* am I here?"

Whit said nothing for a minute or two. Then, under the din of the crowd, he said quietly, "I need the Duke of Marsden to arrange an extraction."

"The duke is unavailable. He also has a life."

"One hears rumors to the contrary. It seems no one has actually seen or heard from Marsden since his rather token appearance after the death of his brother."

"My point exactly. He's not available to do your dirty work."

"This particular extraction is actually quite civilized compared to some of the duke's past excursions. In fact, it is only because this mission requires a journey to Paris that it even qualifies as such. The party being extracted is quite willing to leave, and the party in possession of the package is just as eager for the operation to take place, having plans to relocate his own family to more hospitable environs."

"If everything is running so smoothly, why do you need the duke? It sounds like a simple matter of documents and transportation."

"Just so. Except that the White Terror is raising its flag throughout France, and the Royalists have been somewhat indiscriminately executing those who served Napoleon—especially his generals."

"Ah…so, you need someone to spirit one of Napoleon's generals out of France. I'm assuming this general is the one who provided such valuable information before Waterloo?"

"You know how I feel about assuming anything, Edgewood, but yes. In this you are correct."

"Still, it all sounds like a perfectly straightforward mission. Why do you need Marsden to extract the general from France?"

"It is not the general who is in need of the duke's escort. It is the general's *mistress*." Whit paused with an annoyed sigh. He hated explaining himself.

"In order to maintain the charade that is their cover,

I have need of the duke's rank along with his innate air of superiority and his insufferable arrogance."

Whit hesitated for a moment. "I also need his skill and experience. This *should* be a simple mission, but considering the current state of affairs in Paris—throughout the country, really—and in light of some intelligence I have recently received, it has the potential to become perilous."

"Nevertheless, as I said—"

Whit interrupted. "The mission also has a personal connection for me."

Edgewood raised an eyebrow. "Really? How personal?"

"An old friend. I've known her since she was born. The lady has worked diligently for us over the past two years, but now it's time for her to come home. I need someone I can trust to fetch her."

"Fetch her? You make her sound like a bone, which, I must say, doesn't bode well for the appeal of this mission or offer much incentive to save this damsel in distress."

Whit laughed. "If I were you, I would be careful about saying things like that in front of her. You might find your family jewels handed to you on a plate."

Edgewood shifted uncomfortably at the implied threat.

"Why me? You have plenty of men—and women for that matter—who could do the job admirably."

Whit watched the dancers whirling around the Haversham ballroom in their sparkling ensembles, laughing and talking in anticipation of the new year—now just minutes away.

When he finally answered, the duke spoke clearly

4

and said perhaps the only words that would ensure his friend's complete and total cooperation.

"It's Henrianna, Edgewood. She's in danger."

Chapter 2

Haversham House, two years earlier

As second-in-command to Britain's spymaster, the Earl of Edgewood knew better than most that the upcoming year held the promise of more peril than peace.

Napoleon was insisting on conquering everything that stood in the way of his becoming Emperor of Europe—possibly the world—and so, the British would most likely be joining with the Prussians and others in a strange alliance of bedfellows that precipitated a whole new set of problems for the continent, as well as for England. Those in charge could only hope and pray that the ancient saying held true and that the enemy of my enemy was, in fact, a friend.

Wandering the corridors and balconies above the dance floor at Haversham House, the famous home of Lord and Lady Haversham, renowned throughout the *ton* for its lavish and sometimes unconventional but always sensational entertainments, Edgewood had an excellent bird's-eye view of the goings-on below. This restless roaming had become something of a habit of his over the last few months—mainly because it allowed him to avoid marriage-minded mamas and their always eligible daughters, but also because it let him steer clear of sticky situations, such as the one playing out below him where the Earl of Battenburg and Viscount Sutherstone were obliged to exchange holiday pleasantries in the presence of polite company—even though their animosity toward one other was legend.

Surveying the far end of the grand ballroom, Edgewood frowned at a trail of evergreen needles that drew his attention. His frown quickly turned into a smile, and he congratulated himself again for being above the fray as he witnessed the spectacle of a guest who had made the unfortunate choice to attend Lady Haversham's seasonally themed celebration as a fully decorated Christmas tree. The lady's hair was styled as the top of the tree—complete with a glowing Christmas star—and she was, without a doubt, the leading contender for "Most Unusual" costume. Fortunately, the lady did have the sense to leave the candles among her branches unlit; unfortunately, those same branches were leaving a trail of debris as the costume in question slowly disintegrated. One hoped the lady wore some sort of gown under the branches, for certainly the balsam boughs would not outlast the fifty-five minutes until midnight.

For it was then—right on cue—that the giant, heavily carved front doors of Haversham House would be thrown open, and, in spite of the unusually frigid temperatures, guests would gather in the front entryway, each holding a glass of the finest French champagne, which they would raise in a toast to welcome the new year. Just after the final stroke of midnight, a first footer—the dark, handsome "stranger" whom Lady Haversham had engaged for just this moment—would cross the threshold and bid the assemblage a happy 1814, and Lord Haversham, in one of his rare appearances, would formally welcome the newcomer with a short poem of good tidings and best wishes to all for health, happiness, and prosperity in the new year.

At the rear of the sprawling mansion, the back doors would also be opened, allowing the old year to slip away, taking with it all the troubles of the past twelve months. Servants would remove all previously prepared food, along with Christmas greens, flowers, and other decorations. Bags of old clothes had already been collected to be distributed to the poor. Even the ashes from the fireplaces would be removed and replaced with newly laid fires in every room of the great house.

Back at the front of the house, another set of servants would enter through the front doors to place fresh flower arrangements throughout the public rooms and to lay out a lavish buffet of tantalizing savories and tempting sweets in the well-appointed dining room. As the guests made their way back from the great hall to form the supper queue, then—and only then—could Edgewood finally slip away to one of the tiny guest cottages in the woods where latecomers to Lady Haversham's house parties were accommodated.

For anyone else, the cottage would have been an inconvenience, as it necessitated walking somewhat of a distance to the main house for meals, entertainments, and all other social interaction. But for Edgewood, who tonight craved no one's company as much as his own, it was a blessed reprieve from all the clamor and gaiety of Lady Haversham's New Year's Eve gala.

In his mind's eye, Edgewood could see steam rising from the hot bath he'd paid a footman handsomely to ensure would await him in front of the fire in the cottage. He could almost feel the warmth seeping into his bones.

Shaking his head to clear the rapturous vision,

Edgewood turned his mind back to the problem of how to pass the next fifty-five—no, fifty-three—minutes. Unlike most of Lady Haversham's guests, he was only pleasantly relaxed from the excellent champagne being served—certainly not foxed enough to enjoy gossiping with the more inebriated gentlemen. They would insist on talking of nothing but their skills in hunting—both the wild game that roamed Haversham Forest as well as the more common species of domesticated female. It was too late to join a game of chance—although perhaps he could watch others in the process of losing *their* fortunes—and it was too early to join the clock watchers.

Edgewood considered but reluctantly discarded the idea of seeking out a companion for an evening of private entertainment. However convenient Lady Haversham's house parties usually were for sampling exotic fruits, tonight's gathering had a distinctly aristocratic bent. He had no desire to embark upon a flirtation that might well end up in a more permanent arrangement, facilitated by a pretty young miss and her overly ambitious mama. There was a reason why Lady Haversham's gatherings were known as the birthplace of many a *ton* wedding.

Even so, starting the new year with a willing partner in his bed did hold a certain appeal, and he might have pursued the matter more seriously except that, in less than forty-eight hours, he would be on his way to the Iberian peninsula on a mission for the Duke of Whitley. From his vantage point, Edgewood could see that very gentleman, seeking the attention of the very beautiful and very elusive young lady who had recently made her mark as one of London's most talented actresses. Edgewood could also see the fluttering fans that identified those among the *ton* who were shocked to find themselves at the same social event as an actress—no matter how beautiful or talented—and were even more dismayed to see the woman being actively pursued by the eminently eligible duke.

Edgewood raised his glass in mock salute to his friend. Whit was determined to have the charming Miss Allen as his new mistress. It was a worthy goal and one in which Edgewood wished him the best of luck—mostly because, to put it bluntly, the long-celibate duke had become a royal pain in the arse.

Beneath the growing excitement of the guests anticipating the midnight hour, Edgewood felt the steady pulse of the grandfather clock that stood watch beside him. Its chimes at the eleven o'clock hour had reminded him of a very similar clock guarding his father's study at their family estate near Perth. The piece had been custom made for the fourth Duke of Marsden, and Edgewood had often watched, fascinated, as his father's butler executed the solemn duty of winding the timepiece every Saturday night. The clock standing beside him in Lady Haversham's upper hallway could easily be its twin— perhaps his hosts claimed a bit of Scottish blood in their lineage.

Casually, Edgewood looked to his right and then to his left. Would anyone notice, he wondered, if he gently moved the hands ahead into next year?

Sighing for what must have been the hundredth time, Edgewood took another sip from the crystal flute he held and lazily watched the crowd begin to sort itself out for the next set. He was quite fond of dancing— especially the waltz and especially with a skilled partner—but the upcoming set was the supper waltz and would require that he escort his partner, not only through the twenty-minute dance, but also through all of the new year rituals, and then to the partaking of the midnight feast.

With any luck, by the time this crowd settled down to their soup, *he* would be settling into a blissfully deep tub with a glass of Haversham's best cognac.

Edgewood leaned against the column that supported his secluded balcony. No, it was much better to be here, above the crowd and ready to make his exit at the first acceptable opportunity. He lazily scanned the swirling gowns of the ladies, noting that all the colors of the rainbow were accounted for, with perhaps an over-abundance of rich reds and forest greens to represent the yuletide season. The gentlemen in their white-tie elegance had dutifully embraced their role as mere backdrops for such multihued beauty.

But, soft! What light through yonder crowded room breaks? Like the first snowflake of winter, a lady in a sparkling white gown floated among the other revelers.

Edgewood followed her progress as she captured the arm and attention of a tall man in the scarlet, gold-trimmed uniform of an officer in the King's army. The soldier greeted the lady with gusto and a full embrace and allowed himself to be drawn into a nearby alcove and out of sight.

Edgewood frowned. He was not happy with the disappearance of his entertainment and not wholly comfortable with the soldier's ungentlemanly behavior. He rationalized to himself that it was the lady who had detained the officer, but still, he was relieved when, just a few minutes later, they both came back into view, talking with a great deal of animation. Obviously on his way out, the soldier had delayed his departure long enough to talk to the snowflake. Sure enough, after only a few more minutes and another embrace, the officer made his way toward the stairs leading up to the front entrance of Haversham House.

Edgewood turned his attention back to the snowflake, who was now weaving her way through the crowd, presumably back to her escort or chaperone. She was not so far away that he didn't notice her brushing away what appeared to be tears. Had she just said goodbye to a lover? But the man had seemed surprised to see her. Whoever he was, their parting had made the snowflake sad.

Edgewood followed the circuitous progress of the snowflake, watching her exchange greetings with other guests, until she reached the far end of the room. He was only slightly surprised to see her slip out the frost-covered doors for what was undoubtedly a moment of quiet and a breath of fresh air.

The natural décor of frost on the floor-to-ceiling windows of the ballroom made it difficult to see how far beyond the doors the snowflake ventured. However, Jack Frost had yet to emblazon the top third of the glass and in a just a few minutes Edgewood could see a white-clad figure at the entrance to the famous Haversham gardens that started just beyond the terrace.

The little idiot! Where the hell was she going without a cloak? People died in this kind of cold—and those were the people dressed in furs and great coats and covered in lap robes and blankets. Just for the walk from his cottage to the house he had worn almost his entire wardrobe and, even so, had grown quite chilled. How long did she think she could stay outside in just an evening gown?

Edgewood strained his eyes to see if the white figure was returning. Was he the only one to see her leave or to understand the danger she was in? He looked around and saw that all the servants and most of the guests were busy making preparations for the midnight celebration. Presumably, her friends would be looking for her— although not if they believed she was still with the soldier who, of course, would be under the impression she had returned to her party.

Edgewood glanced at the grandfather clock. She had been outside now for almost five minutes and no one had gone after her. He doubted anyone had seen her leave except him. Which meant…

Bloody hell. He had to go and fetch her.

Chapter 3

"All I'm saying is that you might have written that you had joined up," said Henrianna. She was supremely annoyed with her twin brother—not an unusual circumstance.

Newly commissioned Captain Hill Barbour allowed his older sister—by a mere twenty-two minutes that she never let him forget—to pull him into an alcove off the magnificent ballroom at Haversham House and wrapped her in a bearhug.

Hugging him almost as tightly, Henrianna at last extricated herself with a breathless, "Let me go, Hill! I can't breathe!"

Released from her sibling's enthusiastic embrace, she put her hands on her hips and frowned up into the face that mirrored her own gray-green eyes and chestnut-brown hair. "How would you like it if I joined up and didn't have the courtesy to mention it to you?"

Hill snorted. "They don't accept women in His Majesty's army."

"Which probably explains why they're having so much trouble dealing with one rather short Corsican. When were you going to tell me?"

"Truly, it all came about rather suddenly," said Hill. "There was no time to tell anyone. I'm leaving in just a few minutes—I actually report for duty tomorrow morning. I wasn't trying to keep it from you, Hen, I—"

"Don't call me that."

"What?"

"I hate it when you call me by that horrible nickname you and Avery created." Henrianna punched him in the arm.

"Ow! Since when? I thought it was *Henrianna* you didn't like. What am I supposed to call you then? Henny? Hank?" Seeing his sister's stormy face, Hill wisely took a step back and regrouped.

"I wasn't trying to keep it from you, Henrianna. I just didn't want to tell Mother, since she would have told Elvin, and he would disapprove. I don't need my dear stepfather thinking he has any say-so over my life." Sarcasm dripped from Hill's words. There was no love lost between his mother's second husband and himself.

"I couldn't believe my eyes when you walked down those stairs," continued Hill. He looked his sister up and down and smiled. "You look good, Henrianna. Really, I mean it."

"I'm not sure that's a compliment, coming from you, seeing how we look so much alike," said Henrianna. "It's like looking in a mirror—just like Mother always said."

Hill was silent for a moment and then asked the question that hung between them. "How *is* Mother?"

"She's well…" started Henrianna. Then she amended her answer. "She's as well as someone who lost the love of her life can be—especially upon realizing she has remarried a rather poor substitute."

"She didn't have to marry Rudder. It was her own doing. I would have taken care of things."

"Yes, but you weren't there, Hill. Neither was I. She would have done anything to make sure you finished at school. I know she didn't want you having to come home just to take care of her and the estate."

"She should have asked me."

"Please, let's not get into that argument. I agree with you, but I also think there were extenuating circumstances that perhaps we weren't privy to."

"Such as?"

"Such as I think, before he died, Father made her promise to marry again. And I think Mr. Rudder took advantage of that and of his land's proximity to ours to press his suit and undermine her confidence in managing things by herself. I can't prove it, but I wouldn't be surprised to find out that he was the cause of some of the problems she had on the estate. What I *do* know is that he bombarded her with all sorts of stories about widows losing everything after their husbands died."

"She should have said something."

"I agree, but she still sees us as children. Anyway, it's all water under the bridge now. It was her decision, and she did what she thought was best at the time."

"Is he at least a good husband to her?"

When Henrianna didn't answer, Hill looked over at his sister in concern. "Hen? Is he a good husband?"

"He's not Father," said Henrianna softly, "and he knows it. And at times that makes him very angry, and he takes it out on others."

"Is he abusive to Mother? Tell me the truth."

"No," said Henrianna quickly. "Truly, I don't think he is, but then, Mother is giving him no reason to be angry with her. She's in kind of a daze. She still misses Father so much."

"If he doesn't take out his anger on Mother, then on whom? The servants?"

"No! Neither Mother nor I would ever allow that."

"Who, then?"

Again, Henrianna paused a little too long. Hill's face turned dark with rage. "Henrianna, did that man harm you?"

Henrianna laughed as she turned away. "I didn't give him the chance. That's why I'm here."

Hill's voice was almost a growl. "I'll kill him. Tell me what happened. All of it."

"Nothing happened. Mr. Rudder told me he was planning to match me up with one of his sons. He told me he had left it up to them to decide who would marry me. I laughed at him and told him he was delusional, which made him angry. He'd been drinking a great deal, and he started ranting and raving about how I thought I was so much better than his sons and how I'd better change my tune if I knew what was good for me."

"He threatened you?"

"At the time, I thought it was just because he'd been drinking, but then last week when Mother was out making calls, he found me in the library and told me that two of his sons would be arriving in the next day or so. He said they wanted to get a look at me before deciding who would take me. I told him there was no way on God's green earth that I was going to marry *any* of his imbecile sons and..." Henrianna paused for a quick moment, remembering and editing out her stepfather's infuriated response.

"You really said 'imbecile'?" Hill grinned approvingly.

"...and then I ran up to my room and locked the door. Mother came to my room later that night and told me she'd made arrangements for me to go to London and stay with Lord and Lady Matthas for the season. I arrived in London yesterday. Beth and Jane Ellen were very excited to see me, and when Lady Matthas read mother's note, she just swept me up in her arms and hugged me. They were already packed and planning to come here to Haversham House for the New Year's Eve celebration, so they brought me with them, and here I am. I had no idea I would see you, but I think maybe Mother did. She told me if I ran into you in London, I was to give you her love and tell you not to worry—that she was managing just fine."

"I should go back and give that man a thrashing."

"And be arrested for assault? Absolutely not. It would just make things worse." She gently touched her brother's arm. She could tell he was not satisfied with her answers. "I think we have to trust Mother to handle things."

Henrianna paused, letting her feelings and thoughts mingle with Hill's in the silent conversation that had always existed between the twins. Then she smiled and with a bit of forced gaiety said, "Enough talk about the past. You look very dashing in your uniform. Do you know where you will be assigned?"

"No, and even if I did, I couldn't tell you. How long will you be in London?"

"I believe the idea is for me to find a husband so Mother no longer has to worry about Elvin's sons staking a claim. Lady Matthas is already making plans for Jane Ellen's debut and said she would just slip me in as well. Beth is already out, of course, so it promises to be a whirlwind season. I'm to have new gowns made next week. Beth let me borrow this one for the evening, though. Isn't it lovely? Jane Ellen said Lady

18

Haversham's balls always have themes and the theme for tonight was Signs of the Season."

Hill made a point of looking his sister over from head to toe. "So…you're…what? One of the heavenly host of angels at the birth of the Christ Child? You're so white. And fluffy. Wait, are you one of the sheep being watched by the shepherds?"

"*Très amusant*, brother. Very droll. I am a snowflake. A dancing snowflake. See how my skirt flutters and floats when I twirl? Just like falling snow."

"More like a bloody blizzard, if you ask me," said Hill to no one in particular as he watched his sister pirouette.

Henrianna smacked him on the arm with her lace fan. "By the way, Beth said I should bring you back for a dance. She seems to be inexplicably attracted to anyone in a uniform."

"If I recall, Beth is mostly attracted to Beth," drawled Hill as he turned his attention toward the stairs at the entrance to the ballroom. "Anyway, I have to go. They're waiting for me."

He looked his sister over once again, and then frowned in the general direction of the revelers in the ballroom. "I should stay just to fend off the legions of gentlemen who are starting to circle. I can't believe I'm saying this to my own sister, but you look stunning, Hen—Henrianna. You're easily the most beautiful lady here tonight. I guess I'll just have to trust you to take care of yourself. Somehow you always do. I'm glad I got to see you before I left. Now, give me a kiss so I can be off. I would hate to start my career by being tossed in the brig for being absent without leave."

Hill leaned down and kissed her cheek as Henrianna

wrapped her arms around the neck of the man her brother had become. "Please be careful," she whispered in his ear, "and come back safely. Write and let me know you are well."

Reluctantly leaving her embrace, Hill stepped back to regard her with suspiciously damp eyes. "Take care of yourself, little sister," he said, smiling at the immediate frown his words provoked.

And then he was gone.

Chapter 4

The army! No wonder she hadn't heard from Hill. It all made sense now.

"Miss Barbour?" Her hostess, Lady Haversham was waving at her from across the floor. Henrianna pasted a smile on her face and made her way over to the attractive woman who was holding court at one end of the ballroom.

"Miss Barbour, are you acquainted with Baron Cabot?"

"No, my lady. I have not had the pleasure."

"Lord Cabot, I would like to make known to you Miss Henrianna Barbour. She is in town visiting my dear friends, Lord and Lady Matthas. Miss Barbour, Lord Cabot lives on the other side of the shire. Lord Haversham invited him to join us tonight, and he has brought his friend, Viscount Glenly."

Henrianna faced the two gentlemen with a curtsy. "How lovely to meet you both."

Baron Cabot stepped forward to bow over her hand and kiss the tips of her fingers, his eyes lighting up at the expanse of decolletage visible from that particular angle. "Very lovely, indeed, Miss Barbour." The baron took his time raising Henrianna from her curtsy, holding on to her hand quite a lot longer than was proper as he looked her up and down as if assessing a racehorse.

Lady Haversham raised an eyebrow at his

Carolina Prescott

inappropriate behavior and cleared her throat.

With his eyes still on Henrianna's bosom, Cabot said, "Miss Barbour, may I present my friend, Lord Glenly? You have an eye for beauty, Glenly. Have you ever before seen such a delectable tidbit as Miss Barbour?"

The viscount's obvious boredom with the evening did not abate with the introduction. After bowing his head only slightly in the briefest of acknowledgements, he turned his back to the ladies and made a show of surveying the ballroom before replying to his companion. "For once you are correct, Cabot," said Glenly, not bothering to modulate his voice. "She is most attractive. A much appreciated change from the other ladies I have met this evening, I must say."

Lord Glenly was quite a bit taller than Henrianna and quite powerfully built. He sported long sideburns and tousled blond hair in the current fashion, attractive in an oddly compelling way. Baron Cabot, on the other hand, was short—and, for lack of a better word—oily, both in his manner and his appearance, which seemed to exemplify the complete opposite of attractive.

"Might I hope you have room on your dance card for a waltz later, my dear?" The baron smiled, and Henrianna could smell his fetid breath even from where she stood. The man made her skin crawl, and she had no intention of allowing him to get close enough for a dance.

"I regret that my dance card is full this evening, my lord," she said. Was it her imagination or did Lady Haversham relax considerably with that news?

"But of course. I should have guessed that the most beautiful lady in the room would be inundated with requests to dance. Perhaps when we meet again?"

"Perhaps," murmured Henrianna. "And now I must beg you to excuse me, for I see my chaperone signaling to me."

Both gentlemen bowed as Henrianna curtsied again and hurried off. She was certain she did not mistake the twinkle in Lady Haversham's eye when Henrianna turned and proceeded in the direction opposite from where Lady Matthas was chatting with old friends.

Henrianna had thought to find Beth or Jane Ellen, but suddenly a wave of loneliness washed over her. Everyone had someone special to talk to—everyone except her. If only Hill could have stayed—at least long enough to wish her a happy new year. She missed him terribly, and it only made it worse to have found him just to say goodbye. And now, in addition to missing her brother, she would be worried about him, too. The war on the continent was not going well for the enemies of Napoleon. If that was where Hill's regiment was to be deployed, then he would be right in the thick of things and in a great deal of danger. The thought of her twin injured—or worse—made Henrianna catch her breath.

Brushing back the tears that unexpectedly welled up, she looked around for a place to gather herself. The ladies' retiring room was all the way on the other side of the ballroom. Besides, it was not exactly the place to go for a few minutes of solitude. She looked around for a secluded alcove, desperately needing to be somewhere quiet, somewhere away from the heat of so many perfumed bodies crushed together—just for a moment or two.

The ballroom's great floor-to-ceiling windows were decoratively etched in frost, and the promise of a breath or two of fresh, clean, crisp air drew her toward doors that were closed but hopefully not locked. Henrianna smiled as the latch turned easily, and she slipped out into the cold December night.

****

The cold air took her breath away, but the comforting calm of the dark was exactly what she needed. If only she could get somewhere and see the stars. Henrianna took a few tentative steps onto the terrace and looked up. Even bare, the trees obscured the sky, so she carefully followed the snow-covered path out to a clearing near the entrance to the Haversham gardens.

At last.

Above her, the stars twinkled brightly in the velvet night, sparkling like diamonds in the clear, cold air. Henrianna took a deep breath and shivered. Keeping her eyes on the heavens, she slowly turned in a circle to find her favorite constellations. She easily spotted the plough in Ursa Major, Cassiopeia's sprawling W, and then the three stars in Orion's belt. She smiled as she greeted her old friends and let the dark quiet soothe her. After another minute, she shivered. It was much colder than she'd first thought—she should return to the inside festivities.

"Bollocks, man, not here! If anyone hears you, we'll both be hanged for treason."

Sounds traveled easily in the cold, crisp night air, and the voices startled her. Henrianna stepped back into the shadows as a familiar voice reprimanded his unseen companion.

The other man's voice was also familiar and confirmed their identities as the gentlemen she had just met. "Then when? I told them I would have something for them tonight!"

Both men sounded angry. They clearly would not appreciate being overheard—no matter how innocently—by a third party.

"I said *not here*," hissed Viscount Glenly. "We can't take any chances. There. We can detour through the gardens."

"Who'd be daft enough to be out in the freezing cold anyway?" grumbled Cabot.

Heavy footsteps crunched the frozen grass as they headed in her direction.

"The Ice Duke, of course," laughed Glenly.

Cabot snorted. "Not tonight, he ain't. He's too busy chasing after that bloody actress…not that I blame him. I wouldn't mind an act or two with her. Did you make any progress with the others?"

Glenly's reply was muffled.

Henrianna didn't wait to hear more. All thoughts of the cold vanished as she slipped deeper into the dormant Haversham gardens. She darted down a path to her right, quickly turning the corner and crouching behind a hibernating shrubbery.

"What was that?" said Glenly.

The footsteps stopped for a moment.

"It's just a rabbit or some such creature. How much farther, then? I'm freezing my balls off!"

The sound of footsteps came closer and closer. Henrianna clapped her hands over her mouth so the men wouldn't hear her panting. There was nothing she could do about her pounding heart.

The footsteps were right beside her now, and then…

They passed by, and the sound of shoes crunching on the gravel began to recede. After a few seconds more, the only thing Henrianna could hear were low muffled growls as the two men continued their conversation on the other side of the garden, toward the forest.

Henrianna stood up slowly and released the breath she'd been holding. Inhaling deeply, she took a relieved step toward the brightly lit house. But her relief turned to panic as someone tugged at her gown. She cried out and frantically turned to face her captor.

Chapter 5

Edgewood deposited his empty glass on the tray of a wandering footman and hurried down the stairs at the far end of the ballroom. He thought about sending a footman for his great coat, but then decided his plan did not include being outdoors for more than a minute or two. He would simply shepherd the lady back inside and call for two warm brandies. He would then introduce himself, discover her identity, and gently chide her on her decision to be outside in such frigid weather. The whole damn business should take no more than ten minutes.

He closed the heavy door behind him and looked around the deserted terrace. All remnants of civilization had been removed for the winter. The snow had been swept from the paved surface, exposing treacherous patches of ice that promised a fall to those not paying close attention. Looking everywhere except down, Edgewood slipped and, cursing, caught himself on an abandoned urn.

Where was she? She had to be close by.

He stepped gingerly to the far side of the terrace and paused at the edge. Dancing pumps were not the worst choice for navigating slippery surfaces, but they wouldn't last long on the frozen grass. From inside, strains of a waltz rose to a crescendo as he made his way down the flagstone walk toward the gardens.

The entrance to Haversham House's formal gardens was a circular clearing that featured a large bronze sundial and offered a choice of paths to the various garden walks. The stars were shining brightly, but the moon was waning and provided little illumination. The snowflake lady was nowhere to be seen.

She couldn't possibly have gone far. Most likely she had returned to the ballroom through another door. Edgewood was about to turn back when he noticed footprints in the broken blades of frozen grass—*someone* had come this way.

Damn it, where *was* she?

"My lady?" he called, hoping his voice would carry in the still night. "My lady, you must come in. It's freezing cold!" He walked slowly past the sundial gleaming like an oracle and decorated in icicles. With neither sun nor moon to cast a shadow, it was doing its best with starlight on this clear, cold night.

"My lady? Can you hear me? You must come in. If you stay out much longer, you will be in grave danger. Hello?"

A muffled response turned him in the opposite direction. He walked quickly toward a disembodied, feminine voice.

"Hullo? Oh, thank goodness! Please, could you offer your assistance?"

"Where are you?"

"I think just on the other side of the hedge from you. I went down the first path on the right from the sundial and I'm…I'm unable to move!"

Edgewood quickly retraced his steps to the sundial circle and took the first path on his right. Only a few yards in, he was met with the amazing sight of a lady being held captive by the wicked thorns of an ancient climbing rose.

"T-th-thank you s-so m-much. I am s-s-so embarrassed, but I seem to be caught on th-th-the th-th-thorns. This dress is not mine, it belongs to m-m-my friend—and I have been trying so hard to b-b-be careful. I almost had it free, b-b-but then the wind came and tangled me up again, and now m-m-my fingers have gotten so s-s-stiff with th-th-the c-c-cold…"

While the lady in white did her best to offer an explanation through chattering teeth, Edgewood worked to untangle the glimmering snowflake gown from the treacherous rose bush.

"There. That's the last of it," he said finally, gently pulling the lady away from the wall by her bare arm. You're as cold as ice!" He slipped off his frock coat and draped it over her shoulders and then offered his arm to guide her back to the house. "Whatever made you decide to take a stroll on such a cold night?"

She shook her head as she took his arm. "I only meant to be outside for a minute. Just for a b-b-breath of f-f-fresh air. It was so hot and so crowded and loud inside. Th-th-thank you for coming to my rescue. It nev-v-ver occurred to me that I m-m-might be accosted by a shrubbery." She tried to laugh but her teeth chattered.

"You need to get into a hot bath—the sooner the better," said Edgewood. Disregarding all propriety, he put his arm around her, over his own coat, and hugged her to his side. He could still feel her shivering violently.

"Th-th-that would be lovely, b-b-but I d-d-don't think anyone will be getting a hot b-b-bath for quite a while."

"I beg your pardon?"

He looked over at her with a question on his face. She was difficult to understand with her teeth chattering so much, but surely he had misheard her. Since when was it difficult to get something as simple as a hot bath at the home of Lord and Lady Haversham?

"New Year's-s-s Eve?" she offered. "You know, out with th-th-the old and in with th-th-the new? If past is p-p-prologue, it won't be until very much later before the f-f-fires are relit and hot water becomes available, but I'm s-s-sure I'll be fine if I can just get b-b-back inside…"

Was it his imagination or were her words fainter than before? He felt her weight drooping against him. "My lady? It's not too much farther." But it was actually quite a bit farther than he wanted to admit. It was then he realized how very close they were to his own cottage. A cottage where a steaming hot bath sat ready and waiting.

Just as Edgewood had made up his mind to convince the snowflake to accompany him to the closer safety of his cottage, the lady's full weight slumped against him. Without missing a beat, he caught her up in his arms and turned down the path to his abode. The path was familiar, and he could already see the light that Haversham's footman had left in the window. Not wasting any more of his energy with another word, Edgewood carried the unconscious snowflake inside.

Chapter 6

A delightful warmth enveloped Henrianna, along with the very clean, masculine scent of balsam. She opened her eyes and saw that she was in a small but charming kitchen. A man—the one from the garden—knelt before her while someone else wrapped yet another blanket around her shoulders.

The warmth seemed to touch only some parts of her—like her nose and shoulders—but stayed just out of reach for the rest of her body. It was as if a thin layer of ice had formed over her. She had never felt so cold or so tired.

The man who had rescued her in the rose garden was obviously a gentleman. He was dressed in formal evening attire with an elegant white silk shirt and an exquisitely tied, silk cravat over a starched, white brocade waistcoat. She wondered where his frock coat could have gone until she remembered he had given it to her. Long cuffs tickled the foot he held in his ungloved hands. *Her* foot. Her *bare* foot.

"Can you feel this? My rubbing your foot?" the man asked, looking up at her.

Henrianna blinked her eyes and only stared at him. The cold seemed to have numbed her brain as well as her body. All she wanted was to close her eyes and sleep.

He asked, "Can you feel anything in your foot?"

"Ouch!" Her eyes flew open and she scowled. "I felt

that. It hurt."

"That's good," he replied. "If you have feeling in your toes, it means you don't have frostbite and we can use warmer water. Bring the basin and some cold water as well," he said to someone over her shoulder. "We don't want it too hot. It must be done gradually."

Henrianna watched as a footman, resplendent in Haversham livery, came into view and slowly poured both hot and cold water into the basin. She knew she should be feeling more warmth from the water, but as yet she only felt a sensation of movement. The blankets draped around her were very heavy, and she let her head drop down, thinking to rest her chin on her chest.

"Oh, no, you don't," said the man in front of her. He reached up and gently patted her cold cheeks. "Stay awake." He looked above her head and said, "Bring her some brandy. She's still so cold."

On his knees but sitting back on his heels in front of her, the gentleman pulled off her gloves and took her hands in his own. He vigorously rubbed them both, his big hands completely engulfing hers. "Can you tell me your name?"

Henrianna shook herself mentally. It had been an extremely trying few days, and the idea of sleep was a very good one. But he was right. She did not even know the name of the man who was now massaging her fingers. The same person who, presumably, had taken off her slippers, stockings, and garters. Introductions were definitely in order. She struggled with the words.

"I…I am Miss Henrianna Barbour. I am here with my f-f-friends, Lord and Lady Matthas and their daughters."

The man inclined his head and brought her

fingertips to his warm lips. "At your service, Miss Barbour. I am Edgewood. I am only slightly acquainted with Lord and Lady Matthas, but Lord Haversham is a cousin on my mother's side. Can you feel me rubbing your fingers?"

"Some of them…I think."

Edgewood reached up to take something from the footman, and then put a glass of amber liquid in her hands. He cupped his own hands over hers to help her hold the glass.

"Drink this. It will warm you inside and out."

Henrianna took a large gulp and promptly choked.

"It's probably best that you sip it," said Edgewood standing up to pound on her back until she finally took a deep breath.

"Yes, of course," she said, still coughing a little. "I see now that probably would be best. What is it? It's quite lovely. I do feel much warmer now—at least on the inside. Might I have some more?"

Edgewood looked at her empty glass in surprise and then nodded at the footman.

"I'm sorry, my lord, that was the last of it. I had planned to bring a new bottle back when I returned with your supper."

Edgewood looked over at the fire where a huge kettle steamed. "The rest of the water is heating?"

"Yes, my lord. The bathtub is almost full and needs only toppin' off with one more bucket of hot water."

"Good man. Bundle up and go back up to the house. Bring back another bottle of cognac and something for us to eat—preferably something warm—and fetch Miss Barbour's cloak and my great coat and outdoor things. And mind the time. I promised Lady Haversham you would be available for the midnight doings."

The footman donned his coat and wrapped a scarf around his head before dashing out the door. The gust of cold air that blew in set Henrianna shivering again. Edgewood frowned and went to the fireplace to bring back more hot water, which he poured slowly into the basin.

"M-m-might you tell me where we are, my lord? I don't remember c-c-coming into this room. It looks very small to be the kitchen at Haversham House."

"This is one of the guest cottages where Lady Haversham stashes latecomers to her parties. As it would happen, I had asked for a hot bath to be ready upon my return, right after midnight. And, as you said, it will be hours before you can get hot water up at the house, so I brought you here. And the reason you don't remember entering this room is that you lost consciousness just as we left the garden. I carried you the rest of the way."

"Are you saying I *fainted*? That's impossible. I n-n-never faint. I have witnessed everything f-f-from a compound fracture to a calf being born. I never faint."

"Well, perhaps you simply stumbled, collapsed into my arms, and chose not to get up, but I did, in fact, carry you from the garden wall."

"I s-s-suppose I must believe you, but it is rather embarrassing, I m-m-must say. And I am quite disappointed in myself."

Edgewood laughed. "I don't think you should be so hard on yourself. People faint all the time and in less strenuous conditions than you found yourself during those last few minutes alone in the garden."

"Have *you* ever fainted?"

"No, I can't say that I have. But then again, I've

34

never found myself in frigid temperatures dressed only in a very thin gown while being harassed by a hibernating rose bush. If I had, I feel quite sure fainting would not have been out of the question."

Henrianna giggled and then shivered again.

"What?" he said, reaching around her to pull a shifting blanket closer.

She smiled. "I just had a v-v-vision of you in my gown, with your unstylish beard and very broad shoulders, thwacking at that poor rose bush."

"I'm sure I would look very dashing. It is a lovely gown, and you look like a snowflake fairy in it. But why do you say my beard is unstylish? I had it trimmed just this morning."

"Because it is. All beards are unstylish at the moment. All of London's f-f-fashionable gentlemen are wearing the t-t-tousled look of Mr. Brummel. If they have facial hair at all, it is in the g-g-guise of long s-s-sideburns. It's a p-p-pity, too, because I do like the look of a man in a well-trimmed beard. Do you really think I look like a snowflake fairy?"

"Well, not at the moment, of course. Right now you look rather like a quilt rack."

Henrianna burst out laughing. "What a terrible thing to say!"

"Well, it's true. I've piled every blanket and quilt in the house on you, and you are still shivering." He bent his face closer to hers. "And why are your lips blue? Are they still cold?"

As if to answer his own question, Edgewood put his lips on hers. He lingered there for a long moment—much longer than was needed to determine their temperature. A soft pink blush spread upward to flame her cheeks,

35

warming her from the inside out.

"There," said Edgewood with a satisfied whisper. "That's better, but you're still cold. Come here." He pulled her to stand up against him, her feet still in the basin. He put his arms around her, drawing her into a tight embrace.

His warmth was intoxicating, and Henrianna leaned forward against him, pressing her cheek against his chest and feeling his heart beat beneath the silk shirt. Everything about him was hard—his arms, his chest— and her whole body was aware of being held so close. She sighed as she relaxed into his embrace, which for some reason made his heart beat even faster. She stood there, motionless, for what seemed like both an eternity and an instant. When she felt his lips on her hair, she pulled back slightly so she could see his face, but it was the look in his eyes that drew her. He looked like he was seeing her for the first time, yet oddly with a sense of recognition as if greeting a beloved friend. But there was something more—something primitive that was both fierce and satisfied all at once.

She shivered but did not look away. And when he bent to kiss her again, it was the most natural feeling in the world.

At first, he softly caressed her lips with his— tentatively at first, and then more persistently, varying the pressure as though he was seeking the best possible position for a kiss. Taking his time, he nibbled and caressed her bottom lip, sending a sigh of pleasure through her.

That small sound from her seemed to encourage him, and he lightly traced the seam between her lips with the tip of his tongue, tasting, testing, teasing. When she instinctively parted her lips, he moved one hand to cup her face, his thumb slowly caressing her cheek as his tongue continued to explore. He stepped closer, pulling her tightly up against him, and she responded by tangling her tongue with his as he plunged into her only warmth. She reveled in the heat spreading throughout her body— heat that seemed to emanate from her very core—but when she felt his hand moving inside the quilts down her back, she gasped in surprise.

Edgewood froze at the sound and after a brief moment took a step back, holding her gingerly by the shoulders at arm's length.

"I...I beg your pardon, Miss Barbour. I should not have pressed my advantage like that. I don't know what came over me. Please forgive me." He released her and bowed slightly, moving quickly to pick up a fallen quilt.

"On the contrary, Lord Edgewood. It was my fault. You are quite warm, and it felt nice to feel such...such heat." Her explanation faded to a murmur as she sat back down. "I'm sure no apology is necessary. You were simply trying to warm me up as best you know how, and for that I am greatly appreciative."

"Yes, of course," mumbled Edgewood. "I'll get more hot water."

Chapter 7

Bloody hell! What was he doing?

It was bad enough to have her here alone, but he didn't have to seal his fate by kissing and fondling her. She seemed quite ready to make excuses for his unacceptable behavior, though. He should thank his lucky stars she wasn't screaming accusations at him. It was a close call, and a good thing he'd come to his senses when he did.

So then why was he so desperate to hold her again? And why was he disappointed that his inappropriate behavior had been so graciously excused? It was almost as if he *wanted* to be forced into offering for the chit.

He should be grateful that she seemed disinclined to call out his ungentlemanly behavior, but instead he was trying to figure out how he could go back and do it again.

He'd never experienced such intensity, such *arousal* with a simple kiss. It certainly made him rethink that characterization. There had been nothing simple about the kiss he had just experienced.

A simple kiss was a peck on the lips or a pressing of the lips to a cheek or forehead.

A simple kiss was a greeting or a farewell, done without thought, and certainly done without such feeling.

This kiss was the complete and total opposite of a simple kiss. It had drawn him in like a blazing fire on a cold evening, making him crave a closeness he had never before experienced. At the same time, it made him feel as if he were standing on top of a mountain, taking his first real breath after a difficult climb. And it had all struck him in a flash—like lightning—in the course of a single kiss, a kiss that was anything but simple.

And a kiss, he noted with some satisfaction, that had been returned with mutual fervor.

When he put his mouth on hers, he'd felt her cool—no, cold—lips immediately warm and soften. And when he had moved his lips over hers, reveling in their softness, she had relaxed against him, sinking into his arms. When she'd timidly kissed him back, he actually felt the warmth transfer from his lips to hers…and back again, like a molten river of fire coursing between them. He'd instinctively pulled her closer, taking the kiss deeper and tracing the fullness of her plump bottom lip with his tongue, schooling himself even then to be satisfied with simply caressing that satin fullness. But when she responded, parting her lips and pressing back against him and making that small sound of pure pleasure, that's when he was undone.

Edgewood had been with enough women to recognize the sounds of pleasure they made during tender moments. In fact, he himself was usually responsible for the ladies' making those sounds, and it never failed to arouse him. He liked knowing he was responsible for the pleasure his lady was receiving, and he enjoyed watching his partner's look of surprise as her body responded to him in such wanton ways. Granted, this usually happened rather further along into the lovemaking process—not with just a kiss.

Perhaps Miss Barbour's sensuality was heightened by her brush with danger? But then how did he explain his own primal response? He wasn't a boy stealing his first kiss behind the barn, but he'd had to step back and turn away from Miss Barbour so neither of them would be embarrassed by the unmistakable evidence of his desire. Mumbling an apology, he'd turned quickly to the fireplace, wondering briefly about the location of his long frock coat that might disguise his condition and groaning inwardly as he remembered its location around the lady's shoulders. Fumbling with the buckets and kettles over the flames, he tried conversation as a distraction.

"I know you said you went out onto the terrace for some fresh air—which I most definitely understand— but why did you stay outside so long?"

Henrianna flexed her feet in the still-warm water. "Orion's belt."

"You mean the asterism?"

"Yes." She paused and looked over at him. "I don't know anyone named Orion in real life, do you?"

Edgewood chuckled. "No, I can't say that I do, although I do know a Cassiopeia. And, had she been a male, she might have ended up with the name of Orion. Could you not see the stars from the terrace?"

"No, the trees were too close. There was a clearing just beyond the lawn, so I decided to try to see the sky from there."

"And could you?"

"Yes. All of the stars were bright, but I could see Orion's belt and sword quite clearly."

"Then why didn't you come back in after that? I saw you leave the ballroom. You were gone for quite a while."

"I didn't mean to stay outside," said Henrianna. "I

was already freezing, but just as I was turning to come back inside, I heard two men talking rather loudly—actually, they were arguing and they sounded angry. Then one of them told the other to be quiet because someone might hear them and…well, I thought it best they not realize that I *had* heard them, so I turned onto the first path I saw and waited until they passed by. That's when I realized my gown was all caught up on the rose bush. I had almost gotten myself free when a gust of wind came through and tangled me up all over again. The more I tried to get free, the more trapped I became. That's when I heard you calling. I am ever so grateful you came to my aid."

"Why were you looking for Orion's belt?"

Henrianna looked down at her feet still in the warm water. "It's silly."

"I promise not to laugh."

Henrianna sighed, but after a moment, continued. "My father was a great amateur astronomer. He first showed my brother and me Orion's belt when we turned three years old. He told us there was one star for each year we had been alive and it was our birthday present. Whenever I see Orion's belt, I think of him. I was missing him tonight, so I went to find the stars he gave us."

"You and your brother are twins?"

"Yes. I'm the elder by twenty-two minutes, which he absolutely hates."

Edgewood laughed. "I would too. The only way I maintain any type of control over my sisters is due to the fact I am clearly older than they are."

"Evidently I was rather obnoxious about it as a child. My mother says I always claimed seniority and lorded it over my brother our entire childhood—at least until he grew bigger and much taller than me. Then he just laughed when I tried to order him about."

"Did you do that a lot?"

"What?"

"Order him about."

Henrianna laughed. "No more than he needed."

"I expect he saw it differently."

"You don't even know him and you're taking his side?"

"Is he here tonight?"

"He was, but he had to leave."

"Ah, yes. Was that the man in uniform you embraced before you disappeared out onto the terrace?"

"You were *spying* on me?" Henrianna narrowed her eyes, but Edgewood looked only slightly guilty as he shrugged his response.

"Yes, that was my brother. He just bought a commission in His Majesty's army and he reports to his commanding officer tomorrow morning. I was hoping… Well, none of it matters now. I promised myself I wouldn't cry, and I won't, but I'm going to miss him very much. He wouldn't even tell me where to write him because he said his assignment was secret."

Edgewood saw the sadness in her eyes and turned to check the water, allowing her time to gather her feelings. "Perhaps it's best you not know," he said after a few minutes. "Napoleon's spies are everywhere, and if your brother is involved in the Crown's secrets, the less you know, the better. I'll give it just a minute more."

"So, I'm curious, my lord. Where were you that you could so easily observe everyone's comings and goings?"

"Promise you won't tell?"

Henrianna made an exaggerated show of looking to her left and to her right. "Whom exactly would I tell?"

Edgewood smiled as he brought over the bucket of steaming water and poured it slowly into the basin. "Point taken. I was up on the second-floor balcony in an alcove, avoiding the other guests."

"Why?"

Edgewood set down the bucket. "I'm not sure," he confessed. "I, too, am reporting for duty soon—although not until the day after tomorrow—so maybe I'm already starting to separate."

"Separate? From whom? Are you here with family? Friends?"

"As I told you, Lord Haversham is a cousin somewhere on my mother's side, and Lady Haversham is always kind enough to invite me to her New Year's Eve festivities. This is the first one I've ever attended. I was to meet up with a friend here, but he has been rather...occupied. And I arrived rather late, hence the cottage as opposed to a room in the manor house. But to be honest? I'm rather enjoying the peace and quiet."

"And now I've invaded your solitude. I *am* sorry. I should go." Abruptly, Henrianna sneezed.

"Miss Barbour, at the risk of sounding like a nursemaid, you're not going anywhere until you've warmed up properly."

"I think, my lord, under the circumstances, you may address me by my Christian name."

"Henrianna?"

Henrianna sighed. "Yes. And before you ask, it was my mother who decided I should be named for both her mother *and* her father, while my brother was named after my father, a very lyrical, very respectable Hubert Hill Barbour."

"I think your name is quite…uh…unusual—I've met several *Henriettas* before, and one or two *Georgiannas*, but never a Henrianna."

"It's a case of trying to please everyone and pleasing no one," said Henrianna. "As I understand it, my grandfather Henry was not a very nice man, and his wife, Analise, was the very essence of primness and propriety. My mother and father ran away to get married, and I think naming me after her parents was an attempt to broker peace. Of course, my parents didn't want to leave anyone out, so my middle name is Rose, after my paternal grandmother, whom I adored. If only I'd been allowed to go by Rose… It's quite lovely, don't you agree?" She sighed. "Much better than Henrianna. My brother shortened it to *Hen,* and he and his best friend teased me constantly, following me around making chicken noises."

Edgewood grinned at the picture she painted, but quickly covered his smile with a cough when Henrianna narrowed her eyes and glared at him. He was saved by a knock at the cottage door.

"Ah, excellent timing! Here's Stuart with supplies."

Edgewood threw open the door for the heavily laden footman who carried—in addition to the earl's greatcoat, hat, and Henrianna's cloak—a huge basket that he placed in the middle of the table.

"There's cold chicken, cheese, mushroom tart, fresh bread, apples, and a crock of hot soup," said Stuart, "and Mrs. Weaver's sponge cake frosted with chocolate icing. Mr. Kerby put in a bottle of champagne along with the brandy. Will you be needing anything else, my lord? I promised I'd be right back to help with the fireworks once the first footer's come through."

"This will do famously. Thank you, Stuart. Let me just write a note to Lady Haversham apologizing for my absence."

"Might I write one to Lady Matthas as well?" asked Henrianna. "I'll tell her I've retired for the evening with a headache. I don't want her to worry."

"Indeed," replied Edgewood. "Stuart, you'll see these delivered? And be careful of the fireworks, lad— we wouldn't want you to lose any fingers."

"Yes, my lord. I mean, no, my lord. I'll deliver these, my lord, and keep a watch on my fingers."

Closing the door behind the footman, Edgewood turned to Henrianna. "You do realize your reputation will be quite ruined should anyone find out you are here alone with me?"

"Yes, I suppose that's true," she mused. "Although I don't suppose it will do your reputation any good either. I expect the best thing is to make sure no one finds out, so I'll just go straight upstairs and slip into my room."

She gave him a coy smile. "And if anyone finds out, I promise to do the honorable thing by you."

Edgewood chuckled, but then frowned as her saucy reply was punctuated with another sneeze.

"Well, right now, you're not going anywhere. You're still shivering—we need to get more of you warmed up." He looked over at the steaming tub. "I think it's time for a bath."

Chapter 8

In hindsight, it wasn't quite as difficult as it should have been to convince Henrianna to disrobe and step into the bathtub. She had a delightful practical side to her that—at least temporarily—overcame her modesty and the impropriety of the situation.

"I daresay," she pointed out, "my reputation will be of no use to me if I succumb to a chill."

Using a sheet from the tiny linen cupboard, Edgewood managed to fashion a sort of privacy screen from the hat rack to the mantel, and, after testing his discipline by helping Henrianna with the hooks on the back of her gown and the laces on her corset, he obligingly turned his back and crossed to the other side of the room, congratulating himself on his self-control.

Felicitations were premature, however. The sighs of pleasure from Henrianna as she sank into the steaming water were enough to unman him. Trying to ignore his uncomfortably aroused state, he busied himself with unpacking the hamper from the main house. But his mind, usually so disciplined and so focused on the task in front of him, refused to contemplate anything except the beautiful woman in the steaming hot bath not six meters away. He imagined her soft skin now pink from the hot water and pictured delectable curves and valleys glowing in the light from the fire.

He argued with himself about the ethics of the whole

situation and then—after deciding that there really was no way he could, as a gentleman, pluck her from the tub and ravish her right there on the fur rug in front of the fire—he turned to the more critical debate about whether or not he was actually a gentleman. Just as it seemed certain that his lesser angels might win the day, he rallied, deciding to fall back and regroup.

"We need more wood for the fire," he called out in the direction of the privacy screen. Hastily donning his coat, he fled outside into the bitter cold with hopes of regaining some semblance of control.

Several brisk laps around the cottage later, Edgewood came back inside with an armful of wood just as Henrianna was stepping out of the tub. She proceeded to dry off using the heavy towel he'd set out to warm in front of the fire along with one of his nightshirts, some woolen socks, and his dressing gown. Unfortunately, the shadow of her on the makeshift screen was like an erotic fantasy. He watched, spellbound, as she bent to dry her legs and feet and then as she stood, arching her back to dry her backside. Her silhouette showed off her figure in magnificent detail, right down to the pointed tips of her full breasts. Too late, she brought the towel back around to her front, blurring the shadow and leaving him harder than he had ever been in his life.

Edgewood dropped the logs to the floor and headed back out into the cold. Fires always needed more wood.

Chapter 9

"You'd best hurry or you'll miss the beginning of the new year."

Edgewood eased out the champagne cork and filled two glasses he'd found in the sideboard. "It's only two minutes before midnight."

"Where did all this firewood come from? You must be anticipating a very cold night."

The voice behind him was closer than he'd expected—although, with all the blood rushing to various parts of his body, it was a wonder he could hear anything at all.

Edgewood turned and sucked in his breath at the vision before him. His mind went blank and his mouth went dry.

"Will I do, then?" Henrianna executed a graceful turn in front of him. "Maybe I'll set a new style. It's not high fashion, and I'd have to tuck it up a bit to waltz, but the velvet is so soft and lovely, and it *is* my favorite color."

Without a doubt, Henrianna Barbour was the most beautiful woman he had ever seen. She stood there waiting for his approval, her cheeks pink from the heat of the bath and her hair still styled for the evening, with curling tendrils kissing the nape of her neck. She was completely covered by his emerald-green velvet dressing gown—the same verdant green as the McDaniels tartan—but she'd wrapped it almost twice around herself and secured it with a satin tie in the back, creating a short train and showing the tips of her toes warmly ensconced in his best woolen socks.

Wrapping the velvet so tightly around her had created a high neckline that completely covered her décolletage, but it also outlined her figure and the graceful lines of her legs, which, without the usual layers of petticoats, were clearly visible beneath the soft, green fabric.

Edgewood swallowed hard as he tried to remember his own name. "I think…" He took a deep breath and started again. "I think you look beautiful." His eyes, traveling downward from her tentative smile, caressed her every curve.

Her laugh was like liquid silver as she made an awkward curtsy. "I thank you, my lord. I am happy to provide you with the name of my modiste for your lady."

Gathering his wits, he responded with a bow of his own. "Alas, I have no lady. At least not at present." Was it his imagination or did her eyes light up at this information?

"A man of your character and charm—not to mention that you are quite pleasant to look at? Whyever not? Is it the unfashionable beard? Surely the right lady would be able to look beyond the overabundance of whiskers."

He was saved from responding by the sound of fireworks coming from the main house. "Ah, it appears we have made it to 1814 at last. Happy New Year, Miss Barbour." He handed her a crystal flute of champagne and touched it with his own.

"Happy New Year to you as well, Lord Edgewood."

She smiled and took a sip of the sparkling wine.

"It is tradition to kiss the lady you're with at the start of the new year. May I have the honor?"

Henrianna's cheeks blushed a deeper pinker. "Far be it from me to defy the ancient ways, my lord."

Edgewood took a step toward her and bent his head to brush his lips over hers. Her eyes closed, and he felt her lips part slightly. He inhaled the faint balsam scent that Stuart had put in the bath meant for him, and when Henrianna leaned ever so slightly toward him, he quickly reclaimed their wine glasses, setting them on the table before pulling her to him and cupping her face in his hands to resume their kiss. Her arms went around his waist and the notion of a quick holiday buss disappeared like frost in the rising sun.

Edgewood bent his head reverently and covered her lips with his, gently tracing her bottom lip with the tip of his tongue, tacitly asking permission for a more intimate exploration. Her sigh was the same pleasurable sound he'd heard when she stepped into the bath, but his body's reaction this time was much stronger. He moved one hand behind her to keep her close while with the other hand, he caressed his thumb over her soft cheek. Feeling her relax into his arms, he deepened the kiss, exploring her lips and her mouth with his own. He trailed his fingers down her back, caressing the soft velvet of his dressing gown while reminding himself that his robe was all that stood between his hands and her bare skin.

She was returning his kisses now, frantically pressing her soft lips to his lips, his cheeks, his nose, and then more adamantly back to his mouth. Her arms were now around his neck and he could feel her breasts pressed to his chest. When she parted her lips, he pressed his advantage, invading her mouth with his tongue, exploring the taste of her and tangling his tongue with hers.

He simply could not get enough of her, and somehow he knew that, before this night was over, she would be his—permanent consequences be damned.

Chapter 10

It was only after many minutes of kissing and touching and *feeling* that Henrianna realized the fireworks—at least the ones coming from Haversham House—had stopped. In fact, it was the sound of the silence that pulled her back to the reality of the moment. Left to her own desires, she most certainly would never have returned.

Flustered, she stepped back onto her unwieldy velvet train and promptly lost her balance, stepping quite heavily on Edgewood's foot before being steadied by a firm grip on her shoulders.

"I beg your pardon, my lord. I did not mean to trample your toes!"

"It was a very slight trampling," Edgewood said huskily as their eyes met. "But I am pleased to know there was no malicious intent on your part." He turned from her and took a deep breath. "Shall we sit? Stuart was able to procure quite a sumptuous repast—especially on such short notice. I'll just unpack the rest of the hamper, and then we can eat. Do you want to sit closer to the fire?"

"Perhaps later. I am quite warm now. From the bath I assume, but also from this lovely robe. It is indeed warm. My robe is not as warm as this one, but I think I might have one like this made. I don't think I have ever felt velvet so soft. Did I tell you that green is my favorite color? It used to be red, but I think green is more calming, plus I think it goes better with my coloring—especially my hair—although blue is nice too."

Goodness! When had she become such a chatterbox? It was as if her mouth had gone off without her, trying to distract from all the feelings flooding through her right now.

This man was a stranger. She had literally known him little more than an hour. She was alone with him in his rooms. At night. Wearing only a robe. She knew she was in a very dangerous situation, but to be honest? Right now she would gladly do anything he asked of her, without question.

Clearly she needed to put some distance between herself and this...this wildly attractive man.

"Would you care for more champagne?"

And *clearly* she did not need to imbibe any more champagne, much less more of that delicious brandy. That would truly be her undoing.

"Stuart also included a bottle of Haversham's cognac."

But as clear as the messages from her head were, her heart was saying something else entirely.

"Yes, please. I have always adored champagne, but I must admit that the brandy you gave me earlier was quite lovely. I know it's not the thing for ladies, but I confess I could easily become a convert."

"We will have some after dinner, then. Although I would be remiss if I did not warn you that Haversham is an afficionado of cognac, and his cellars are some of the best in all of England—perhaps the world. You may, in fact, become quite addicted."

"How do you know that? Wouldn't you have to be

an afficionado yourself?"

"Fair point," agreed Edgewood. "I will confess to being somewhat of a snob when it comes to brandy. Like Haversham, I prefer cognac. Unfortunately, with all the trouble Napoleon is stirring up in France, poor substitutes abound right now. Anyone serving fine brandy today is in league with a smuggler or, like Haversham, has deep cellars."

Henrianna sat primly in the chair Edgewood held for her. "How much longer do you think Napoleon will be in power?"

Edgewood looked at her in surprise. "Are you interested in the war?"

"Isn't everyone?"

"Most ladies—even most gentlemen—are loath to talk about it at all, much less bring it up while dining."

"I do beg your pardon, then. What shall we talk about?"

"No, no. I am happy to discuss the situation. It's just that I've not met a lady who wanted to know more about it."

"It's not my favorite topic, to be sure, but especially since my brother is, by all evidence, going to be in the thick of it, I'd like to know more. And you also said you were involved in the war effort, isn't that right?"

"I've actually been working for the Crown for several years now, but I start a new assignment this week."

"Do you mind if I ask what you do? And why are you not in uniform?"

"Like your brother, I am sworn to secrecy when it comes to these affairs, so I'm afraid I cannot divulge any details of my service."

"Of course. Is it possible for you to discuss the situation on the continent without betraying confidences?"

"Yes, I suppose so. Most events are public knowledge. Even the *Times Observer* has reported that it will take an alliance of all the like-minded countries to defeat Napoleon. The question is, which countries will be in that alliance? And another, when will they start behaving as one force to oppose the emperor? Do you read the London papers?"

"I do—at least I used to, before I returned home." She took a sip of champagne before continuing. "My father died several years ago, and my mother remarried. My stepfather insists there is no reason to subscribe to the London papers when we have a perfectly good local newspaper. It *is* a good rag, as local papers go, but it never concerns itself with anything beyond the county borders, much less the world. I had a chance to look at the *Times Observer* on our journey down from London. I hadn't realized until then how much I missed knowing what was going on in the outside world."

"You said you went away to school?"

"Yes, I did. My mother and father thought it as important for girls to be educated as boys, so when my brother went to Eton, I was sent to Miss Gruben's Seminary for Young Ladies in Switzerland. I loved it— in particular, history and geography and learning about all the places in the world. Miss Gruben is a great believer in teaching girls the same curriculum as boys, including math, sciences, philosophy, religion, politics, and especially languages."

"Do you speak a language other than English?"

"Je parle couramment le Français, l'italien, et le

portugais, et je connais un peu l'espagnol. Je peux traduire du grec et du latin."

"Very impressive. Does 'fluent in French' mean you studied in France?"

"No. Sadly, my knowledge is only from the classroom and from living in Switzerland—they do speak French there, although it's a different dialect. I have always wanted to travel to France, to Paris, and to Italy—which is probably why I was so eager to learn those languages."

"And Portugal and Spain? Are those places also destinations of interest?"

Henrianna laughed. "I would not turn down an opportunity to travel almost anywhere, but unless I marry an ambassador to another country, I'm afraid my traveling days are over—especially with Napoleon on his rampage."

"Languages have always fascinated me as well. *Dae ye ken Gaelic and Welsh and aw?"*

Henrianna giggled. "My roommate at school was from Edinburgh, so I learned a bit of Gaelic from her. But to answer your question, I can understand some Gaelic, but Welsh is a total mystery to me—they have so many letters in their words! Do you speak it?"

"*Nae.* My mother—her name was Eleanor—her family hailed from the Highlands. Her great-grandfather was a clan chief, but my father's family were lowlanders, from north of Glasgow."

"Is Scotland as beautiful as everyone says it is? I have wanted to go there ever since meeting Margee—she never stopped talking about it. In my second year at Miss Gruben's, I was supposed to go home with her at holiday, but—"

Henrianna stopped abruptly. Her eyes, sparkling with excitement only moments before, dulled, as if a shroud had been drawn over her face, replacing the light with a deep sadness. She took another, much longer drink of her champagne and then slowly started again.

"When my father died, I came home to help my mother. We have an estate in Northamptonshire. My mother was devastated by my father's unexpected death, and I ended up helping our steward run the estate for a while."

"Did your brother not come home as well?"

"He wanted to, but mother was adamant that he stay and finish school before coming home. We were both in our last year. But then, not even a full year after my father died, my mother suddenly married the landowner whose property meets ours. I still don't know why she did it—I thought it quite odd, considering how in love she and my father were. Hill and our stepfather were at loggerheads from the start. After the wedding, my brother and my stepfather quarreled, and Hill hasn't been home since. He went down to London and stayed with friends for a while, and now he's an officer in the army." Henrianna sighed, recalling the constant friction between her brother and her mother's new husband.

"When my stepfather moved in, I assumed I would return to Switzerland and finish my last year of school, but he wouldn't allow it. He said I'd had more than enough 'schooling' and the only thing I needed to know was how to please a husband and have babies."

Henrianna looked down at her soup, avoiding Edgewood's eyes. Those were not the actual words her stepfather had said to her, but she would never repeat his degrading words and crude remarks.

"If I may say so, your stepfather sounds like an unsophisticated arse."

"He is, rather," said Henrianna, taking another spoonful of the delicious oyster stew. "He told me he had decided I would marry one of his sons. He said it didn't matter which one and that he would let them decide who would be my husband."

Edgewood scowled. "Might I ask who the lucky gentleman turned out to be?"

Henrianna scoffed. "None of them are gentlemen. And luckily for me, my mother bundled me off to Lady Matthas before they arrived. If I hadn't come to London, I would have run away—most likely to Scotland to stay with Margee."

"Where are these sons now?" Edgewood's voice was hard, as if he planned to find the sons of her stepfather and pummel them into small pieces.

Henrianna shrugged. "As long as they are far away from me, I don't care where they are." She cavalierly buttered a piece of fresh bread, acting as if the threat of imminent marriage was of no consequence, but in truth, the danger was very real. It was not without possibility that her stepfather had already sent his imbecilic sons to London to find her and take her back to Brockway House. She knew she was safe here and in the Matthas home, but who was to say they might not kidnap her when she was out shopping?

Amidst her musings, Henrianna realized Edgewood had asked her a question.

"I beg your pardon, my lord. What did you say?"

Edgewood looked at her for a long moment as if he were reading her thoughts. Then he repeated his question. "I asked if your stepfather was also the reason you were not in London for last year's season? I keep trying to figure out how it is we never met before. I am certain I would have remembered you."

"My stepfather told my mother that there was no reason for me to have a season in London because he had already found a husband for me, so you are correct. I was not in London last season. But wait—how would you know if I was present or not? You who spend all of your time hiding behind potted palms! Correct me if I'm wrong, but aren't you the same gentleman who took refuge tonight on Lady Haversham's second floor balcony as far away from the guests as possible?"

"I'm not *always* on a balcony," said Edgewood defensively. "Sometimes there's a secluded terrace. And for the record, I wasn't hiding. And I never said anything about potted palms."

Henrianna laughed, then leaned forward as if to impart an important piece of information. "For future reference," she whispered, "a full-leafed dieffenbachia makes a better blind than a potted palm." Grinning, she sat back in her chair, her eyes twinkling at him. "Truthfully, Lord Edgewood, can you say with all honesty that you have never employed a potted plant to help you avoid a particular gentleman or lady?"

Edgewood face fell with the look of a child caught with his hand in the biscuit tin. "I cannot," he confessed feigning guilt. "I confess that most nights, like tonight, I am more inclined toward a hot bath and a peaceful evening with a book."

"And I have repaid your kindness by robbing you of both," said Henrianna, suddenly embarrassed. "I should go." She made an effort to stand, only to find that her unwieldy evening frock was held fast under the legs of her chair. She sat back down with an ungraceful flop and a startled, "Oh!"

Edgewood came to his feet when Henrianna started to rise, and now he knelt at her side, trying to hide his smile at her awkward landing, and failing miserably. "Please, madam. I cannot have you injuring yourself while under my protection. And truly, I find I no longer crave solitude as much as I desire your presence."

"But that doesn't seem fair, with all you've done for me..."

"Very well then. My payment is your presence and..."

"And?"

"And honest answers to any questions I may ask. Only then will your debt to me be satisfied."

Henrianna narrowed her eyes. "Very well," she agreed. "I will answer your questions, but only if I am allowed to ask questions of you as well."

"Done," said Edgewood coming to his feet and holding out his hand to help her rise. "Although I do reserve the right to fabricate my answers as necessary so that I appear to be more fearless, more intelligent, more agreeable, and better looking."

Giggling, Henrianna took his hand. The sound came like a happy brook trickling over smooth stones after a spring rain. "Never fear, my lord. I doubt you'll have much fabricating to do in that regard."

"Let us settle ourselves in front of the fire, then, and we will commence the interrogations."

Chapter 11

While Henrianna padded over to the fireplace, Edgewood gathered the cognac and two snifters. Joining her in front of the flames, he smiled at her nest of quilts. She sat in the middle, leaning back against the settee with her eyes closed and a faint smile on her face, but he thought he could see little lines of worry on her brow and he longed to smooth them away. In the light of the fire, her hair gleamed a rich chestnut brown that reminded him of his brother's favorite horse.

She opened her eyes as he was still staring down at her. "I know. I must look a fright."

"Nothing could be farther from the truth," he replied. "I was just thinking that the color of your hair reminded me of my brother's prized stallion."

"You're comparing me to a horse?"

"A *prized stallion* that my brother loved until the day he died."

"The horse died?"

"No. My brother died. As far as I know, the horse is still living." Changing the topic quickly, Edgewood said, "I believe *I* am the one who should be asking the questions, my lady. Would you care for some cognac?"

"Oh, yes, please. Is this what you gave me earlier?"

"Yes, this is cognac."

"I thought you gave me brandy."

"Cognac is a type of brandy. All cognacs are

brandies, but not all brandies are cognac." Edgewood placed a half-full snifter into her hands and settled down on the quilt beside her.

The liquid in the snifters glimmered gold in the firelight, casting a magical glow over the room and its inhabitants. Edgewood stole a glance at the lady who had enchanted him—the one who made his old dressing gown look like high fashion and the one who had made him laugh more in the past hour than he had in the past year. He was determined to learn everything about her.

"Cognac comes from a very specific region in France."

"Would that be the Cognac region?" Her eyes twinkled as she favored him with a teasing smile.

"Oh, right. Fluent in French. Yes, the Cognac region. Only grapes grown in the Cognac region can become cognac. The grapes are made into a white wine and distilled twice—unlike other brandies which are distilled only once. Then it is aged in oak barrels. Cognac is rich and sweet and contains notes of dried fruit and spices, even toffee."

"Why didn't you warm it with a flame like people do with other brandies?"

"One does not warm cognac with a flame. It takes a personal touch. To release the magic of cognac and experience all of its pleasures, you need only to warm it with your hands—not unlike releasing the pleasure in a beautiful woman."

Henrianna rolled her eyes at him, but Edgewood enjoyed the rise of color that stained her cheeks as she pretended to ignore his sensuous words.

"You don't believe me? It's true. You can tell when the cognac is ready because it turns a lighter shade of caramel. When a woman is ready for her lover, she flushes a soft pink."

"And tell me exactly how are you able to ascertain such slight changes in hues in the dark or by firelight?"

"Ah, that is where the practice comes in." Edgewood leaned back against the sofa, slowly swirling the contents of the snifter in his right hand.

"I imagine you have had years of practice and a great number of teachers."

"Would you?" Edgewood sat up and raised an eyebrow at her sassy reply, waiting for her to realize the suggestive nature of her remark.

She blushed, but then narrowed her eyes at him. "Don't look at me like that. I meant teachers who were teaching you about cognac, not teaching you about…the other."

"The other?"

"You know what I mean."

"Yes, *I* know what you mean. The question is, do *you* know what you mean?"

Henrianna's soft pink coloring deepened. Edgewood was enjoying seeing her flustered and found himself somewhere between totally fascinated and extremely aroused.

"I grew up with a twin brother, remember? And his best friend. I know many things that, depending on your point of view, a young lady should not know."

"Such as?"

The dark pink returned to her cheeks. "Such as never you mind, my lord."

Chuckling, Edgewood returned to his relaxed position, stretching his legs out toward the crackling fire and swirling the contents of his glass. "As the cognac warms in your hands, its bouquet becomes more apparent. Put the glass down in your lap and take a sniff."

Henrianna sat up straighter and rested the glass on her thighs, cupping it like a beggar. She inhaled and immediately a smile lit her face.

He smiled too. "See? Didn't I tell you? I am always surprised at the strength of what they call the *montant* odors at such a distance. Now, slowly raise the snifter to your nose as you continue to inhale. First, you'll smell the floral or fruity bouquet—violets, roses, apricots, pear…"

"I smell violets," said Henrianna. "It's lovely."

"Now lower your glass a bit and swirl it gently to stir the aromas. Bring the snifter up to your nose again and tell me what you smell."

"Oh, it's quite different," said Henrianna, closing her eyes so she could focus more completely on the mélange of fragrances wafting up from the golden elixir. "It smells less floral and more spicy than before. More solid."

"Good. Now lower the snifter and swirl it again, and then put it back up to your nose. Each time you sniff the bouquet, it's different."

"Oh, it is! It doesn't exactly change to something new, it just adds new things—now I smell…nutmeg?" Henrianna looked up at him in wonder and surprise as the liquid in her glass presented her with a different arrangement of its bouquet.

He smiled at her delight. "Each woman has her own scent—a mixture of her perfume and her essential self. A fine cognac also has its own bouquet. Each time you take the time to appreciate it, you will find something different. Now it's time to taste."

His eyes fell to her mouth. He cleared his throat, but his next words still came out as a growl. "Lick your lips."

The sight of Henrianna, wrapped in his dressing gown in front of the fire, made a sensual picture that had kept him hard since she first emerged from behind the makeshift screen. The sight now of her licking her lips at his command had him struggling to keep his voice modulated. He made himself take several deep, even breaths.

"Take a small sip to prepare your mouth." He could see the small movements of her lips and throat as she followed his directions.

"Now, take a drink and hold it in your mouth. You should immediately have a sense of the cognac and be able to say if it's round or short or long *and* you should be able to taste all the things you previously smelled."

When she looked at him, her eyes were wide with surprise and pleasure. The earnestness with which she followed his every instruction was incredibly erotic.

"It works best if you hold it in your mouth for a moment while you taste it all," he said, not at all sure he was still talking about the fortified wine. He shifted his position to accommodate his growing desire, but, instead of changing the subject to a safer and less fraught topic of conversation, he continued the verbal seduction. "Now swallow it—all of it at once."

Even the motion of her swallowing was sensual. When she licked her lips to gather the lingering drops, Edgewood thought he would lose his mind. Without another word, and before he came to what little sense he had left, he put their snifters aside and pulled Henrianna into his arms. His lips covered hers, tasting the eighty-year-old wine as he nipped and tugged at her bottom lip.

He pressed into a deeper kiss, exploring her mouth with his tongue as his hands traced the line of her back through the velvet robe. She caressed the side of his face with one finger, stroking his soft beard as she returned his kiss with matching ardor.

Without breaking the kiss, he turned and laid her back on the quilts she had arranged. Only then did he, reluctantly, part from her lips and sit back on his heels to behold his beautiful snowflake.

Her hair still clung to its once elegant coiffure—a narrow white ribbon appeared randomly, seeking a path among the curls. Her dressing gown—*his* dressing gown—enveloped her, but it had fallen open enough to frame her slender throat and shoulders with a careless vee that pointed the way between full, rounded breasts. As he continued to gaze upon the vision before him, she nervously clutched at the garment, instinctively trying to protect her modesty. He gently forestalled the movement by taking her hands and raising her fingertips to his lips. She responded by pulling one hand free and caressing the frown on his forehead.

"Why are you scowling at me? What do you see that makes you so serious?" Her smile had changed to concern…for him.

He studied the picture she made for a moment longer, and then, folding her hand to his heart, he bent to softly kiss her lips. When he raised his head, he looked into her eyes and smiled. "I see you, and I see my future," he whispered.

Her answering smile was all he had hoped for, and her words left no room for doubt. "As do I," she whispered. But then she furrowed her brow as if considering an insurmountable problem. "What do we do now?"

"That's simple. You marry me."

The frown vanished and her smile lit the room. "Well, that's certainly one solution, my lord." She laughed and then added, "Perhaps you should convince me of its merit."

"Exactly what I had in mind."

Chapter 12

She should be cold. The frigid night that had brought
them together had not abated except inside the guest
cottage that was set farthest from Haversham House.
There, the blazing fire warmed the air, as desire and
passion and cognac warmed the bodies that moved
slowly together upon the makeshift bed.

Slowly, almost reverently, Edgewood spread open
the dressing gown that covered Henrianna, kissing each
bit of newly exposed skin until she lay bare before him.
He trailed his tongue along the same path as his lips,
teasing her as she arched and sighed in frustrated
anticipation. When he caressed the underside of her
breast, she held her breath, not believing she could
continue much longer without bursting into flame.

Her breasts were flushed a rosy pink, except for the
taut, darker tips. When he touched his tongue to one of
those tips, she gasped, writhing beneath him as he
slowly, slowly circled the first firm peak and then
nibbled before taking all of it into his mouth to suck. He
brushed his thumb across her other breast, as if preparing
it for his mouth. She started to reach up to pull him
closer, but found herself entangled in soft, emerald
material, her arms pinned beside her.

Edgewood sat back and grinned at the granting of
his every fantasy, watching as she realized the velvet
gown that once covered her was now a backdrop upon

which she was displayed for him. She quickly stopped her struggles and, raising her eyebrows, returned his grin.

"So, my lord," she said in a low voice, "now that you have me, what are you going to do with me?"

"You're rather cheeky for someone in your position, don't you think?" Edgewood reached for the glass still containing a small amount of Lord Haversham's finest cognac and then settled himself back on top of her, straddling her thighs. "Perhaps I'll have another taste."

Dipping his forefinger into the liquid, he touched it to his tongue. "Mmmm...delicious. But I see a better way to enjoy it." Dipping his finger again, he leaned over and painted the wine on the tips of her breasts, first one and then the other. The cooling wine and the caress of his finger drew them into hard points. After dripping several more drops onto her breasts, Edgewood put the snifter aside and bent forward so his mouth could find and taste each drop—licking, sucking, and drawing hard as she moaned and moved beneath him.

"Your nipples are very sensitive," he whispered into her ear. "I wonder if I can make you come just by doing this. Shall we try?"

"Try what? Come where? Just keep kissing me, please?"

Edgewood froze.

"Why did you stop?" Her tone was accusatory, but when her eyes met his looking down at her, her face flamed. "Did I...Did I do something wrong?"

"No, never, my sweet. You didn't do anything wrong. It's just...I didn't realize... Henrianna, are you a virgin?"

"What? I... Does it make a difference?"

"I need to know, darling."

"If I say no, will you go back to kissing me? Please?"

"Henrianna, tell me the truth."

"Must we talk about it *now*?"

"Especially now."

Hearing the determination in his voice and seeing his stern face, she closed her eyes and breathed a very deep sigh. Pushing him away, she sat up and reached for a soft white blanket at the edge of her nest and wrapped it around her, wiggling to find a comfortable position.

"Of course I'm a virgin," she said crossly. She pulled the blanket tighter. The room was cold without Edgewood's warming embrace. "How could I be otherwise? I went from my childhood home to a secluded boarding school and then back to my mother's house. The only men I've known during that time were either relatives or servants or the men I met tonight at the ball. I am a twenty-three-year-old virgin who still has not had her official debut into society. Other women my age are having their second child. When was it that I had the opportunity to take a lover? Did you think you were seducing a woman of the evening?"

Edgewood's head was swimming. This was not the blushing confession of chastity he had expected. Henrianna was clearly annoyed. At *him*. And for what? For *not* taking her virtue?

"You needn't worry," she continued, adjusting the wrap. "I know everything there is to know about coupling. As I told you, I grew up in the country with my brother and his best friend, who treated me like one of them. My father even bred horses for a while, so there is nothing I don't know about the process.

Although…earlier…when you were…"

At this point, Henrianna seemed to recall something from the activities that had preceded this conversation and he watched, fascinated, as a deep flush crept up her neck to her cheeks.

"When I was what?" prompted Edgewood. He was amused that Henrianna considered herself to be such a woman of the world and yet blushed furiously at the mere thought of his passionate kisses. The idea of introducing her to all the pleasures that she had yet to experience was incredibly appealing. And the fact that no one else had been there before him aroused him as nothing else could.

"Tell me," he said in a husky voice.

"When you were kissing my breasts…all over. I didn't know it would make me feel like it did," she confessed softly, looking up at him and then looking quickly away. "I always thought this was a rather interesting pastime for men, even if it was a bit odd and messy. And, of course, it *is* a rather clever way to procreate. It's just that I had no idea it could be so…"

"So *what?*"

"I had no idea it could be so…nice."

"Nice? That's how you would describe it? *Nice?*"

"Is it not nice for you, my lord?"

Edgewood rose to the challenge. He pushed her back down and covered her with his body, holding his full weight on his hands and knees. Bending his head, he pressed a kiss to her lips and then whispered in her ear, "Allow me to show you just how nice it can be, my lady."

Chapter 13

Edgewood felt Henrianna tremble beneath him as he tenderly kissed her lips and then caressed her face with his thumbs. The passion that had been building before came roaring back to flame as he kissed his way down between her breasts.

He stopped there, taunting her with only the tip of his tongue as he tasted the last remnants of cognac on the crest of one nipple and then blew softly on the wet, sensitive peak. As he took her into his mouth, she caught her breath and arched her back, offering more of herself to him. The soft sounds she made were almost too much to bear.

"Tell me how it feels now," he whispered. "Do you still find the feeling nice?"

"Actually, it's…it's rather more than that."

Edgewood suspended his downward explorations to retrace a path up to her lips. "I intend for it to be much more than that, my love. There are so many ways I want you to find pleasure tonight."

"There's more than one way?" Henrianna blushed at her own innocence.

Edgewood chuckled. "Oh, my darling, you have no idea…" He was interrupted as she pulled him down for an extended kiss.

Between kisses he murmured, "I love making you blush."

She broke the kiss and pushed him away, frowning. "I can't help that I blush so much or that it always happens at the most inopportune times."

"I love it," said Edgewood, "because you don't just blush on your cheeks, you blush all over—at least, I believe it's everywhere." He started kissing his way down her flushed body, narrating his progress. "Yes, I believe I *am* correct. You're pink here…"

He kissed the hollow at the base of her neck. "And here…"

"That tickles." She sighed.

Moving down her body, he placed a gentle kiss on her belly. "Aye, and here as well."

Mesmerized by his words and his gentle caresses, Henrianna shivered and caught her breath at the sensations. She reached out to touch his face and he took her hand in his, kissing her fingers before continuing his journey.

He kissed the inside of one smooth thigh and then tangled fingers in the silky, dark curls at her apex, caressing and separating the soft folds that hid the tight bud at her center. Shifting so he could see her face, he slowly stroked one finger down her opening, pausing for only a second before pressing inside to find her hot and wet.

Henrianna gasped, but it was he who moaned. "You are almost ready for me, love." He used her wetness to slowly stroke her again and again.

"Talk to me, Henrianna. Tell me. How does this feel?" He circled the tight bud with the pad of his finger.

"I don't know," she gasped. "I can't…I've never… I've never felt this way before." She moved her hips to get closer or maybe to escape the persistent stroking, but his hand stayed with her, not letting her avoid the building sensation.

"Henrianna, I want to make you come, my love. Let me take you there."

"What do I do?" she whispered.

"Just relax and let me help you. Look at me, Henrianna...my Hanna. Look at me, darling."

Wide-eyed, she found his gaze.

"That's right, love, just look into my eyes." As he gentled her with his words, he continued stroking, feeling the tension in her build as she moaned and moved against his hand. When he gently but firmly touched the very tip of his finger to her center, he felt her whole body stiffen and shudder. As she cried out and fell over the edge of her first climax, he pulled her into his arms and held her tight.

****

When Henrianna at last took a deep breath and let out an even deeper sigh, Edgewood tipped her chin up so he could see her eyes. He grinned at the wonder in their dark depths and kissed her nose. After only a few seconds, she pulled away.

"Well, that certainly was... It was..."

"Nice?" he offered innocently.

She narrowed her eyes at him. "You are a wicked, wicked man," she said, "and someday you will regret making fun of me. In fact, you may regret it this very day."

"I seriously doubt that I will ever regret anything that happens today, my lady."

"Hmmm...perhaps not. However..." Henrianna scooted to sit up. She pulled the emerald robe around her. "However, since I seem to be lacking some basic information about these types of situations, I think I should do a bit of research on the subject."

"What do you suggest?"

"Well, my lord…"

"You must call me Grey."

"Very well, Grey, as I was saying, since you have seen me—all of me—it seems only fair that I get to see all of you."

"That can certainly be arranged," said Edgewood, sitting back and pulling at the buttons on his waistcoat.

"No, no, no! Stop!" said Henrianna. "That's not what I meant. I don't want you to take off your clothes…"

Edgewood's disappointment was obvious. "I see."

Henrianna looked up at him with a sly smile. "I don't want *you* to take off your clothes, my lord, because *I* want to take off your clothes. Slowly. So I can have a look at what I've gotten myself into."

Edgewood's grin showed what he thought of that idea. "Do let me know if I can offer any assistance, my lady."

Henrianna sniffed. "I believe I can manage, thank you. Shall we start with your waistcoat since it is already undone? There. Now, show me your cuffs so I can take out the buttons. These are lovely, by the way." As she reached for his sleeves, her robe fell open, allowing him an unobstructed view of her breasts.

"They are indeed," said Edgewood, trying to appear nonchalant and failing horribly. "Oh, you mean the cufflinks. Yes, they were given to me by my father when I turned twelve."

"Now your necktie. Do you know, Hill has still not learned how to tie a neat cravat for himself? Even at his age. I hope they don't punish him for that in the army."

Edgewood reached over to tweak a bare nipple and grinned when Henrianna yelped. "I would greatly prefer that I be the only man you think about while you are seducing me, madam."

"Is that what I'm doing?"

"It would appear so—except that you're talking entirely too much, which is distracting you from the task at hand."

"Well, if you haven't already noticed, I tend to talk when I'm nervous. And there are certain parts of you that are making me extremely nervous."

"Oh? And which parts might those be?"

"Never you mind! Put your arms up. I think after I…take…off…this…shirt, you should…" Henrianna threw the silk fabric upon the settee. "You should lie back."

Henrianna pushed him none too gently to his back and then threw one leg over his hips to straddle him, the green robe streaming out behind her. He smiled as she seemed to fixate on the impressive bulge in his trousers, a bulge that only grew as she fumbled with the buttons at his falls. It was some new kind of torture, he decided, gritting his teeth and then groaning as she inadvertently fondled his already stiff length. When she finally tugged his trousers down, it sprang free in front of her.

"What…what is this?" she said, unable to pull her eyes from his fully erect member.

"I thought you knew all about coupling."

"Yes, well, we've established that I don't know *everything* about it, but I have seen Hill and Avery swimming without clothes many times, and they had nothing like…like this. It was nowhere near this big."

"I'm sure that is something neither gentleman would like bandied about." Edgewood caught his breath as Henrianna proceeded to examine him, stroking up and down and measuring his girth with her finger and thumb. He groaned as she continued exploring at the base of his already pulsing shaft, kneading gently.

"Does that hurt?" Abruptly she stopped all movement, and he groaned again.

"I cannot tell, my lord. Is this a *nice* feeling for you?"

"Yes, it is. Please don't stop." He put his hands over hers and showed her how to move up and down on his hardened length as he grunted and tensed beneath her. "That's right. That's the way."

Still moving her hands the way he'd shown her, Henrianna furrowed her brow. "I know where this is supposed to go, but it won't fit at all. Must we wait for it to get smaller?"

Dangerously close to losing all control, Edgewood quickly reversed their positions, rolling her onto her back and kneeling between her thighs.

"Nothing's getting smaller," he growled as he took her mouth, thrusting and exploring with his tongue. With what was left of his willpower, he broke the kiss and looked down at her.

"I can't wait any longer to have you, Henrianna, but I need to make sure this is what you want. Is it? Shall I continue?"

With her hands on either side of his face, Henrianna pulled him back down to kiss him with an intense passion. He felt her heart beating wildly, and the tiny sounds she made were driving him mad. Pulling back from her again took everything he had left.

"I want you to say the words, Henrianna. I need to know that this is what you want."

"Yes. Yes, it is what I want. *You* are what I want. Please, Grey. Please."

He covered her pleas with his mouth and sent his fingers down between them, teasing her curls and sliding along her opening until she parted her legs and let him in to stroke her wet heat. With her writhing beneath him, he helped his achingly stiff erection find the molten satin between her thighs. He pressed steadily into her, feeling her tension build. She was so tight and hot. When he reached the barrier to his path, he stopped and pulled back a bit, and then bent to whisper in her ear, "Relax, love, and hold on tight to me. I need to be inside you now."

He waited until she had put her arms around his neck and then with one strong thrust, he pushed deep inside, burying himself up to the hilt. He covered her startled cry with his mouth, kissing her deeply as he held himself still within her. After a few more moments, he felt her relax. He broke the kiss and watched her face as he started to move inside her. He willed himself to go slowly, but when he felt her responding with her own movements, he slowly increased the speed of his rhythm. Her eyes were huge and dark with desire, and he felt her clenching and tightening around him as he thrust harder and deeper, riding the building waves of tension and need.

"Hanna, I want you to come with me. Let yourself go, darling, and just relax. That's right. That's right…just relax. Now." She cried out his name, and he felt her whole body tense and pulse around him. He moved faster now, deeper and harder until, with one final thrust, he shouted his own release and emptied himself into her scalding heat.

****

The memory of the sharp pain was already fading, replaced by a feeling of such intimacy that it made her heart ache. He'd seemed to feel it almost as much as she had. If a quick sharp pain was the price to pay for such an exquisite joining—this feeling of closeness—she was more than willing to pay it.

Grey put his lips to her ear as he gathered her to him. "Next time will be easier, my love. The pain is only with the first time."

Henrianna leaned back to look up at him, her face full of concern. "I'm so glad. I wouldn't want you to hurt so much every time."

"Me?"

"Yes, you groaned a great deal at the end. I can only imagine how it felt."

"You are worried for me?"

She nodded.

He pulled her close against his chest, kissing the top of her hair. "Hanna, *mo leannan*, I wasn't groaning from pain, I was groaning because it felt so good to have you, to be inside you and feel you come around me." Slowly he disentangled from their embrace so he could look into her eyes. "*Your* pain is what I was talking about. Does it still hurt?"

"It's just a tiny ache," she said. "Truly, it is nothing."

"Lie back and let me take care of you." Edgewood rose and disappeared into the darkness, returning with a soft, wet cloth that he used to soothe between her legs. The coolness felt wonderful, but when she felt his insistent fingers, stroking her once again, she started to protest.

"Hush, my love," he said. "This is just for you. Trust me. This will relax you. Just lie back and let me do this for you."

The soft, rhythmic caresses at her core were different from the hard, frenzied thrusts she had craved just a few minutes before. He persisted with long firm strokes that started the excitement building again. As she caught her breath, he slowly guided her into a rhythm that took her up and up and up and...finally...over a waterfall of release.

As she floated back down, he held her close as if he would never let her go. He covered them both, and then, curled together in the bed of quilts in front of the well-stoked fire, they slept.

Chapter 14

Edgewood awoke with a feeling he had experienced only twice before. It was the feeling that things were changing in his world such that his life would never be the same again.

The first time he experienced this feeling was when he lost his parents at the too-young age of twelve. Even then he was aware that the carriage accident depriving him of a mother and father would also take away his playmate and companion by thrusting his older brother John into his new role as the Duke of Marsden.

The next time Edgewood felt this way was when he met his best friend. He'd known then that his life would never go back to the way it was before he crossed paths with the Duke of Whitley, and he soon came to measure his adult years in terms of before or after meeting Whit.

Last night, after making love with Henrianna, he'd had the same prescient feeling. There was no accompanying sadness as there was with the death of his parents, nor did he feel the overwhelming sense of purpose he'd felt upon meeting Whit. Instead, there was a complete and total feeling of rightness and utter happiness.

Only yesterday afternoon he'd blithely told Whit that he had no need of a mistress or—God forbid—a wife. He routinely decried all efforts to involve him in any sort of relationship. He vastly preferred short, less complicated interactions with the opposite sex. But now? Now he could barely remember *not* feeling this way. As with the other times, he knew without a doubt that his life was about to change forever—and he could hardly wait.

****

Henrianna had never felt so happy—so safe and so…satisfied. Her body ached in a marvelous way in a myriad of places, and the solid warmth at her back confirmed that her dreams were not dreams at all, but wonderfully real. She carefully turned over to have a better look at the man who had completely altered her life.

At some point during the night, Edgewood had carried her to the bed that took up most of the bedroom and had donned his long shirt. But a great gaping vee allowed her to glimpse the golden-red curls that covered his muscled chest. Wanting nothing more than to play with that soft fur, she scooted closer and crept her fingers just under the edge of the vee. After just a short minute of twining her fingers through the springy tendrils, Edgewood's large hand shot out to capture hers, holding it close to his chest.

"Enough of that, lass," he growled, his eyes still closed. "We've many things to talk about and many plans to make, and if you keep toying with me that way, we'll get none of it done."

Henrianna snatched her hand back, but then stubbornly resumed playing with the curls. "Have you ever noticed that your brogue is more noticeable at some times than others?" she mused. "When we met, you had only a trace of it, but then last night when we were…"

"Ma brogue is na' the only thing thickening, Miss

Barbour," said Edgewood, recapturing her hand as he pushed back against the pillows and sat up. "Now stop distracting me and sit up here so we can talk."

Henrianna sighed. It was almost certainly going to get complicated from here, and truthfully, she'd just as soon put that off as long as possible. She looked up to see Edgewood regarding her intently, and like a puppy, she closed her eyes and cuddled up to his side, seeking warmth.

"First things first. Say you will marry me." Edgewood waited a minute for a response. "Henrianna? I want you to say that you will marry me."

Without opening her eyes, Henrianna furrowed her brow. "Is this what I am to expect in the future? Incessant nagging until you get your way?" She opened her eyes and smiled up at him. "I believe I promised last night that I would not allow your reputation to suffer, and I also agreed to marry you. Must I repeat myself over and over again?" She scooted closer, nudging his arm around her as she put one arm across his chest.

"As I recall, madam, you agreed to several things last night, but none of them was marriage to me."

Henrianna's eyes flew open and she sat up. "I'm sure I said yes... Did I not?"

With a wicked grin, he said, "Many times, *mo leannan,* but not about our betrothal. I want to make it official."

"Well, that was certainly remiss of me. I meant to give you an answer."

"Then you may do so now. It is not complicated." It was as if he had read her thoughts. "Not unless we make it so. I love you. You said you love me. We've had the wedding night, now all that's left to do is have the wedding."

"When you say it like that, it *does* sound easy," said Henrianna, "but are you sure this is what you want? I don't want you to feel that you're just doing your gentlemanly duty to save my reputation. As I told you, there's not much to save, and—"

"Henrianna, you were not my first lover, but I know I was the first for you. For some, that would be reason enough for a wedding. But the real reason is that I love you and I don't want to live my life without you. By some quirk of fate, our paths crossed last night. I'm not a gambling man, and I try to take only reasonable chances, but I'm not going to walk away from such a gift. Maybe our meeting was destined or maybe it was just a coincidence. It's what happens next that matters. We can throw it all away because of some arbitrary reason like we've only just met, or we can seize the chance to be as happy as we are now for the rest of our lives."

Henrianna watched Edgewood as he spoke. She knew nothing about this man—nothing about his family or friends, whether he was rich or poor, or even where he was from, except that he hailed from Scotland. What she *did* know was that she loved him as she had never loved anyone before and could never hope to love again. It was a most calming feeling to have such certainty in the midst of so many unknowns.

She smiled up at him. "Could we be married here?"

"You mean in bed? Don't you think that might be asking a bit much of the clergy?" He laughed at the face she made.

"Seriously, do you not want to marry from your home?"

"No. Not with my father gone and not without Hill.

My stepfather would just try to stop everything. Or worse, he would insist on giving me away. Just come and get me when you return. You can meet my mother then. Perhaps we could come back here to Haversham House to be married."

"Done. I'll speak to Lady Haversham before I leave, and when I return, I will procure a special license for us."

"Shall we wait for the gardens to bloom or have a winter wedding?"

"I think that depends on whether or not other things are blooming. I did not take the precautions I should have when I made love to you, Henrianna. Seeds that were planted last night might well be blooming in nine months."

Henrianna blushed bright pink. She'd not even considered that possibility.

Edgewood smiled at her flushed cheeks. "You blush so easily, my love. You would make a terrible spy. You realize that you will never be able to keep secrets from me." He kissed her pouting lips and then whispered huskily, "A child with you is not something I'd mind. Would you?"

He looked so smug that Henrianna rolled her eyes. "Of course *you* wouldn't mind. You're a man. It's nothing for you." But she let her eyes twinkle at him and snuggled closer as she considered the prospect. "I would be happy either way, although I might enjoy a little time getting used to the idea of a husband first. But let's not wait to be married. That way we don't have to pretend— and we don't have to sleep apart."

In the end, they decided to marry as soon as Edgewood returned from his assignment. He would still be on active duty, but neither of them wanted to wait any longer than the month he planned to be away. They also decided to keep their plans secret from everyone except Lady Matthas, her daughters, Whit, and Henrianna's mother. If Hill had not been deployed, Henrianna would have told him as well.

"There will be time enough to announce our plans when you return," she insisted. "I don't want to have to answer everyone's questions by myself. They will think I've gone quite mad and that I imagined the entire thing. Sometimes I think that myself."

"I want you to have this." Edgewood pulled off the small emerald signet ring he wore on his pinky finger and solemnly slipped it on the ring finger of her hand. "The Romans believed there was a direct connection from this third finger to one's heart," he said. "When you think it's all been a dream, just look at this and it will remind you of today. It isn't the family ring I would normally have given you to seal our betrothal, but it's all I have right now. It belonged to my mother, which makes it dear to me. I think she would like that you have it."

"It's lovely," Henrianna said, smiling up at him, love shining in her eyes.

"Keep it safe for me," he whispered, and they kissed to seal their promise of love to each other.

Chapter 15

They spent the first day of 1814 together, talking and making love so many times that Henrianna truly lost count. Stuart, the footman, obligingly came by to take away the remnants of their New Year's Eve feast and brought a new basket of tempting treats—including another bottle of Lord Haversham's favorite cognac. He also carried two hastily written but reassuring notes back to the main house to their respective hostesses, explaining their continued absences and allaying any fears.

The sun set early during the short days of winter, and up at the house, lamps were lit to stave off the darkness. The first day of the new year was waning.

He woke her during the night, needing her again. This time he pulled her back against him and entered her from behind, slowly, barely pushing inside. He held her bottom against his belly to keep her from moving as he brought her to climax over and over again, stroking the sensitive folds of her sex and applying just the right pressure to the place they protected. He callously ignored her pleas for anything else, prolonging her pleasure by denying them both. When he finally entered her fully, he felt her inner muscles clench and hold him as she came immediately at his command. And when her shudders started to calm, he took her up once more. This time as he felt her nearing the edge, he drove deep, riding her hard to the most powerful release he'd ever known. Afterward, still aroused, he stayed within her as they fell into an exhausted sleep.

She awoke not an hour later to the delicious feeling of him growing big and filling her from the inside out. This time their lovemaking was achingly slow. Her own release came as languidly as slow waves upon a beach. And when he finally came in his own climax, she felt his hot release in every part of her body.

****

The sky in the east was growing lighter. Henrianna was tucked up against him with one arm possessively over his chest, breathing softly. God, she was beautiful. Edgewood closed his eyes and tried to doze off again, but to no avail. He was surprised that he'd slept at all—he seldom did before a mission, usually because his mind was whirling with plans and logistics. This morning, however, his mind was oddly calm and content.

As the first rays of the winter sun broke through the morning clouds, he kissed her nose. "Hanna? It's time to take you back to the house, love."

Henrianna answered quickly. She must not have been asleep after all. She caressed a finger down Edgewood's chest, stopping to feel the slight ridge of an old scar. "Is it very dangerous? Where you will be?"

Edgewood moved her finger to his lips and kissed it lightly. Pulling her into his arms, he spoke into her ear. "You know I cannot tell you about it, but I *can* tell you I will not be at the front or on the battlefield."

Henrianna held him tightly. "Having Hill in harm's way is awful enough, but the thought of you in danger as well…"

"I will be fine, don't worry. I've been on many

missions that were much more dangerous. Come now, *mo leannan*. We must go."

The sun was almost fully above the horizon. Back in her snowflake gown, Henrianna donned her cloak and walked beside Edgewood back up the path to Haversham House. She bit her lip and brushed at the tears that insisted on welling up.

"Let me go in alone," she said. "I don't want to talk to anyone and I don't want anyone to see us together."

Edgewood nodded. "I'll see you to the edge of the trees."

Stopping where the path cut across the grass, he pulled her cloak more tightly around her, but couldn't let go of the fabric. He bent to kiss her. "A month is not so long," he whispered. "I love you."

"It's an eternity," she replied. "I love you too."

Chapter 16

"Edgewood! Where the devil have you been?" With a scowl on his face, Whit hailed his friend from the path that led from the stables up to the house. He gestured to a stable boy to bring out his mount.

"Looking for you," Edgewood called back, as he waited for his own mount. "I was about to leave you a message. I have to go. I've arranged to meet a transport at Port-Town. Are you off then, as well?"

"My rather anxious employer has called me to London with yet another omen of disaster." The Duke of Whitley rolled his eyes. "If His Majesty would simply let me do my job, then there might be less reason for anxiety. As it is, I'll spend the evening trying to convince him that we shouldn't shutter the whole kingdom and start speaking French. Where did you get to? I don't recall seeing you since late on New Year's Eve."

"I'm surprised you noticed my absence. Were you not yourself engaged in entertaining Miss Allen?"

Whit smiled, looking quite proud of himself and also quite relaxed. "Yes, my…ah…mission with the charming Miss Allen was an unmitigated success. She is in rehearsals and left for London yesterday. If I can get away from my other engagement, I have plans to join her later this evening."

"And well into the morning, I presume?" Edgewood grinned at his friend. He was glad the game of cat and mouse with the beautiful actress had ended in victory for the cat.

"Most likely—unless she's grown tired of me already."

The two friends chuckled at that unfathomable possibility. Whit's expertise in the boudoir had achieved legendary status, thanks in part to early lessons at the hands of a rather infamous paramour.

"So, where were *you*? You were nowhere to be found at midnight. Miss Allen and I had to take our supper alone."

Edgewood laughed. "I'm sure you didn't miss me."

"Don't tell me. You put a hole in Lord Haversham's whiskey cellar and then had to spend the first day of the new year in bed?"

"As a matter of fact, I *did* have my share of cognac, and I *did* spend a great deal of time in bed, but not, I think, in the way you imagine."

"Indeed?"

Edgewood hesitated for just a moment and then casually said, "Actually, congratulations are in order. I'm to be married. I celebrated the new year and spent yesterday and last evening with my betrothed."

"Don't even joke about a thing like that, Edgewood."

"It isn't a joke."

"Have you hit your head, then? Or maybe you're still foxed?"

"Neither. What I am is very much in love. I met her just before midnight on New Year's Eve."

Edgewood could almost see the chill as it moved across the duke's countenance. This was Whit's professional demeanor—the Ice Duke—and as such, he showed no surprise, no anger, nor any other emotion. When Whit spoke again, it was in the Ice Duke's calm, cold voice—the same one he used when he questioned prisoners.

"This is all rather sudden, is it not?"

"Very much so. No one was more surprised than I at how events unfolded."

"Do I know the lady?"

"I don't believe so, but I am eager to introduce you to her." Edgewood was annoyed that this conversation with his friend was beginning to feel like an interrogation. "She is from up north and is in London visiting Lord and Lady Matthas and their daughters."

"Have you spoken to her father?"

"Her father is deceased. She was at school in Switzerland but returned home after he died. She was unable to return and finish her schooling and has been at her home with her mother since then."

"Good God, man! How young *is* she? Have you debauched a virgin, Edgewood? Is that why you have to marry?"

"I would never force myself on a lady, Whit. You know me better than that."

"Yes, well, I thought I did, but obviously I was mistaken. Perhaps *she* is the one who did the seducing?"

Edgewood took a step back. He did not like his friend's implication. He'd always admired Whit's ability to intimidate the enemy, but he did not care for it at all when those talents were focused on him.

"Is that what happened? Did she trap you into this?"

"She did not trap me. If anything, I was doing the luring, but in fact, it was a mutual decision."

"So she could be carrying your child?"

A sudden vision of Henrianna's luscious figure, her belly swollen with his child, made Edgewood catch his breath. He put the image aside and said flatly, "I told you we just met on New Year's Eve."

Whit cocked his head, waiting for further information.

Edgewood shrugged. He really should have been more careful with Henrianna. He could ill afford to be distracted on this mission. His vision of fatherhood would have to wait.

"I suppose, technically, it's possible…"

Whit's icy interrogation continued. "Is she aware of what you do?"

Edgewood had had enough. "You mean have I broken my oath to keep secret my activities on behalf of you and the Crown?"

"That is precisely what I mean."

"Then you should say so and have the balls to ask me directly whether my cover has been jeopardized."

"Has your cover been jeopardized?"

"You are such an ass!"

"You did not answer the question, Edgewood."

"And if I do not?"

"Then I shall have no other choice but to assume that you, your cover, and your investigation have been compromised, and I will immediately abort the mission, take measures to mitigate the damage to those you work with, and take you into custody to be imprisoned in the Tower on charges of high treason against king and country."

"I'd like to see you try it," snapped Edgewood, falling silent as the stable boy appeared with Edgewood's mount and handed him the reins before scurrying back into the barn. Edgewood quickly mounted the dancing horse, who sensed her master's tension. He wheeled her in a tight circle before turning back to Whit.

"In answer to your question, *your grace*, no, I did not tell my fiancée who it is I work for or what it is I do. I only told her that I was leaving today and would be away for several weeks until the middle of next month. We are to be married upon my return."

The two friends glared at each other in silence until at last Edgewood nudged his horse forward, missing Whit by only the smallest of margins. Anger made even a nodded farewell impossible.

In spite of the icy roads, Edgewood broke into a full gallop as soon as he cleared the yard. Back at the stable, the Duke of Whitley mounted his own horse and stormed off in the opposite direction, toward London.

After the men were gone and the dust had cleared, the stable boy hurried to find the gentleman who had offered to pay for any information about the duke or his friend.

Chapter 17

Henrianna walked to town to pick up the post, but waited until she was on her way home to look at the gilt-edged card with a silly verse from Hill. The missive reminded her that tomorrow was Saint Valentine's Day and that it had been six weeks since the first day of 1814, when she had fallen in love with a veritable stranger.

It had been five weeks and six days since she had promised to marry the man and anxiously bid him farewell on his month-long sojourn, and it had been two full weeks past the time he'd promised to return.

It had also been, Henrianna noted with a rising sense of panic, two full months since her last courses.

Every day since the beginning of February, Henrianna kept one ear open, hoping to hear the first sounds of an approaching horseman, and every day, so far, she had gone to bed disappointed.

When Henrianna broke the news of her whirlwind engagement to Jane Ellen, Beth, and Lord and Lady Matthas, they were surprised, suspicious, but eventually delighted. Lady Matthas was adamant that Henrianna allow her the honor of providing a wedding gown—in lieu of, her mother's friend explained, all the gowns she had planned for Henrianna's season in town. Henrianna agreed to a single gown and was thrilled when the talented modiste whom Lady Matthas patronized agreed to fashion what turned out to be a stunning wedding dress from the beautiful snowflake gown.

"It never looked right on me," said Beth with sincere flattery and obvious relief. "And it is absolutely beautiful on you."

A week later, Henrianna wistfully bid her friends goodbye, with promises to see them again after the wedding. Now she wondered if she had been premature in telling anyone anything. In fact, there were times when Henrianna wondered if she had simply imagined the entire interlude. Only the gold-and-emerald ring she wore on a ribbon around her neck spoke to the reality of her imagination.

At the last minute, Henrianna had reconsidered the decision to tell her mother about Edgewood. "Homesick" was the response she gave when pressed for the reason she'd left London so abruptly, but something kept her from revealing the whole story and her future plans. Time enough, she decided, to announce the news when Grey came for her. Until then—well, until then there were other things to occupy her.

Upon her return to Brockway House, she had been more than a little surprised to find that her mother was increasing.

"That was one of the reasons I sent you to London before Christmas," her mother confided. "The women in our family have easy confinements—except for the first two weeks at the beginning of their third and sixth months. During those weeks they have horrible morning sickness that lasts all day long. I had it with you and Hill, my mother had it with me and my brothers, and *her* mother had the same thing with all six of her children. I'm sure you'll have it too, when you have your little ones."

Her mother turned away but added, "I knew if I were sick, I wouldn't be able to protect you." Straightening her shoulders, she turned back to look Henrianna in the eye. "We need to find somewhere else for you to be before the middle of March, darling. I'll be too sick again, and Elvin is… Well, he's still insisting that you marry one of his sons, and that's not what your father would have wanted for you."

"Mother, why did you—"

Her mother interrupted her. "He's not a bad man, Henrianna, not really. Except when he drinks, and then…" She turned away again, but Henrianna had seen the tears in her eyes.

As the days passed, Henrianna's well-controlled panic grew. What if Grey were injured? What if he had been captured by Napoleon's army? Or worse, what if everything he'd said to her was a lie?

Henrianna wasn't naïve. She knew there were men who took advantage of young women and then left them ruined in the eyes of society. She knew about those men—she'd probably flirted with some of them. Grey was certainly not the first man to have noticed her. He wasn't even the first man to kiss her—although he was definitely the best. And of course, he *was* the first man she'd known in the "biblical sense"—that phrase always made her smile. Who would have guessed there was such ecstasy in scripture?

At night, in her room, when she could look into her heart of hearts, she could still convince herself that Grey would come for her, that he was different from those other men. For one thing, he was the only man Henrianna had ever imagined herself marrying. Others who had flirted and flattered her or stolen a kiss—she'd never seriously considered marrying any of them. Her friends had all had romantic crushes on scores of men, both real and imagined, but Henrianna never did. In fact, before New Year's Eve, she wasn't totally sure she wanted to be married at all.

Grey had changed all of that for her. She'd never met anyone like him. He talked to her as if she were a person—without the overtones of a protective brother that her conversations with Hill and Avery always wore. Grey actually listened to her. He even solicited her opinion as if her ideas and thoughts mattered. When she'd told him she wanted to travel and see the world, he didn't dismiss her dreams. Even her father had laughed when she insisted she would see the Great Pyramids and find the Northern Lights. But Grey listened, and then they made plans to do those things together.

They had talked about everything—how Henrianna wanted to go to Paris, how much Grey loved the Scottish hills where he grew up…

"They're almost as beautiful as you, Hanna," he said as he lay in her arms after making love. "But they can be deceptively dangerous."

"It sounds as if I have a lot in common with those hills."

"You? You don't have a deceptive bone in your body. If you ever tried to hide the truth, your blushes would give you away." He'd chuckled then and tried to steal a kiss, but she'd blushed and swatted him away.

She told him about losing her father while she was away at school and the sense of betrayal she felt when her mother remarried. She confessed how worried she was about Hill being on active duty in the King's army. He recounted the dark days after his mother and father were killed in a carriage accident and his older brother became the Duke of Marsden. He confided how devastated he still was about his brother's death just two years ago.

"I'm certain he was murdered," Edgewood said with a fierce anger, "but I haven't been able to figure out who did it or how. The coroner ruled it an accident, but he didn't talk to the servants or even interview the people who had been with John. Someday I'll find out who was responsible for his death."

Henrianna remembered holding him close for a long time after that particular conversation.

Henrianna had kept her promise to send him a letter every day—even though he'd warned her that he would be unable to write from his out-of-town location. They were silly, innocuous, inconsequential letters that contained memories of their brief time together and narrations of the days' events intertwined with whispers of love and giddy anticipation of his return. She never missed a day—even as the day for his anticipated return came and went.

Oh, Grey, where are you?

Deep down inside, Henrianna knew with absolute certainty that he would never willingly have left her waiting, which left only one conclusion. Something must have happened to him. Something she might never know.

And that was what she feared most.

Chapter 18

The pain came in great waves that ebbed and flowed between burning streaks of a sharper, shooting pain. There was a constant undertow of dull throbbing, an ache that never stopped, as if he were being dragged over jagged rocks. In a faraway part of his mind, he knew he needed to try and understand what had happened to him, but more than that, he needed to not feel the pain. His body knew best, and he lost consciousness again.

The next thing he was aware of was his dry mouth. He couldn't swallow, and he made gagging sounds that seemed loud to his ears. From out of nowhere came a wet rag on his lips, and he gratefully let it moisten his cracked skin as he faded back into darkness.

The pain woke him again, but this time there was room for a quick breath between the waves—room for him to think for a moment. And there was light—bright light—from a nearby window. Nothing was familiar. He had no clue about where he was or how he'd gotten there. More troubling was the fact that he had absolutely no idea who he was.

The only thing he could remember was being shot.

No, he remembered *hearing* a shot—shots—and then feeling excruciating pain. And then falling into blackness. The pain he felt now was not the same as that initial searing pain. This was a more civilized pain, but it was pain, nonetheless, and it made thinking difficult. He closed his eyes again.

He started when he heard a door open. He opened his eyes and saw a child—a boy—come into the room and stand by his bed. The boy leaned over and peered into his face, curiosity in his dark brown eyes. He tried to speak to the child, but his voice was raspy and barely audible, even to himself.

The boy rushed out of the room calling out, "Mama! *Avó*! The man who is hurt is awake! He made a noise, and he opened his eyes and looked at me!"

He heard footsteps and heard the door open. He forced his eyes open. The child was there, but behind him trailed two women, one with gray hair, carrying an infant, and the other with black hair, held back from an unlined face in a long, thick braid. Both women were beautiful, but the older woman's beauty was weathered and spoke of many years of hard living. The younger woman's beauty was not unmarked by time, but her thin face and the circles under her eyes were superficial and her smooth olive skin had not yet been etched by the passage of many years. The younger woman moved to the bed and sat in the chair he had not noticed beside him.

"You're awake. That is good. How do you feel?"

She spoke in heavily accented English, which he understood, but he could find no words to describe how he felt. With every breath, he felt pain in his chest, but that was second only to the throbbing in his head. He tried to sit up and realized that his left leg had been bound and immobilized. His mouth was dry—images of sand and rocks came to him—but he managed to croak out a single word.

"Water?"

"Yes, of course," said the woman.

He heard the trickle of liquid from a pitcher and soon felt the cool wetness of the water against his parched lips. He held the water in his mouth for a moment before swallowing. "Thank you," he said, and she put the cup to his lips again.

There was a bandage wrapped around his head, which would account for some of the painful throbbing.

"We were wondering if you would ever wake up," the woman said.

"Where...?" The one word took all the effort he could muster. He'd searched his brain but found only pain.

"On our farm near the village of Azurara."

He looked at her blankly.

"North of Porto."

He furrowed his brow.

"Portugal," she added, concern creasing her brow. "Do you not remember?"

He started to shake his head but caught his breath at the pain it caused. "No."

The older woman stepped forward and spoke quietly to the first woman in Portuguese as she transferred the baby to her arms. After the younger woman and the baby left, the older woman sat down beside the bed.

"My name is Maris. My grandson found you at the bottom of the cliffs at the beach." Her English was slow and also spoken with a heavy accent.

"I speak Portuguese," he said, forcing the words from his mouth. Somehow it was an important thing to know.

Maris smiled and continued her explanation more easily in her native tongue.

"My English is not easy," she said, "but since you

are from England, I did not know if you also speak Portuguese."

"I am from England?"

"Your clothes. The book you carried is in English. You have papers that say your name is John Marsden, which is not a Portuguese name. And when you were delirious with fever, you spoke in English. Do you not remember any of this?"

This time he shook his head slowly. "No, nothing."

"Is John Marsden your name?"

He searched his confused mind for an answer, but found nothing. "I...I don't know. I can't seem to remember."

"You were unconscious when Sebastian found you. We brought you back here on a donkey cart, and my daughter bound up your side and your head as best she could. You were shot twice. The first bullet went through your body, but the doctor had to remove a second one from your shoulder. He also set the bone in your leg and brought morphine for the pain. He said you had several broken ribs from the fall, as well as other injuries, but he was most worried about your head wound. And, of course, fever from infection."

"How long?" he croaked.

"How long have you been here? We found you on the first day of February and this week is Carnaval, so almost three weeks. You've had a fever for almost a week. It broke last night."

"What did I say when I had the fever?"

"You were very confused, but you did keep calling for *mo leannan*." Maris paused. "You were also very angry at one point and said the English word 'bastard' over and over. I think that is like our word *bastardo*?"

As she spoke, Maris found a cool cloth and wiped his brow of beads of sweat created by the effort of talking.

"Yes, it's the same. I apologize—it's not a word that should be used in polite company."

"Do you remember why you were here? In Portugal?"

"No. I wish I did, but I can't remember anything."

The woman stood up. "I will bring you some broth and send word for the doctor to come when he can. He said to let him know if you woke. You rest now."

****

The doctor was encouraging about his memory. "I've seen other cases like this, and in most of them, the patient regains most if not all of their memory. Since you seem to have made it this far without infection, I think you will make a full recovery—except for maybe your leg. I have set it as best I can, but it was badly broken. It will be several months before it can heal completely. Perhaps by then you will remember what brought you here."

He heard the doctor's words and felt a compelling urgency to go…somewhere. He was starting to remember little bits and pieces of things—he knew that his name was not John Marsden, but he also knew that the name had meaning for him. He was British—possibly from Scotland, because he often had flashes of a rugged landscape that featured mists and mountains and lochs—lakes. The harder he tried to remember, the less progress he made. But in the times when he was resting or right before he went to sleep or right after he woke up, he remembered snippets of memories floating through his mind like a jumbled collage of his life.

It helped, he found, to know things that had

happened since he'd been injured. It was as if he was teaching his mind how to remember.

"How did Sebastian find me?" Now that more of the pain was gone, he could sit up in bed. The women took turns keeping him company when they could.

"He was being naughty," said the younger woman, Sofia, of her son. She laughed. "He is *always* being naughty. I had taken him to look for shells along the beach and he ran away. Big rocks had fallen from the cliffs, so it was easy for him to hide from me. It can be dangerous because we never know when another big rock will fall. When he called me to come see, I scolded him about running away, but this time I am glad he did because he found you." She smiled at him.

"So it seems I owe my life to the fact that Sebastian disobeyed his mother?" He liked it when he could make Sofia smile. Like her son, she had beautiful brown eyes.

"I suppose that is true, but you must never tell him that. He is already much too headstrong. He says I have too many rules to follow." She sighed. "He is a good boy, but it is hard to raise a boy without his father."

"Where is your husband?"

"He was with the guerrilla fighters, fighting so Portugal can be free and not under Napoleon's rule. That was more than eight months ago. He never saw his daughter." Sofia brushed at a tear that appeared and quickly changed the subject. "The doctor says you should try walking with a crutch. He says it is time for you to start building up your strength. I think you should try tomorrow after breakfast. Mother can mind the children and I can help you. Maybe walking around will help you remember."

"Can you bring in the crutch now? I'd like to

practice getting out of bed with it."

"No, not unless someone is here to help you. You don't want to injure some other part of you, do you?"

He let out a frustrated sigh. "Sebastian is right. You do have too many rules. What else can you tell me about where or how he found me?"

"It was clear you had fallen from the top of the cliff. Probably after you were shot. Marauders from Napoleon's army have been trying to recruit some of the Portuguese fishermen. There has been fighting up and down the coast. That devil may take over the rest of Europe to be his empire, but we will never let him take Portugal."

Sofia's flashing eyes told him this was a personal as well as a political stance, but her words triggered something in the recesses of his mind. Apparently, he was a soldier too—also fighting against Napoleon. He seemed to know a great deal about the diminutive Corsican and his plans to dominate Europe. "I am a soldier," he said quietly. "I remember that now."

Sofia smiled. "I am glad you are helping our country, *meu amigo*."

"How can you be certain that I am not one of Napoleon's men?" he said half in jest, half in earnest.

For a moment Sofia looked thoughtful, but then she smiled. "You are much too tall to pledge your allegiance to such a little commander."

He chuckled. "I'm glad." Somehow the idea of working for Napoleon was repugnant.

Chapter 19

It was time to face facts. Tomorrow was the first day of March and Grey was not coming for her. She had to accept that. She had to accept that, for her, there would be no happily ever after.

It had been two months since that wonderful, scandalous, delirious, magical night on the cusp of the new year when she had fallen so in love with a man whom she'd trusted with her life, her love, and her reputation. But now it was time to accept the fact that he had taken advantage of her. It was a tale as old as time. Sad, but true. She was not the first girl to be seduced and abandoned by a handsome man, and she would not be the last. But how could she have been so foolish, and so wrong about a person?

In town, she posted what would be her last letter to him. It was a goodbye letter—the last time she would ever write the words "I love you."

She promised herself she would not cry. Again. She was so very tired of crying, and it made her head hurt. And yet, when she looked up and saw a stormy sky the same blue-gray as his eyes, she couldn't stop the tears that welled up.

"I wonder," she asked the yellow forsythia blooming riotously by the lane, "did all those other girls still love the men who abandoned them? Did they hold out hope in spite of everything that their true love would return? Did their hearts feel this same pain when they broke in two?"

Henrianna took a deep breath and tried to turn her mind to other things. The day was mild for the end of February, and already there were signs of spring in the swollen branches of the bare trees that lined the driveway to Brockway House. Camellias were in full bloom, and soon daffodils and hyacinths would emerge to herald the end of winter.

She had been home for almost two months now, and, at least so far, her stepfather had kept his distance from her in an uneasy peace. But if family history held, her mother was about to become very ill as she entered the beginning stages of her sixth month of confinement. The last thing she needed was to be worrying about Henrianna. And, once her mother was indisposed, her stepfather was bound to take advantage.

In fact, just yesterday he'd announced that two of his sons would soon be arriving at Brockway House. The stated purpose of the visit was vague, but Henrianna knew he had plans to force her marriage to one of them. He was determined to keep control of Henrianna's not insubstantial dowry, which included half of the land he now farmed. Knowing first-hand what her stepfather was capable of, she would not be surprised if he planned to use his sons to put her in a compromising position so he could insist she marry one of the louts. Or—more likely—simply look the other way as one of them forced himself on her.

For just a moment Henrianna smiled to herself. What would her stepfather think if he found out she was already carrying another man's child?

Speak of the devil.

"Are your ears stuffed with cotton, gel? I've been calling you." Elvin's loud voice carried out across the lawn for anyone and everyone to hear. "Where have you been? I've news you'll want to hear."

Reluctantly, Henrianna stopped to let her stepfather catch up with her at the beginning of the driveway.

"My boys will be here next week," said Elvin puffing from his exertion. "George says there's still a fortnight before planting, which leaves plenty of time for a wedding." He chuckled. "Mind you, they still haven't decided which one of them will take you, but they're to sort it out afore they get here. What do you think about that, Miss High-and-Mighty?" He laughed at the horrified look on her face and then added, "Knowing them, I'll lay a bet you're breeding before EasterTide. They take after their old man!"

Henrianna said nothing, but turned and hurried up the drive, eager to be as far away from the man as possible. She would have to leave very soon.

Chapter 20

A carriage waited at the top of the driveway under the portico. Stable hands from Brockway House were tending the pair of matching blacks, but the fact that they had not unhitched the team indicated the owner was not staying long. The coach itself had no emblem or coat of arms. It was plain black, but still a very elegant and obviously expensive carriage. Surely this was not Elvin's sons here already?

Henrianna veered quickly, thinking to take the path that led to the kitchen and the servants' entrance, but she paused when she heard Simpkins, her mother's butler, call her name. Evidently he had seen her approaching the house.

"Miss Henrianna? There's a gentleman to see you, miss. I took the liberty of putting him in the front parlor."

"Did this gentleman give you a name, Simpkins? I was not expecting anyone…today."

Simpkins proffered a silver salver holding a single calling card and whispered, "The Duke of Whitley. And he's been waiting almost an hour."

"Where is my mother?"

"She has not come down yet, Miss Henrianna. Her maid said the mistress was not feeling well."

Henrianna frowned. The Duke of Whitley was the half-brother of Avery, Earl of Hammond, their neighbor and Hill's best friend. She had met the duke once or twice but did not know him well. Deciding it was not the thing to keep such a personage waiting any longer, Henrianna preceded Simpkins through the front entrance and sighed at her image in the hallway mirror. She made a futile attempt to pat the wind-blown strands back into place, and then followed the butler into the parlor.

"Miss Barbour, your grace." Simpkins announced her and then backed out, leaving the door to the parlor open.

"Your grace?" Henrianna sank into a quick curtsy as Whit turned to face her.

"Henrianna Barbour! You've certainly changed from the girl who tried to give Avery a black eye!"

Henrianna smiled, well remembering the incident during which she had first come to the notice of the Duke of Whitley. "He deserved it, your grace—you know he did. He and Hill threw my bonnet into the well."

"Yes, but as I recall, that was only after you left them tied up for almost two hours."

"They kept saying girls couldn't set traps or tie knots as well as boys."

Whit chuckled. "I think you made your point. To this day, Avery is quick to admit that you tie the best knots he's ever seen."

"It's gratifying to know his lordship learned his lesson. Please have a seat, your grace. Shall I ring for tea? I'm afraid Mother is indisposed and not receiving visitors just now."

"No. Thank you, no." Whit hesitated. He was obviously struggling with something. "I'm sorry to hear that your mother is ill, Henrianna, but the fact is, I've come to see you. On rather unpleasant business, I'm afraid."

"Your grace?" Henrianna looked steadily at the duke, willing herself to take steady, calming breaths. "Is it Hill?"

"No, no. It's not your brother. Shall we walk in the garden, Miss Barbour?" Whit looked pointedly at the door leading to the hallway. Even from where she stood, Henrianna could see the shadow of someone standing there. "It's cold, but the sun is warm if we are out of the wind." His next words were just above a whisper. "What I have to say is for your ears alone."

Henrianna's heart beat faster, and the queasiness that had been hovering all day threatened to disgrace her. She forced herself to make her response light. "Certainly, your grace. I'll just go and get my cloak and bonnet and meet you in the front hallway."

Ten minutes later, Henrianna found herself on the duke's arm, strolling along the paths of the still-dormant rose garden in the thin sunshine of late February. They had descended the front steps briskly, but once they were far enough from the house, the duke slowed his pace. He stopped in front of a carved stone bench warming in the sun and cleared his throat.

"Perhaps you should sit down, Miss Barbour."

Henrianna frowned at Whit's uncharacteristic hesitation, but perched on the edge of the bench.

"I'm not quite sure how to start," said the duke.

"If it's any help, I find it's usually best to begin at the beginning," she offered, wishing he would just get on with it.

"Right. Were you aware that I was at the recent New Year's Eve celebration given by Lord and Lady Haversham?"

Henrianna flushed at his words. What did he know

of her night with Grey? Might Whit know where he was? She answered slowly. "No...I did not know you were there, your grace."

"I didn't think so. It doesn't surprise me. I was somewhat less than social at the time, as I was intent upon pursing a young lady, and you, I have come to learn, were...uh...occupied with a friend of mine. Lord Edgewood?"

Henrianna stood and suddenly took an avid interest in dead-heading the climbing rose that had bloomed at Christmastime. She plucked at the withered blooms, her back to Whit. "Lord Edgewood is a friend of yours? How lovely. Yes, I met him at Haversham House. Have you seen him lately?"

"I have not, which brings me to why I am here today. These are yours, I believe."

Henrianna turned to see Whit holding out a bundle of letters tied with cotton string and addressed in her hand to Edgewood at his residence in London. She took the bundle. It seemed all of her letters were there. One or two had been opened. "Yes, these are mine. May I ask why *you* have them?"

"I have them because Edgewood's landlord gave them to me. Edgewood has not been home for over two months, and his landlord is...an associate of mine. After several weeks, when Lord Edgewood failed to return home from his scheduled trip, his landlord thought there might be something important in the letters that had come daily to a man who—until now—had received nothing at all through the post. Knowing Edgewood and I were friends, he brought them to me. I opened a few and read them, which is why I am here today."

"I don't understand. What do my letters have to do

with you?"

"Nothing directly, but once I found out about your connection with Edgewood, I felt I owed you an explanation of his disappearance."

"You don't owe me anything, your grace," said Henrianna, turning back to the faded roses. "And neither does Lord Edgewood. He and I had...a...a pleasurable interlude at Haversham House. That is all. He gave me his direction in London, and I wrote inquiring about his health and his trip. He had mentioned he would be away on business for several weeks, and I thought to invite him to visit here at Brockway House if his travels ever brought him this way. Since I heard nothing back from him, I assumed he was no longer interested in furthering our acquaintance."

"Your letters would suggest there is more to the relationship than that."

"Surely you cannot begrudge a lady her romantic fancies. It was nothing."

"That's not how he explained it to me."

"He spoke to you about me?"

"I didn't know it was you at the time, but he did tell me he'd found the love of his life and the woman he planned to marry. I have never seen him so happy—hell, I can't say I've ever even seen the man *smile* before, and he was grinning ear to ear."

"When did he speak to you?"

"The morning before he left." Whit took her elbow and turned her to look at him. "Miss Barbour... Henrianna, Edgewood worked...works...for me. I'm the one who sent him out of town on...business. And yes, I expected him back at the end of January—early February at the latest."

"Do you know where he is?" Her voice was low and desperate. "Is he…" She couldn't finish the sentence. She closed her eyes and swayed against the waves of fear and nausea that broke over her.

Whit steered her back to the bench. "Sit down," he commanded. "And put your head between your knees. I've no wish to create a spectacle by causing you to faint."

"You've never worn stays, have you, your grace?" mumbled Henrianna, bowing her head as low as she could.

"I beg your pardon?"

"Never mind. I'm fine, truly. Just please tell me. What has happened to him?"

"That's just it. We don't know. I don't know. He seems to have vanished."

"I don't understand. Where did his business trip take him?"

Whit hesitated again and then heaved a great sigh as he sat down on the bench beside her. "Henrianna, Edgewood works for the Crown. He assists me in gathering and providing information to British military operations in the fight against Napoleon and other enemies of England. As such, on January third, he went on a mission for me to the continent. You do not need to know the nature of his assignment or his destination, but what you should know is that he never returned. I can only presume he has been captured or killed."

Henrianna sat very still for a few minutes. She heard the words Whit spoke, but they didn't register in her head. She didn't know how to respond.

"We're looking for him. And we will continue to look for him until…"

"Until what?"

"Until we have evidence one way or another of his disposition. But I want to be honest with you. We have found no trace of him. Nothing that might lead us to believe he is still alive." Whit hesitated again. "Edgewood is a highly trained professional. He would above all things figure out a way to make contact with us if he were alive, unless he were badly injured or unless…"

"Unless what?"

Whit said nothing for a moment. When he spoke, his voice was cold and devoid of any of the feeling he'd shown earlier.

"It's possible that Edgewood does not *want* to be found. For example, if he found himself in an untenable position with you and regretted his hasty offer of marriage. Perhaps he thought it would be easier just to disappear rather than face the consequences of his actions. Or…" Whit's face turned to stone. "It's also possible he's been convinced to work for the other side."

"You can't believe that."

"It's a possibility, and one I must consider."

Henrianna looked at Whit and then back out over the faded garden. "But you don't believe it, do you?" she asked softly. "You don't believe he would betray you, do you?"

"Truthfully? I don't know what to believe."

Chapter 21

The garden was eerily quiet for a late afternoon. Even in February there was always some activity, but today the entire world seemed to be holding its breath.

After a moment or two of silence, Whit cleared his throat. When he spoke, it was in the icy, slightly arrogant tone that Avery had always made fun of—the tone that earned him the moniker of Ice Duke. "What I believe is irrelevant, Miss Barbour. I can only deal with what I know. Whatever has happened to Edgewood, I felt you deserved to know he was missing. I am counting on you to keep our secret."

Henrianna stared down at her hands. She'd forgotten to wear gloves, and her hands were freezing. She flashed on the memory of Grey rubbing her hands and how they prickled in the warmth of the cottage.

"I read what you wrote to him, Henrianna. I know you had feelings for him. I know that this was more than a casual encounter to you."

"But you think I might have been only a casual encounter to *him*?"

Another moment of silence and then Whit sighed. "No. Actually, I do not. Edgewood was not that kind of man. He was not one to have lady friends all about town. He was my best friend, and from what he told me, I believe he loved you and planned to marry you just as he promised."

"Then why did you say what you did about him regretting his actions?"

This time it was Whit who turned away. "Because I don't know what the hell happened to him! I keep trying to find a less damning reason for him to have vanished."

"Are you worried that he... Do *you* believe he has turned to the other side?"

"Truthfully? No, I don't. But it is a possibility. We all have vulnerabilities and secrets and limits—but no. I think he would die before he would betray his country. Or me."

"You think he is dead."

It wasn't a question, but rather a restatement of accepted facts. Nevertheless, Whit responded. "I think that is the most plausible explanation, yes. I am sorry, Henrianna."

She nodded but said nothing. Her mind, already reeling from the realization she'd come to just that morning, was spinning with questions and no answers. Her life was about to change drastically—that was inevitable. Her only option was to try and direct the change as best she could. It was clear she could not stay at Brockway House. Her mother seemed happy about the coming of a new baby, but her stepfather would not allow Henrianna to stay—especially once he knew of her condition. At best, he would send her away. At worst, he would still force her to marry one of his sons.

"Henrianna? Are you all right?"

She had almost forgotten the duke was there. She stood up. "We should return to the house now, your grace. I...I have things I must figure out."

Whit stood beside her. "Is there anything I can do for you? If Edgewood is gone, then as his friend, I want to help you in any way I can."

"Thank you, no. I'm sure I'll be fine."

"I will send word of any news, if you like."

"Yes, thank you. Actually, no, I won't be here for long. Would it be acceptable for me to send you my direction? I'm going to be traveling abroad—Switzerland, I think."

Whit frowned. "Certainly, that is acceptable, but are you sure it's wise?"

"Yes, I'm sure. Unless, of course, you know of a position for a spinster whose betrothed, a man she'd known for less than forty-eight hours, went missing after the couple had anticipated their vows." Henrianna laughed a little hysterically. "I am in a literal no-man's land—no man wants me. I'm not married, so I'm not a widow, but I'm no longer a virgin, so I'm used goods and not fit to marry anyone else. I can't stay here and be a daughter to my mother because my stepfather will either molest me or marry me off to one of his idiot sons, perhaps both. And now I find that I'm—"

She stopped abruptly. She was not ready to tell anyone her most intimate secret. She brushed angrily at the tears spilling down her face without her consent. She looked up at Whit, her eyes dark with anger. "If I had been born a boy, I could bloody well go off and fight that cursed Corsican who has destroyed so many families and killed so many brothers and sons and sweethearts. Or I could work for the Crown, gathering information like you and Grey. As it is, my only path is to leave here as quickly as possible and pray that my old school friends will take me in."

She looked up at Whit and saw her own pain reflected in his eyes. He was also experiencing loss, grieving his friend whom he had known much longer than she. Henrianna took a deep breath and put her hand on Whit's arm. "I'm so sorry, your grace. You lost him too. I know this is difficult for you as well."

Another wave of nausea threatened to engulf Henrianna, and she convulsively tightened her grip on the duke's arm.

"Henrianna? What's wrong? You look very pale. Perhaps you should sit down again."

Whit gently pushed her back down to the bench and then sat beside her, taking her hand. "When I asked Edgewood if he was getting married because he had to, he admitted that there might be…uh…repercussions from the time the two of you spent together. Are you…? That is, might you be…? Not that it's really any of my business, but if…"

Henrianna patted Whit's hand and leaned back on the bench. "Actually, your grace, the answer is yes. I believe that I am with child. I wasn't sure, but according to my mother, if I am, I am about to experience two weeks of rather intense morning sickness. Evidently it's a family trait that the women on my mother's side have a fortnight of horrible nausea when they are increasing. The first time is at the beginning of their third month and the second time is at the beginning of their sixth month. My third month would start today—which might explain why I've been unable to keep anything down since breakfast. And, if my mother is correct, it's only going to get worse. That said, I need to leave Brockway House immediately. Tonight, if at all possible. So, if you don't mind, your grace, I should get back to the house to—"

"You're sure you don't want to stay here?"

Henrianna smiled. "I make my stepfather furious

even on the best of days. Once he finds out about my condition... Well, I'm sure I won't be allowed to stay. And because my mother is also *enceinte*, I really can't depend on her to intervene as she did before. If I stay, there's a very good chance I'll end up killing my stepfather, and then I will hang for his murder."

Whit's eyebrows rose. "That wasn't exactly the answer I was expecting. I thought perhaps I would bribe the man or call him out on your behalf, but it seems I shall have to procure a situation to protect your stepfather from you." He looked thoughtfully at Henrianna. "You mentioned travel to Switzerland. Have you traveled outside England? Have you ever been to Paris?"

"Yes...I mean, no, or rather..."

"It's not a difficult question, Henrianna," said the duke raising a single eyebrow and looking down his nose at her in his all-too-familiar condescending manner.

"It's not that the questions are difficult, your grace, it's that you ask so many of them at once. Yes, I'm thinking of traveling to Switzerland. I went to school there for several years before my father died, so yes, I have traveled outside of England. But no, I've never been to Paris. Why do you ask?"

"And you have contacts in Switzerland? Someone with whom you could stay?"

"Yes. I've kept up a correspondence with two of my teachers from school. They invited me to visit whenever I could."

"Excellent. Let's go back to Brockway House. Have your maid pack whatever you need to be away for the next few months. I will take you back to London, and you can stay at my townhouse while you are..."

"Casting up my accounts all day long?"

"Exactly. Once you have exited that particular phase of your...uh, condition, I have an errand for you to do that will give you a companion to Paris. She can put you on a train from there to visit your friends in Switzerland. You're certain your friends will let you stay with them?"

"Yes, I have already heard back from one friend, and the two of them are thick as thieves. But your grace— Whit—I can't just go to London and stay at your townhouse. I know I don't have much of a reputation left, but it would never do to have your name linked to mine, especially given what is going to happen in another seven months. Everyone would think that you...and I..."

"Not at all. My Aunt Charlotte is in residence at my townhouse, with all of her extremely overpaid staff. She flits in and out of the city, visiting friends and using the townhouse as her base. I stay in rooms at my club for the most part. It will all be quite proper, and you will have people to wait on you hand and foot while you are indisposed. Then, before anyone is able to figure anything out, you'll be on your way to Paris and on to Switzerland. You can send for your trunks once you are settled. I will make sure you have whatever funds you need to go wherever you want to go."

"I...I don't know what to say, your grace. Thank you, but I couldn't possibly impose on you or take money from you. I'm sure I can—"

And there was the tone again.

"I'm offering you employment, Henrianna. You just said to let you know if I knew of a position that suited, and I do. You said yourself you cannot stay here. Your brother would not want it. Edgewood would not want it. And from what you've told me, it will be a relief to your mother not to have to worry about the perils of your being here. You can write her once you are settled in Switzerland."

"But what do I tell her?"

"Tell her the truth—at least part of it. It's easier that way. Simply tell her you're going to stay with friends. I shall return for you at noon tomorrow. I'll stay at Terra Bella tonight. The Duke of Easton is good company, for all his quirks."

"I don't know… I'm not sure I—"

In an almost unheard-of show of tenderness, Whit leaned over to kiss Henrianna on the cheek. "It's the very least I can do for my best friend, Henrianna. Please let me do it."

Henrianna looked up at the man beside her, trying to gauge his thoughts. Then she sighed. "I don't have many choices, do I? Thank you, Whit…your grace."

"Go in now before you catch a cold as well. You need to pack. I'll take my leave by the side gate."

The duke walked briskly toward the garden exit and in just a few minutes was out of sight. Only then did Henrianna bow her head, closing her eyes to let the waves of sadness, loneliness, and grief wash over her.

He really was gone. In the blink of an eye, her true love had come into her life and just as quickly vanished, like a dream from which she'd been abruptly awakened. She balled her hands into tight fists as another round of nausea overtook her. Slowly she breathed, in and then out…in and then out, until the nausea receded—at least temporarily—leaving her with an overwhelming sadness. It was only marginally better, but it was all she could manage at the moment, so, for now, it would have to do.

In the months ahead, she would need every bit of courage she could muster, and even then, it wouldn't be nearly enough. But knowing she wasn't totally alone would help. And perhaps knowing she hadn't lost all of Edgewood would give her the strength she needed to endure and the courage she needed to go on without him, even with her broken heart.

Chapter 22

The channel crossing was smooth. It was Henrianna's stomach that was churning.

At least seasickness was an acceptable excuse for her malaise. Luckily, the other passengers had no way of knowing that Henrianna had been "seasick" for the past thirteen days, most of which was spent on solid, dry land at Riverdown, the Duke of Whitley's Mayfair town home.

Her last visit with Whit had been short and only a little more enlightening than their conversation in the garden. "You understand that you must never, ever, tell anyone what you know?"

"I don't know anything," protested Henrianna.

"You know more than you think, and if our enemies believe you know things, they will try to make you tell them more."

He was careful to tell her only what she needed to know. In this case, that one of Napoleon's generals was a primary source of information for the British. This general was also an aide to the world's most astute and cleverly cynical diplomat, Charles Maurice de Talleyrand-Périgord, Napoleon's on-again, off-again foreign minister whose loyalty to anyone but himself was tenuous. Napoleon's *General de Brigande*, Jean-Luc Demonte, lived in Paris with his wife, Louisa, and worked for Whit. Jenny, the maid who was accompanying Henrianna on her journey, also worked for Whit and would soon be employed in the general's household to serve as a courier between General Demonte and Whit's network of spies on the continent. Henrianna's role was simply to provide a cover for Jenny to get to Paris. As the rather well-to-do Madame Honoria Cheval, a widow taking a trip abroad for her nerves, Henrianna would visit her friend Louisa Demonte in Paris. Once there, Madame Cheval would declare she was no longer in need of the maid's services, and Jenny would be absorbed into the general's household. Henrianna would continue on by train and meet her friends outside Geneva.

It had been Whit's idea for Henrianna to travel as a widow instead of as an unmarried spinster. "It's just easier," he explained. "People tend to avoid a widow—especially if she is still in deep mourning. Whether they do so out of respect or because they are simply trying to avoid any sort of brush with death is unimportant." He cautioned Henrianna again to tell no one about her role or her destination. No one—not her mother, not even Hill—was to know that she had been in Paris or where she was traveling in Europe.

"All you have to do is spend one or two nights at the general's home. He will then see that you get on the train to Switzerland. Do not trust anyone other than the general, his wife, and Jenny. You must never tell anyone anything about me or that you even know me. And nothing about Edgewood—that is critical. People's lives depend on your discretion and your ability to keep a secret, Henrianna. Do you understand?"

Henrianna nodded her head.

"Say the words," insisted the duke.

"I understand. I will tell no one about you or Grey or Jenny or the general."

"Good. And rest assured I and others will be keeping *your* secret. I am the only person who knows about you and Edgewood. Other people may have pieces of the puzzle—like Jenny and her contact and the general and his wife—but, like you, they know only what they need to know for their mission. It's safer for everyone this way. Good luck, Henrianna."

Impulsively, Henrianna went up on her tiptoes and gave the Ice Duke a kiss on the cheek. "Don't worry about me, Whit. You have helped me so much. Because of you I no longer feel helpless. I know you did it for him, but I, too, am grateful."

Embarrassed at being caught caring, Whit drew on his Ice Duke persona. "You see, this is what I was afraid of, madam. You simply cannot go around kissing men willy-nilly. You must play the part of the grieving widow at all times."

He sighed. And then as much to himself as to Henrianna he said, "I don't know what I was thinking to send you on this mission. Please be careful."

****

Jenny had tried everything to alleviate the nausea that, according to the calendar, would plague Henrianna for one more day, but nothing helped. Apples, lavender, even citrus—any scent just made things worse. The only thing that offered the slightest respite was fresh air. Consequently, Henrianna had spent much of her time in London bundled up and sitting outside in the private enclosed garden at Riverdown, with a bucket at her side.

And now, as one might have predicted, waiting in the small, enclosed ladies' parlor near the ship's stern threatened to bring up her meager breakfast of tea and toast. Deciding that public fresh air was preferable to close-quarter privacy, Henrianna wrapped her widow's weeds around her and climbed up to the main deck to stand at the rail. Other passengers, respecting her recent bereavement, left her alone, and for a time, she was able to breath in the fresh sea air that calmed her protesting stomach. The thick black veil draped over her hat danced wildly in the strong breeze and threatened to fly away, so Henrianna took it off and tried pulling it close around her shoulders. But just when she thought she had all the pieces under control, a particularly mischievous gust of wind snatched her hat, scattering pins all around her.

Before Henrianna could do or say anything, a man who had been standing at the rail a respectful distance away sprinted after the black felt-and-feather confection and rescued it just before it flew overboard. Retracing his steps, he presented the wayward chapeau to Henrianna with a small bow.

"I believe this belongs to you, madam?"

"Thank you, sir. You have saved me from having my first stop be at the milliner's."

"I am happy to save you the trouble, although you *do* understand that many ladies go to Paris exclusively to visit the city's many milliners? You and your maid *are* on your way to Paris, are you not?"

It seemed like a rather inappropriate question and entirely too forward. Henrianna didn't know if the gentleman was merely passing the time with a fellow passenger or if maybe he sensed a vulnerable woman because of her widow's weeds. By all standards of mourning etiquette, she should not be talking with anyone outside her family, certainly not with a complete stranger, but, by that same etiquette, she should still be below deck retching her guts out in seclusion in that stifling, windowless room.

Rather than give the man an answer to his odd question, Henrianna employed her cotillion training, which had taught her that—given just the tiniest bit of encouragement—most gentlemen would talk about themselves above all things. And so, she answered his question with a query of her own.

"Is Paris where you are bound?"

"No, my business is in Le Havre. I make the trip from Southampton once a fortnight. But surely you're bound for Paris? Even if not to the milliner's?"

"I am visiting friends on the continent who could not attend my husband's funeral."

The man was immediately contrite. "I do beg your pardon, madam, and my condolences on your loss. I did not mean to be glib in my remarks. I was enjoying the sea air and glad to see someone else doing the same."

"It *is* quite refreshing, and a most definite improvement over the ladies' waiting parlor below deck." Henrianna took a deep breath of the invigorating air, holding her own recently departed hat tightly in her gloved hands. The wind was whipping her hair into a tangle that would take days to straighten out, but Henrianna didn't care.

"You're lucky today," continued the man, moving a bit closer on the rail. "The breeze is strong, but the water's not so rough. It's not usually this nice. Why, just last week the wind was so strong that no one could wear a hat. More than one ended up in the drink, mind you— lost forever. Only some of the bonnets that were tied on survived—and even then they lost all ornamentation save for their ribbons. One lady—she actually looked much like your maid—used a scarf to tie the whole thing—lock, stock, and barrel—under her chin."

Henrianna laughed at the picture he painted.

"Has she been with you long? Your maid?"

Taken off guard by the question, Henrianna hesitated as she recalled the cover story Whit had insisted upon providing even for her minor errand. "Ah...uh...yes, yes, she has. Jenny's family has been with my family for several generations."

Luckily it didn't seem to matter to the man how many generations of Jenny's family had been in false service to Henrianna's family. He was already talking again, warming to the expository opportunity presented to him.

"Indeed? Your Jenny reminds me of a maid who worked for my mother back when my father was doing these crossings. I, myself, am the most recent generation to be tasked with the responsibility of maintaining our company's connection with France."

The man was almost a head taller than Henrianna and quite powerfully built. Like Henrianna, he was dressed warmly against the chilly sea breezes of the crossing, his many-caped greatcoat topped with a thick, royal-blue woolen scarf, the ends of which blew like a flag in the channel wind. He held his hat in his hand, not willing, she supposed, to tempt fate and put such an expensive accessory at risk.

The gentleman appeared to be in his early forties, but it was somewhat difficult to tell his exact age or too much about his appearance because his face was covered by a full beard instead of showing the clean-shaven chin currently favored by the beau monde. Interestingly, his beard was several shades darker than his brown hair, which was showing quite a bit of gray at the temples. He had a pleasant smile that changed his whole face and put small lines at the corners of his eyes. His voice was calm and soothing, almost familiar in its cadence, and had instantly put Henrianna at ease. In fact, she was enjoying the luxury of simply listening without having to hold up her end of the conversation.

"You see, each crossing is different, and I can tell you tales about each one. This year has brought more than its fair share of cold weather—especially these last two months. To date I have encountered snow, sleet, rain, and a gale warning. Yes, indeed, I've yet to experience a clear crossing this year. Interesting fact…"

Henrianna's mind wandered again as she half listened to the gentleman go on and on. She wondered how he would react if he knew she was "in the family way" and that getting that way had meant spending forty-eight hours in bed with a veritable stranger. She could only imagine the horror on his face as she told *her* tale. The thought made her chuckle.

"…you laugh, but I assure you the captain was beside himself. The entire crew had to be replaced upon their return, and there was no one left to unload the cargo. I offered to…"

The man's monotone monologue was starting to make her sleepy. To be fair, she was exhausted. Her nausea did not respect sleeping hours, and she had spent more of her recent nights sitting with the chamber pot than in her bed. Tomorrow should be the end of this first two-week-long period of morning sickness that her mother had unwittingly warned her about. Henrianna was anxious to see how accurate her mother's prediction was. She glanced over at the man beside her, who continued to pontificate about previous channel crossings. It felt as if he'd been talking forever, but he showed no sign of stopping or of even asking her to engage in the conversation. It was only as they approached the docks and bumped gently against the pilings that he gave any indication that he might be wrapping up his soliloquy.

"...and that's why, on my very first crossing as a young lad, I never sat down while aboard the boat. Are you and your maid staying in Paris long?"

Another question out of the blue! Henrianna had stopped paying attention to the man a long time ago. Perhaps it wasn't out of the blue. Perhaps he had been leading up to this question, but it still seemed odd. She turned to address the man. "As I mentioned, my husband—"

A loud bang interrupted Henrianna's answer. She snapped her head around to find the source of the noise. Was someone shooting at the boat? At the passengers? At her? She saw a curl of smoke in the air up toward the bow of the boat and then heard angry voices and the sounds of a scuffle. Passengers who had started to queue up to disembark quickly scattered, blocking her view. On the shore, she saw several longshoremen running toward them.

Henrianna turned back to the man beside her, but he was nowhere to be seen.

Chapter 23

She needed to find Jenny. Whit had said there was very little chance that Napoleon's network would be active at the port, so she had no reason to believe this altercation was anything other than a disagreement among the street vendors who made their living selling to the passengers on the ferries, and the pickpockets who targeted the same. But a gunshot? Surely *that* was unusual. Or maybe it wasn't a gunshot. Maybe it was a signal of some sort.

Where was Jenny?

She had followed Henrianna when she came up on deck, but she soon left to check on their bags and get a better view. Henrianna thought she heard a woman's voice coming from the crowd and tried to get closer. The voices grew louder, and then she heard a huge splash as if something or *someone* had fallen into the water.

Everyone was crowding together—some people were trying to get off the ferry while others were trying to board. Henrianna allowed herself to be moved toward the gangplank along with the other passengers trying to go ashore. She looked up and saw two men—one of them carrying a small bag—moving away from the confusion. They were pushing and fighting their way through the crowd. A dockhand grabbed at one of them, but was shoved into the harbor for his trouble.

As she watched the two men making their way

against the crowd, Henrianna realized that one of them was the gentleman who had stood beside her at the rail only minutes ago. He no longer had the blue scarf wrapped around his neck, but he still wore the caped greatcoat and had that odd full beard. At the top of the hill, he stopped and looked back at the ferry. He seemed to be searching for something. Just then a woman let out a scream of horror. Henrianna saw the man smile. She couldn't tell whether or not he had seen her watching him, but he seemed to have found what he was looking for. The crowd surged forward, and she looked away for a moment to catch her balance. When she looked up again, the two men had disappeared.

Where was Jenny?

Another scream claimed everyone's attention, and from her vantage point, Henrianna saw several people pointing and gesturing at something in the water. Trying to see between the pushing passengers, she saw a blue scarf floating beside the gangplank. With everyone converging on the dock side, the boat listed to port. Henrianna lost her balance again, but was steadied by a strong grip on her elbow.

"Miss Barbour?"

Henrianna started. All of her papers showed her to be Madame Honoria Cheval. Why was this man using her real name? Was she supposed to acknowledge him? She jerked her arm out of his grip and backed away.

The man came closer. "I work for our frozen friend," he said looking her straight in the eyes. "I was supposed to meet you and Jenny to provide transportation to Paris."

Henrianna smiled warily at the man. "Of course. It's a pleasure to make your acquaintance. I am Madame

Cheval. With all the excitement, I fear my maid and I have become separated in the crowd. Have you seen her, Monsieur…?"

The man did not return the smile, but he did grip her elbow again and bent to whisper in her ear. "Roberts, ma'am. I'm Jenny's contact. Or was. Jenny is dead, ma'am, and I need to get you to safety."

The man led Henrianna to a secluded corner of the deck and handed her a hat she recognized as Jenny's. "Here. Take off your veil and hat and wear this one. You're no longer a widow in mourning but a bride on holiday with her new husband. Tie this around your shoulders." He handed her a colorful silk shawl like the ones made popular by the Empress Josephine. "Quickly now. We don't want anyone to see you. And put this on." Roberts gave her an intricately engraved gold wedding band. "They took her reticule, but they'll be back once they realize it doesn't have what they want. They already know she wasn't traveling alone."

"Who knows? Who will be back?" asked Henrianna as she took off her hat and wrapped her veil around it. She handed the bundle to the man, who took two steps and tossed it over the side of the boat.

"I'll explain later. Right now, just come with me." He pulled her hand through his arm and patted it with an intimacy that spoke of lovers. Bending closer to her ear, he whispered, "Pretend we're on our honeymoon—just follow my lead." He casually led her to the front of the boat where the passengers were disembarking.

"Smile at me," he hissed.

She stared at him and then broke into a playful giggle and smiled up at him through flirtatious lashes. An older couple queuing up behind them exchanged looks of understanding and tolerance.

The woman smiled and asked, "Are you visiting here in Le Havre?"

"Just for tonight," Henrianna's companion replied. "We're on our honeymoon trip. Tomorrow we take the train to Rome." He smiled broadly and patted Henrianna's hand tucked into his arm.

"Congratulations," said the gentleman. "I hope you have as long and happy a union as we have enjoyed."

"Are *you* visiting here in Le Havre?" asked Henrianna, trying to keep her voice from shaking.

The lady proceeded to recite their entire itinerary, with periodic annotations from her husband. Henrianna's faux husband seemed fascinated by their every word, but Henrianna saw his eyes scanning the crowd. At last the two couples stepped onto dry land and, after wishing each other a pleasant journey, parted ways.

Henrianna said nothing as Roberts hurried her to an unmarked carriage away from the docks. He said something to the footman as he helped Henrianna into the carriage. Then he put up the steps and climbed inside the coach, barely managing to sit down across from her before the carriage jolted forward. Henrianna heard the driver urging the horses to go faster.

"Please tell me what is going on," said Henrianna, as the man pulled out a pistol and held it at the ready. He shook his head and put his finger over his lips. They rode that way for what seemed like miles before Henrianna felt the carriage cross a bridge. The coach slowed and her companion finally seemed to exhale, nodding as he tucked the gun back into a pocket.

"I'm sorry to be so abrupt, Miss Barbour, but we needed to be sure we weren't followed. Are you unharmed?"

"Yes, thank you, but what happened? And who are you? And how do you know Jenny is dead?"

"We were betrayed," the man said. "As I said, I am—was—Jenny's contact. The men who killed her are working for Napoleon's spymaster, a man named Jones. He also goes by the name of 'The Frenchman.' Do you know anything about him?"

"No, no," said Henrianna, shaking her head. "I just…" She stopped. Whit had said that people's lives depended on her discretion. There was no reason to tell this man any more than she already had. "Why is Jones called 'The Frenchman'? Aren't all of Napoleon's spies French?"

Roberts looked at her approvingly and then replied, "Not by a long shot. Some of Nappy's best operatives are British citizens. That's what makes this man Jones so dangerous. He's English—some think he's from the aristocracy. But because he's English, people just naturally assume he's fighting against Napoleon when, actually, nothing could be farther from the truth. I believe Jones came over on the ferry with you and Jenny. I didn't see him until after you docked."

"The man who talked to me at the rail! It must have been him. I saw him, with another man, running away from the docks."

"Can you describe him? No one seems to be able to come up with a good description of the devil."

Henrianna shook her head. "Not a good one. He was tall, he looked strong, he had brown hair and a darker-brown beard. He was so bundled up against the wind— we both were—that it was hard to notice anything else about him. He did have his hat off, and I saw that he had quite a bit of gray at his temples, so he's maybe forty-five or fifty?"

"Did you notice anything else?"

"No, I… Well, there was something about his voice that was familiar. I almost thought I'd met him before, but I can't imagine where. He had a tiny bit of an accent, just on some words, and you're right, he sounded very upper class."

"That's good work, Miss Barbour. I can see why the Ice Duke felt confident about sending you."

"But, Mr. Roberts, if it was him, then why didn't he… I mean, why didn't he do anything to me?"

"Jenny was their target. There were two men waiting on the dock. I think the plan was to kidnap her. I don't think the other two knew that Monsieur Jones was on the boat, and I think it was sheer coincidence that he was talking to you, but I can't be sure. What I *do* know is that someone in our organization has betrayed us. Someone who knew enough to identify Jenny, but not enough to know about you and the rest of the Ice Duke's plans."

"The man kept asking me if I was taking Jenny to Paris," said Henrianna. "He just kept talking and talking, but I only said what Whit told me to say." Henrianna's voice started to rise in panic. "I didn't stay below. Was that how he— Is Jenny gone because of me?"

"No, no. You did nothing wrong. No, this plan was put into effect long before you entered the picture. There's a good chance that if you and Jenny had stayed below, they would have taken or killed you both. No, this was not your fault."

Henrianna was in shock. "So you think the man talking to me was the man who killed Jenny? And his name is Jones—but he's also known as 'the

Frenchman'—and he is Napoleon's *spymaster*?"

"That's right," said Roberts, easing off his own coat. "His goal—apart from seeing Napoleon Bonaparte as Emperor of Europe and Asia—is to take down the Ice Duke and his network. Word is that Napoleon is not happy with the success of the Allies and blames the Frenchman."

Henrianna was quiet for a moment, taking in all the new information. "Are you sure she's gone?"

Roberts closed his eyes. He leaned back against the well-stuffed squabs and took a deep breath. "Yes. I was standing on the steps when the boat docked. I was not far from her. I saw two men board. They were acting like they were dockworkers and securing the boat. They grabbed her. She fought them off and was able to get off a shot at one of them, and he fell into the water. That's when the Frenchman appeared. In a matter of seconds, he cut her throat and pushed her over the side of the boat. I couldn't get to her in time."

"But if they've already killed Jenny, why would they follow us?"

"Because they didn't find what they thought they would find on Jenny or in her reticule."

"What were they looking for?"

"A map. A map that marked several routes out of Paris."

"If Jenny didn't have the map, then where is it?"

"Did the Ice Duke give you a letter to give to the general?"

"Yes. I have it right here in my reticule. It's only a—" Henrianna froze. She closed her purse and looked at Roberts with huge eyes. "It's not a *letter*. It's a map."

Roberts did not answer. He put his pistol on the seat

beside him and sat back again, closing his eyes.

Henrianna eased herself back against the cushions. She still couldn't believe funny, lighthearted Jenny was gone, and under such brutal circumstances. Was this what had happened to Grey? Did the Frenchman or one of his minions somehow find out that he was on a mission for the Ice Duke?

Henrianna turned the unfamiliar ring on her left hand and felt the engraving on the outside. She took it off and looked at it more closely in the fading light. The engravings formed the initials J and R. She looked over at Roberts, who had closed his eyes but was still tense and alert. "Might I know your Christian name, Mr. Roberts?" she asked quietly.

Roberts opened his eyes and looked at her. His glance flickered down to her hand and the ring and then back up to her face. "Richard. Richard Roberts. My mother liked alliteration. I have a brother Rafael and a sister Regina."

"And the J?"

Roberts closed his eyes again. There was no need for him to answer her question. Quietly Henrianna slipped the ring off her finger and reached across to put it back in his hand. "I didn't know her long, but she was very kind to me. I'm...I'm so sorry."

It was a while later when Roberts said, "You should try to get some sleep. We won't stop again until it's time to change the horses. We'll be in Paris by midnight tomorrow."

Chapter 24

The moon had already set when the unmarked carriage with its weary occupants drove down the *Avenue des Champs-Élysées* in the center of Paris and turned onto a picturesque avenue lined with trees and lit with gas streetlights. Most of the houses were dark at this hour, but Henrianna could see lights inside a few of the sumptuous homes. Toward the end of the street, the carriage finally came to a halt. Roberts opened the door, put down the steps, and handed Henrianna down. Taking her elbow, he urged her up the steps of the house in front of them and knocked sharply on the door. A few seconds later, a butler in full livery opened the door.

"Thomas! Thank God it's you."

"Monsieur Roberts, how good to see you, but we were not expecting you until tomorrow evening."

"Something's happened, Thomas. May we come in?"

"Certainly, sir. At once, sir. May I take your coat? Shall I ring for—"

"No. I will not be staying long. Please go and tell the general I need to speak to him. Tell him it's urgent."

"At once, Monsieur. Would you care to wait in the library?" The butler took a discreet look around. "It is the most private of the rooms on this level."

"Thank you, Thomas. We will wait for him there."

The interior of the townhouse was as luxurious as

the outside implied. Even as tired as she was, Henrianna's head bobbed left and right as Roberts escorted her down a long mirrored hallway to the massive closed doors at the end. Knocking as a mere token, Roberts opened the door to a room with a gigantic desk in the middle. Surrounding the desk on three sides were banks of windows, covered for the night with heavy, velvet, wheat-colored drapes. There was no doubt this was a masculine room, but it felt airy and light, without the usual dark, foreboding ambiance of an English gentleman's library. On either side of the doorway were walls of books that led the eye up to a second-level library which wrapped around the room. A huge marbled fireplace contained only the dull red embers of a fire that had already been banked for the night. With so many windows, the room was already cooling.

"What is the meaning of this?"

The man who appeared in the doorway holding a lamp left no doubt to his identity. His military posture was such that Henrianna knew at once he was her host, Napoleon's *General de Brigade*, Jean-Luc Demonte, the man who was to have employed Jenny as his wife's maid. The general was dressed in trousers and a banyan, and the slender woman at his side wore a thick, quilted velvet wrapper of soft rose pink. Her ginger hair was braided and dangled down her back, giving her an appearance of youth that was quickly contradicted as she turned to issue commands to the butler.

"Thomas, please bring tea at once and whatever you can find in the pantry. Quickly!"

The general gestured to Henrianna and Roberts to sit and then proceeded to stir up the fire. "We did not expect you until tomorrow, Roberts. What has happened?" He raked his eyes over Henrianna's elegant black ensemble. "Surely this is not Jenny?"

"Jenny is dead," said Roberts without preamble. "It was the Frenchman. There were three of them. Two longshoremen attacked her in the middle of the boat docking commotion. I think their plan was to abduct her, but then she managed to shoot one of them. I don't know if he was dead or not, but he fell into the water. Then a third man came from the boat, behind Jenny. I saw him approach her. He was furious. I suppose he was angry that their plan had been foiled—and by a woman, no less. I thought they would kidnap her—she was still struggling with the other longshoreman, and I was trying to get through the crowd to help her. But then the Frenchman came up from behind her. He slit her throat and pushed her into the harbor. She was gone before I could get to her."

"That's the Frenchman's *modus operandi*," said the general. "He almost never takes captives or leaves loose ends."

Roberts paused and put his head down, holding it in his hands. Behind him, the general's wife laid her hand on his shoulder, offering silent comfort. After just a few seconds, he raised his head and continued. "I think they knew Jenny was traveling with someone, but I didn't wait to find out. Most people didn't realize what had happened until a woman saw the bodies in the water and screamed. By that time, we had changed Madame Cheval's disguise from widow to wife. We walked off the boat with the other passengers so we wouldn't draw attention and left as soon as we could. I'm certain we were not followed. We only stopped to change horses. I don't know what will happen when they realize they don't have what they wanted."

Roberts put his head back in his hands. "I just couldn't get to her in time. She was gone before I could help her."

Henrianna had just ridden two days at breakneck speed with this man. He had not said more than a dozen words during the whole trip, but now the sorrow in his words was heartbreaking.

"There was nothing you could have done, Richard," said the general's wife softly. "The man is a monster. He is known for his cruelty and his disregard for human life."

After a few moments of silence, the general spoke matter-of-factly to Roberts, allowing him to put aside his grief for a time. "You said they were waiting at the dock in Le Havre?"

"The two that attacked Jenny were from the docks in Le Havre. I noticed them on shore before the boat docked. But the third man—the Frenchman—must have boarded in Southampton."

"We think he actually spent a lot of time talking to me," said Henrianna.

The general and his wife looked at her in surprise, as if they had forgotten she was there.

"I beg your pardon," said Roberts, grasping for a slight bit of normalcy. "General Jean-Luc Demonte, may I present Madame Honoria Cheval. Madame Cheval, General Demonte and his wife, Madame Louise Demonte. Madame Cheval has the letter from the Ice Duke. Jones killed Jenny for nothing."

"Can you describe him?" asked the general. "No one knows exactly what he looks like—except that he looks like Everyman. He is clever at making small changes to his appearance that draw people's attention. People who have seen him do not recognize him when they see him again. He is of average height, average weight, with an average build and average brown hair. He has been seen as a drunken sailor, a French farmer, and as the lord of an English manor. What did the man who talked to you look like?"

"It's as you said. He was tall, but not too tall. He looked muscular, but he was wearing a heavy cloak—the kind you see everywhere. He had average brown hair and a beard that was quite a lot darker than his hair. He was wearing a bright blue scarf when he was talking to me, but later when I saw him leaving the boat, he was no longer wearing it."

"How did you come to be talking to him. Did he approach you?"

"I was supposed to be below deck in the ladies' parlor, but I was feeling ill and knew I would feel better if I were up in the fresh air. Jenny said she would go check on our cases and then stay on deck to watch our arrival. She said she would come back for me once we docked. I was standing by myself at the rail—everyone leaves a widow alone—when the wind caught my hat and blew it toward the front of the boat. The man who had been standing at the rail some distance away caught it and returned it to me. He started talking and ended up staying beside me until we docked and heard what sounded like a gunshot. I turned to see what it was, and when I turned back, the man was gone. He just vanished. Later I saw him running away from the boat with another man. I kept searching for Jenny, but, of course, she never came back. That's when Monsieur Roberts found me."

A tiny flurry of activity drew everyone's attention as the butler, followed by a sleepy-eyed maid, brought in a tea tray that also contained several thick sandwiches and slices of iced pound cake.

"Please, Richard, eat something," said Madame Demonte. "Let me fix you a cup of tea."

"I think something stronger is called for," said the general, moving to a cut-glass decanter containing amber liquid. He looked over at Henrianna. "Madame Cheval, would you care for some cognac?"

The world stopped.

Henrianna could think of nothing except the last time someone had asked her that question. And for a minute, it was the first day of the new year again and she had fallen in love with a man who loved cognac. It seemed like several lifetimes ago. Had it truly only been a few weeks? So much had changed...

"Madame Cheval?"

"*Pardonnez-moi, General. Merci, mais, non.* Tea will be fine for me."

"Louisa?"

"Yes, *cheri*," said Madame Demonte, perching in front of the tea tray. She poured from the steeping teapot. "Do you take sugar, Madame Cheval?"

The general delivered glasses of cognac to his wife and to Roberts. "Is there anything else you can tell me about the attack? Did you get any indication of where the men were going? Were they returning to England or staying in France? Did they seem to know who you were? And you are certain it was the Frenchman who killed Jenny?"

Roberts sat wearily in the chair across from Henrianna. He took a long drink of cognac and exhaled deeply as he added to the narrative. "I was the first one onto the ferry when it docked. I spoke to Jenny and she told me that Madame Cheval was out on the forward deck instead of below in the ladies' parlor. She was going to fetch Madame Cheval, and I was going to get the bags. I don't think anyone knew I was anyone other than a man meeting the boat from England. And yes, it was Jones. I saw him kill her."

"Let us hope that you are correct and the Frenchman did not recognize you. For now, we must figure out a way to send this information back across the channel. Things are changing very quickly, and the Ice Duke needs to know what's happening. If you are forced to come all the way into Paris every time there is a message, then the information will be out of date before it can be delivered."

"Can London send another operative?" asked Madame Demonte.

Roberts shook his head. "It will take some time. Jenny was pulled from the Bath operation, and I know they already lost an operative at the Portuguese border."

"I don't think we can afford to wait," said the general, "but what choice do we have? Is there someone we can bribe to take packets between Paris and Evreux? You could meet them there, Roberts, *n'est ce pas*?"

"Yes, that would work, but I don't know anyone I can trust. Not yet. Not after what just happened with Jenny."

"Then I will have to make the drops."

"No, General," said Roberts. "It's too dangerous. It could compromise your cover, and it makes you and Louisa too much of a target. The Ice Duke would never approve."

"What about me?"

The words were out of Henrianna's mouth before she had a chance to consider them. "I know the parties involved. I speak French fluently. I could take Jenny's place."

"No," said Roberts. "You're leaving tomorrow for Switzerland."

"But I don't have to. I have no one waiting for me and nowhere I have to be."

"It would never work," said the general, looking her up and down. "No one would ever take you for a maid."

"Then I'll be someone else. I'll be a lady visiting friends and relatives in Paris. Perhaps I could be Madame Demonte's sister."

A silence fell over the room as they considered Henrianna's words. The general slowly shook his head. "No, that would not do. Everyone here knows Louisa's family and they know she has no sister…"

"Fine. Then I can be…your mistress, General. I could pretend to be a widow as well, which would give me all the freedom I need to go about without a chaperone."

"It's too dangerous," said the general.

"I don't think it's wise," said Roberts.

Henrianna looked down at her hands for a moment. They were encased in black, fur-lined gloves, and yet they were still cold. Something had happened to her the night she met Grey. Ever since then, she could not get her hands warm. The last time they had felt warm was the last time he held them. She needed to do *something*. She wanted to do this for him.

"I lost the love of my life to Napoleon," Henrianna said to no one in particular. Then she looked up and stared straight into Roberts' eyes—eyes that were dark and knowing with grief. "Please let me help. I know I can do it."

The sounds of the fire crackling were loud. No one spoke, but each of them looked at her, measuring her words and assessing the situation.

It was Madame Demonte who broke the silence at last. "If you're to have a mistress, husband, then I will be expecting a great many more jewels. As will your new paramour." She smiled. "I can hardly wait for the gossip to start! I'll wager Madame Barrymore will be the first to tell me—with great reluctance, of course—that my husband is keeping a mistress."

"What do you think, Roberts?" asked the general.

Roberts met Henrianna's eyes and slowly nodded. "I think it's an excellent idea, and I think his frozen grace will be furious." He smiled just a bit in anticipation of Whit's response to the new plan.

"Fortunately," said the general, "by the time he learns of the change, it will be a *fait accompli* and too late for him to say anything other than '*Merci!*' " He looked directly at Henrianna. "You do understand the potential danger, Madame Cheval? You do not have to do this. We can find another way. You know what happened to Jenny." His words were deadly serious, and he paused for just a second for everyone to remember.

Henrianna looked at Roberts and then back at the general. Subconsciously she straightened her back as she said slowly and clearly, "I do understand, General. And I still want to do it. Those monsters must be defeated, and if there is any way I can help make that happen, then I welcome the opportunity to do it. That said, there is one other thing I should tell you."

Everyone looked at Henrianna as she continued smoothly. "I am going to have a baby in September."

****

"You said the map was being transported with the girl!" The Frenchman could hardly contain his rage. "I found other messages, propaganda, but there was no map."

The burly longshoreman stood in the middle of the room while the gentleman in the many-caped greatcoat circled him like a wolf. The room was cold, yet the big man was drenched in sweat. He smelled of fear.

"Monsieur, I swear. My contact saw them give the map to the girl."

"Tell me, my friend. What good is paying for information if the information provided is incorrect?"

The longshoreman whipped his head from one side to the other trying to follow the movements of the Frenchman.

"My informant was most adamant, Monsieur Jones. He said the girl would have the map. She was moving to Paris. Her lover is in France, so—"

"I do not care about the girl or her lover or your informant," said the gentleman at his back. "I care only that I have nothing to give to the emperor."

"Maybe they found out about my man and changed their plans. It's not his fault."

"*That* statement at least is correct. It is not his fault. It is yours."

In less than an instant, the Frenchman employed the wire from one of his many pockets. After only a few minutes of struggling, the burly man fell to the floor.

Chapter 25

Looking back, Henrianna was amazed at how easily things came together.

Rather than being an obstacle, Henrianna's condition provided the *raison d'être* for her sudden appearance in Paris. The story she, Louisa, and the general decided to circulate was that he wanted his mistress nearby now that she was to bear his only child—albeit a bastard.

Interestingly, with Paris being Paris—and not stodgy old England—it was perfectly acceptable for the general's mistress to accompany him to the many social events at which his attendance was required. It was also perfectly acceptable for his wife to know about his mistress. In fact, when the general decided that—being such a busy man—he preferred to have his mistress housed in close proximity to his home, no one batted an eye. Happily, such an arrangement allowed Jean-Luc to come and go discreetly, away from prying eyes that might wonder why the man spent the night with his wife instead of his mistress.

Henrianna insisted she be the one to write the coded missive to Whit explaining the change in plans. She wanted to be clear that the choice was entirely hers and that she had not been coerced by anyone. She also wanted to be crystal clear that nothing Whit said or did could dissuade her from her decision.

****

At his desk in the rather opulent rooms at his club, the Ice Duke frowned over the decoded message he'd just received from Alexander's Books, Newspapers, Magazines, and Engravings, one of many London drop points that supported his extensive network of intelligence gatherers. The message was bad news: One of his best operatives had been killed, confirming his suspicions that there was a leak—a traitor—in his organization.

The duke continued to read and then slammed his fist on his desk. What the hell?

"Cooper?" he roared.

"Yes, your grace?" said his secretary, running in from the adjoining room.

"Is Walters still in town?"

"No, your grace. You sent him to Cornwall.

"Then find Jessup."

"He has not yet returned from Bath, your grace."

"Is there no one to deliver a message to France?"

"The messenger left just a few hours ago, but the next batch from Paris should arrive tomorrow. We can return a message then. The new operative is working out well."

"She's not the new operative, damn it! *She's* the reason I need to send the message."

Whit read the message again. Evidently Henrianna Barbour had decided to take the place of Jenny, the operative who had been killed.

"Please understand that I am not asking for your permission, your grace. I will do whatever I can to help defeat these villains. I know you understand."

And she'd signed it *Madame Rose du Bois.*

What the hell was she thinking? She had no experience, no training… She had no idea what she was getting into. When he'd sent her off to Paris with Jenny, it was just a routine cover, a simple assignment, and now…

Bloody hell! If Edgewood *wasn't* dead, he would surely kill Whit when he found out what his friend had done.

****

The details of the arrangement came together splendidly.

"I don't know why we never thought of this before," trilled Madame Demonte as she kissed both Henrianna and the general upon their return from the theatre and another evening of seeding the city with gossip.

Henrianna stayed back to let Thomas help her with her outer garments while Louisa led her husband into the parlor where a cheery fire burned brightly.

"It's so lovely to have someone to accompany you to all of these social events that I detest so much. And I dearly love having a new friend."

"She's supposed to be *my* special friend, Louisa, not yours," the general pointed out dryly. "I don't believe a *ménage-à-trois* would enhance my public image."

"Oh, I don't know, dear," said his wife with a twinkle in her eye. "After all, this is France. They might think even more highly of you because of your peccadillos. I find it all quite titillating."

The general tried to look stern. "Louisa! You are supposed to be disapproving of the arrangement. This behavior is unacceptable."

"I can't help it if I'm ecstatic about your mistress, darling!" His wife's smile changed into a teasing pout.

"Would you be happier if I also pretended to take a lover?"

The general scowled. "Don't even tease about such a thing, madam. I would not allow it."

"So it is perfectly acceptable for *you* to have a pretend mistress, but *I* am forbidden to take a pretend lover?"

"Louisa, I fail to see the humor…"

Madame Demonte smiled but quickly soothed her husband's ruffled exterior with a tender kiss. "Never mind, my love. There's only you. Always, only you."

Pulling off her gloves in the entryway just outside the parlor door, Henrianna couldn't help hearing their loving banter. She listened to her new friends with a hunger that gnawed at her heart. They would never intentionally hurt her, of that she was certain. There was no way for them to know how painful it was for her to witness their little gestures of affection. That they cared for, respected, and loved each other deeply was evident to anyone with eyes in their head, but for Henrianna, it was a special kind of torture.

"Would you care for a nightcap, my dear? Ah, there you are, Henrianna. Come and sit down. There are things we need to discuss. Would you care for a sherry?"

"Just tea, thank you." Henrianna sat in the elegant armchair nearest the fire, leaving the spot beside Louisa for her husband. Just for a moment, she relaxed back into the comfortable chair and closed her eyes, taking a deep breath, her fingers aimlessly tracing the carved swan that made up the armrest. After a minute, she straightened her spine and resumed the correct posture on the edge of the well-padded velvet seat. She was exhausted, but she was also determined to hide her fatigue. She would not provide a reason for anyone to question whether she was able to do the job she had signed up to do—not after finally finding something that made her feel useful again.

"Have either of you ladies thought of how we are to get our information out of Paris? Roberts is going back to his post tomorrow and will no longer be able to come all the way into town."

"We had thought to have Jenny travel to Jean-Luc's parents' house and use that as a drop-point," Louisa explained to Henrianna. "They have a farm in Evreux— about halfway between Paris and Le Havre. We were going to have Jenny pretend to pick up and deliver various items." She handed Henrianna a cup of tea. "And speaking of delivering, have you thought any more about where you would like to have the baby? I wonder if you should be talking to midwives or to a physician."

"Truly, I haven't thought anything about it," said Henrianna, settling back in her chair again. "I've been so focused on playing my part and getting ready for my debut into Paris society." She smiled at Louisa. "Being your husband's mistress is no walk in the park, Madame Demonte. He is quite demanding."

"Oh, my dear, *I* could have told you that," said Louisa. "Have you ever tried to get him to—"

"As much as I would enjoy listening to my wife and my mistress discuss all my shortcomings," interrupted Jean-Luc, "may I suggest that we turn ourselves to solving our larger problem?"

"Very well, darling. If we must," sighed Louisa, giving Henrianna a wink and whispering loudly, "*So* demanding."

She and Henrianna both smiled sweetly up at the general, who just shook his head at them before taking a very long drink of his brandy.

"Is there not something that would make sense for *me* to deliver to your parents? Or pick up from their farm?" asked Henrianna.

"That's what I've been trying to work out," said Jean-Luc. "In normal times, of course, my parents would most likely feel a great deal of animosity toward you. They adore Louisa and would not look kindly on my infidelity."

"You'd do well to remember that, my love, in case all of this gives you any ideas. My wrath would pale compared to the scolding you would receive from your mother!"

Raising an eyebrow at his disrespectful wife, the general continued. "It occurs to me that we might use the farm in a different way. I would most likely insist that you find someone of whom I approve to take care of my child. Perhaps that someone could be my parents. They would be overjoyed to have a baby there. The child would be safe, and you could visit any time you wanted to—it's less than a day's journey from here. Roberts could easily pick up messages from there as well. What do you think, Henrianna?"

"Darling, you really should be using her other name. Remember, we decided on Rose? Rose du Bois."

"*Absolument*. What do you think, *Rose*? Our story would be that I insisted my parents look after the baby once it's born. After all, you can hardly be my mistress if you have to tend the baby, can you? It will also solve the problem of who will care for your baby—at least for a while. We can go to Evreux later this week and I can introduce you to my mother and father. What do you think? Rose?"

Henrianna's head was bowed. A tear slid down her cheek.

"Dearest Henrianna, what is it?" Louisa moved to her knees beside her new friend. "What's the matter, *cherie*? If you are unhappy with this plan, we will think of another."

"No, no," said Henrianna, sniffing and trying to smile. "It's just the opposite." She pulled a lace-trimmed handkerchief from her sleeve and touched it to her eyes. "Having someone else helping me is such a relief. I am so grateful to know there's a place where my baby will be safe. I didn't know what was going to happen, and now you've found the perfect solution." Overcome with emotions, she whispered, "Thank you."

"I wish we could keep the baby here," said Louisa with a sigh, "but I agree with Jean-Luc that it would be too dangerous. Of course, we will have to wait until the infant is old enough to be away from you, but you will adore my in-laws, Henrianna—I mean, Rose. And they will absolutely adore you and will be delighted to have a baby to care for. The only problem I foresee is how much they will spoil your little one."

Louisa reached for her husband's hand and looked up at him as she said, "We haven't given up, but this will be nice practice for them in the meantime."

The general squeezed his wife's hand and brought her fingertips to his lips. From conversations with Louisa, Henrianna knew how very much her friends wanted a child. Louisa had suffered several miscarriages, but they had not stopped hoping. And now, instead of being jealous or resentful of Henrianna's impending motherhood, Louisa and Jean-Luc were providing a solution to her biggest concern and Louisa was taking on the role of trusted friend, sister, and midwife all in one package.

"Then it's settled," said Jean-Luc, rising. "I will write to them right away. Once I hear back, I'll take Henrianna—I mean Rose—for an introduction."

"I'm going to have to order new gowns," said Henrianna. "They are getting too tight in the middle. Not to mention that if anyone were to realize that I've been borrowing from your wardrobe, Louisa, it would destroy our cover."

"You should order several," said Louisa. "And they must be *très* chic and *très* elegant and, of course, *very* expensive. I will give you the name of my modiste. I only wish I could go with you to select the materials. Perhaps you can ask Madame Giselle to give you samples to bring home so that you might consider them here." Louisa clapped her hands in delight at the prospect. "What fun to be dressing the mistress of one of Napoleon's favorite generals!"

Jean-Luc grimaced as he stood up from the desk where he had penned a message to his parents. "This is turning into quite an expensive operation. I certainly hope the British Crown has the resources to reimburse me."

"Oh, and Jean-Luc? Darling, don't forget the jewels," said Louisa, batting her eyes as she smiled up at her husband. "You'll need to purchase more than a few very expensive items if you want to keep both a mistress *and* a wife happy. Lucky for you, I am partial to pearls, but I understand Madame du Bois is quite fond of emeralds."

Chapter 26

While Henrianna Barbour was planning for the care and security of her yet-to-be-born child, Madame Rose du Bois was quickly becoming a Paris sensation.

"From the start, you and I must be constantly at odds," said the general, "with a great deal of bickering and flaunting of norms. That will make it easier to cover up any odd behavior or strange things that might happen. You must be outrageous and pretend to flirt with absolutely everyone. You will be every man's dream…"

"And every woman's nightmare," added Louisa with a smile.

"It's always better to make a big fuss and call attention to yourself when you're trying to hide something," continued the general. "People will be embarrassed for you and will very often look the other way, pretending to see nothing—and actually seeing exactly what you want them to see. And, of course, you can always use your delicate condition as an excuse for anything."

"But you must be head-over-heels in love with Jean-Luc," insisted Louisa. "Your love for him is your Achilles' heel. To him you surrender yourself entirely, but there is one fatal flaw… You are in love with a man who will never belong to you." Louisa clasped her hands and sighed.

Jean-Luc raised an eyebrow and exchanged glances

with Henrianna.

"Louisa," said Henrianna slowly, "how many romantic novels have you read?"

"Am I wrong? Is that not the perfect description for our Rose?"

"Well, yes, it's very good…" started Henrianna, but Jean-Luc interrupted.

"So let me understand this. My beautiful mistress is in love with me, and about to bear our child, but I am still in love with my wife? That doesn't sound very smart of me."

"No one said anything about it being smart," said Louisa tartly. "You are mesmerized by Rose's charm and wit and infatuated by her beauty. She has seduced you and you have allowed it to happen—just like any other man would. No wonder your wife does not welcome you into her boudoir."

"Ah, *cherie*, now I know you are spinning fairy tales," said Jean-Luc with a grin. "My wife is always welcoming and has never turned me away from her bed." In a low voice, he added, "And she never will."

"Jean-Luc!" Louisa's cheeks turned pink. "Henrianna doesn't want to hear about all that!"

Jean-Luc laughed as Louisa pointedly turned away from her husband and continued plotting with Henrianna to craft the specifics of Rose's relationship with the general. Without realizing it, Henrianna drew on the brief time she'd shared with Grey, allowing it to shape the character of Rose. It was the easiest way to summon the kind of icy-hot passion that made her performance as Jean-Luc's mistress believable.

As it turned out, Jean-Luc's temperament had a great deal in common with Henrianna's. Both were undeniably stubborn, so it was not at all difficult for Rose to conjure arguments with her protector. And Jean-Luc was, in fact, quite demanding. He was adamant that they keep as close to the truth as possible so that he had to act as little as possible. As a result, he decreed that Rose—like everyone else under his command—must learn how to navigate the highs and lows of his quicksilver temper. He had also ordained that it was inappropriate for a general to show any public displays of affection, and so, while he and Rose could snipe at and provoke each other incessantly in public, they would always make up in private—at least that was the story they circulated.

For her part, Henrianna decided to fight fire with fire and permitted Rose to display a volatile demeanor that rivaled the general's and led to many loud, passionate interactions. Thus, when the two were late to engagements, it gave rise to a great deal of speculation about what exactly might have kept the compulsively punctual general from arriving on time. Equally of interest was the couple's habit of leaving an event early, sometimes after just a perfunctory appearance, but more often after a particularly heated exchange. If the truth were ever known—that the general simply couldn't bear to be away from his beloved wife any longer than necessary—their entire charade would be at an end.

Henrianna had come to trust and love Jean-Luc like a brother—even though at times he was insufferably arrogant. She enjoyed his dry wit and sharp repartee as much as she admired his loyalty and passion for his wife and for the cause he served. He reminded her a bit of Hill, a resemblance that served her well when she needed to add a bit of sarcasm to her performances. The last time she'd heard from her brother was the Valentine's Day card he'd sent—the one she'd tucked carefully inside her favorite book, hoping that keeping *it* safe would also keep her brother from harm.

She missed her close relationship with her twin, but it was probably for the best that they were not in touch. Just as Hill had done with her, she would have had to keep her real mission secret from him. As it was, the last letter she'd sent to him said only that she had fallen in love with one of Napoleon's officers and was living with him in Paris. It was enough of the truth that it would bear scrutiny and—with any luck—keep Hill from trying to find her.

Chapter 27

"I can do more, if you'll just let me." The baby in his arms smiled and cooed as he spooned bits of mashed peaches from the bowl into her mouth.

"You *are* helping. Someone has to feed and mind Isabela, and I can pick the vegetables faster without her. I'll take the medicine to Senor Flores when I go."

Sofia's mind was made up, and he knew it would be futile trying to convince her that he would be more help in the fields. For one thing, it wasn't true. He still limped heavily on the leg that had been so badly broken. The doctor was encouraging, as always, but the leg would never be as good as it was before the break.

For another thing, his memory was still spotty, at best. He knew the name that was on the papers they'd found, and he recognized it as an important name to him—just not his own. He remembered everything that had happened since he regained consciousness in Sofia's little house, but anything before that came to him only in quick flashes that he couldn't quite capture. It was like looking for a moon shadow or holding a melting snowflake.

One morning at breakfast, Sofia announced, "I think you should go with us to the shore today. Mother is visiting a friend, and I promised Sebastian we could take a picnic to the beach. It's an easy walk if we take the back road and go only as far as the start of the cliffs.

Besides, you need more exercise to strengthen your leg."

"Yes, yes! Please go with us!" Sebastian raced around the kitchen, unable to contain his excitement. "The rocks are very big, but I can climb to the top and you can watch me!"

He laughed. "Very well. I don't see how I can pass up this opportunity to see a world-famous rock climber."

No one was more surprised than he to find that Sebastian had touched a place in his heart. The small boy growing up without a father would soon be called upon to take his place in the household and help support his family. Sebastian's childhood—such as it was—would be extremely short. Not for the first time, he allowed his mind to explore the possibility of marrying into this ready-made family. Sofia was a beautiful woman and he would be lying if he denied an attraction to her. Even baby Isabela had made her choice clear about whose arms she preferred, tugging at his beard until he showered her with baby kisses that made her giggle.

They followed Sebastian down a gentle path that opened up to a stunning vista of the Ave River as it flowed into the Atlantic Ocean. Sebastian was off like a flash, while behind him, Sofia spread a blanket in the shadow of the cliffs and watched Isabela try to crawl on the sand.

He slowly followed Sebastian onto the beach, watching as the boy climbed the big boulders, all of which had, at some point, come crashing down from the cliffs above. Sebastian was agile, as little boys are. He enjoyed watching the child decide which of the boulders was worth climbing and which should be eschewed as too easy.

He turned to look back at Sofia and smiled at the

picture she made with her brightly colored skirt and blouse against the neutral tans and grays of the beach. Sofia smiled back and waved…

And then she screamed.

She pointed and he turned back to see that Sebastian had indeed made it to the top of one of the huge boulders. In doing so, however, he had dislodged less stable rocks on the cliff walls above him. Another of the big rocks was about to fall onto the beach—after it bounced off the boulder where Sebastian had staked his claim.

"Sebastian! Come down here," he called as he started toward the child, waving frantically. "Get down, Sebastian! Come away from the cliff!" But his words were swallowed up by the wind and crashing waves.

Seeing them waving at him, Sebastian waved back, still not noticing the bits of crumbling rock falling down from the cliffs.

Moving as fast as humanly possible, he was painfully aware that his leg was unready for such strenuous movement. It was healing and, at the moment, seemed to bear his weight as he limped through the sand, but he would never be able to climb the boulder in time to get to Sebastian. Maybe…

He reached Sebastian's boulder just as the rock up above began its descent. "Sebastian, jump! Quickly!" Holding up his arms, he prayed the boy would think it all part of the fun and quickly join in. "Jump, Sebastian! I'll catch you. Jump! Now!"

The sudden weight of the boy in his arms knocked them both to the ground. They were peppered by a shower of pebbles that accompanied the descent of the giant rock from the cliffs. As it bounced off the boulder where the boy had stood mere seconds before, Sebastian crowed with exhilaration in the circle of his rescuer's arms.

"Did you see me? I was on top of the biggest rock on the beach!"

He hugged the boy tightly and then gently brushed the sand from Sebastian's back. He allowed the child to pull him to his feet.

Sebastian danced in circles around him. "Can I go up again?"

"I think your mother has our lunch almost ready." Limping slowly, he made his way back to where he had dropped his cane.

Totally unaware of his close brush with death, Sebastian ran off on his own indirect path back to his mother, his sister, and lunch. Sofia met Sebastian halfway and gave him a fierce hug. He squirmed in her tight embrace, and she finally released him. "It was very naughty of you to climb on such a big boulder," she said sternly. "Now go and mind your sister."

He had retrieved his cane and was making his way back across the sand when Sofia came up to him and threw her arms around his neck. "Thank you," she whispered. "Thank you for saving my son, *meu querido amigo*. Thank you."

She stepped back to look at him again and then took his face in her hands and put her lips on his, holding him so close he could feel the softness of her breasts through her blouse and his shirt. His body responded immediately, and he deepened the kiss, but all of a sudden he was no longer kissing Sofia. He was kissing Henrianna.

Edgewood opened his eyes and saw Sofia staring at him, her face etched with concern. "What is it? Did I hurt you? Are you unwell?"

"I remember."

****

With the turning of a single page, Edgewood's whole life story came back to him. Sofia listened as he talked and remembered. The wrenching pain of losing his parents and later his brother. His work and his friendship with Whit. And Henrianna—meeting her, loving her, and leaving her with the promise to return soon so they could marry.

Sofia listened as Edgewood remembered his last day with Henrianna and their plans for the future. She knew that the small ember of love that had sparked for a moment between them had been returned to its proper place of friendship, and she was truly happy for Edgewood. But she was also sad for herself.

"You will be able to travel soon," she told him as he paced around and around the small kitchen. "You must go and find this love of yours."

"But what if she thinks I abandoned her? What if I cannot find her?"

"You will find her, and she will understand, and all will be well. How could she ever stop loving you? She was the one you called for even when you were out of your mind with fever. Your head could not remember, but your heart could not forget."

"And what of you? Sofia, I…"

"Please do not say it. I know. I know that things might have been different for us. But I also know that you belong to Henrianna. I have had the gift of you for a little while, and for that—and for saving my son—I will always be grateful. Go and find her. I know she is somewhere waiting for you."

The very next morning, Edgewood left on a horse he promised to return someday. Maris held Isabela as Sofia and Sebastian waved from the doorway until he vanished around a bend in the road.

Chapter 28

Nothing was right. His intricate network of talented men and women gathering intelligence seemed to be disintegrating right before his eyes.

Things on the continent were in chaos and changing so quickly that he hardly had time to read the newspapers, much less stay current on the intelligence reports coming in from his operatives—at least one of whom, he reminded himself constantly, was a traitor.

Whit was a genius at compartmentalizing—it was a strategy he'd developed early on and it was how he had been so successful as the king's spymaster. Everything—people, information, strategies—was kept separate so that no one, not Edgewood, not even the king himself, knew how it all fit together. Only Whit knew all the pieces and all the players. What he didn't know was which one of his spies was betraying him.

After slamming the ledger books around on his desk again, the Duke of Whitley pushed back his chair and stood to stare out the window. What was he missing? Was there more than one weak link in his chain of operatives?

The chaos in France made him nervous. Napoleon had abdicated only weeks before, but retained the title of Emperor. The man had been given dominion over the sovereign nation of Elba, a place from which he reached out to his supporters and regrouped his forces—even as he was officially exiled from the continent. Most people in France were happy to see the end of Napoleon, but they would not welcome a return to the traditional monarchy.

Louis XVIII—who still had not arrived in Paris to take up his throne—was already being criticized for his heavy-handed treatment of his people. Had the royal idiot learned nothing from the revolution? From Napoleon?

The French people had rebelled before, and guillotines were easy to build. Even the great Talleyrand was having trouble deciding how to maneuver during such a delicate transition—which spoke volumes about the actual state of affairs. As confidant to all and enemy to none, the man had a true talent for choosing the right horse to back—or perhaps just a gift for bribing jockeys and sabotaging the track. Thank God for General Demonte's dedication to the cause, which provided a constant stream of intelligence straight from Talleyrand's mouth.

The allies had already begun celebrating. They assumed, of course, that Napoleon would stay on the island of Elba like an obedient child. Why they thought this to be true was a mystery to Whit. Nothing about the man's previous behavior supported anything close to that particular theory, and Whit had learned the hard way it was best never to assume anything.

"Bloody hell!" Slapping his hand against the window frame made the glass rattle but did nothing to improve his mood.

The door to the hall opened, and his secretary appeared. "Is there something I can get for you, your grace?"

"What?" Whit looked at the man standing in the doorway and shook his head. "No. Thank you, Cooper."

"Very well, your grace."

Whit scowled at the untouched piles on his desk and then called out, "Wait, Cooper?"

"Yes, your grace?"

"Has the post arrived?"

"It was just delivered. The footman should be bringing it up any minute."

"Bring it to me as soon as it arrives."

"Yes, your grace."

Cooper withdrew, leaving Whit to turn back to the garden view that usually helped him put things in perspective. Even though Napoleon had abdicated, the danger to England was far from over. In fact, information was becoming more difficult and more dangerous to obtain.

But all of that was secondary. The more important thing to Whit right now was the fact that, ever since Edgewood went missing, he'd found more evidence of a leak—a jagged hole in his intricate web of spies. He tried not to correlate Edgewood's disappearance with the mounting evidence, but his head kept telling him not to ignore the obvious truth—if Edgewood *had* decided to embrace the other side, there were many options available to him. Whit's instincts told him that Edgewood's disappearance was an unrelated incident, but the leak in his organization was real.

"Where are you, man?" whispered Whit to the curtains framing the outside view. "Can't you get word to me somehow?"

The door opened again and Cooper entered with a stack of letters on a silver tray.

Whit turned from the window to glance at the pile of assorted missives—some several pages thick, others only a single sheet. "Anything urgent?"

"Just the regular reports and invitations, your grace, but they did bring this up with the post. It seems to have been delivered just a few minutes ago."

With his thumb and index finger Cooper held out a grubby chunk of paper that had been folded so many times it fit easily in the duke's palm. "It came by…special messenger."

Whit scowled at the ball in his hand. "What is it?"

"I don't know, your grace. A young boy handed it to the doorman, said it was for the 'cold toff,' and then ran off before the doorman could ask him any questions or even give him a penny for his trouble."

"The 'cold toff'? And I'm supposed to be unoffended that my staff decided it was obviously for me?" Whit looked pointedly at Cooper, who wisely chose that moment to see himself out.

Cooper turned at the door. "As I understand it, your grace, there wasn't even a discussion." He grinned as he bowed and quickly closed the door behind him.

Whit gingerly took the wadded-up ball and sat back down at his desk, pushing his other papers aside. He tried unfolding the paper, but the piece he started with fell off in his hand. Muttering an oath under his breath, he tried unfolding another piece, but it, too, fell off. He frowned but continued to peel the grimy ball of paper like an orange, the tiny pieces coming apart slowly as his fingers gently separated each one from the core. Trying not to cause any further damage to the flakes of paper, Whit carefully peeled the wad of paper down to its very tiny inner core. It was there that he saw, written in pencil on the very last corner of the very last scrap of paper, the letter E with a circle around it—the symbol Edgewood always used in signing messages to Whit.

For the first time in a long while, the Duke of Whitley smiled. Edgewood was alive.

Chapter 29

Madame Rose du Bois leaned forward and whispered to the other ladies in her circle. "*Monsieur le comte* looks a bit haggard this evening, don't you agree?"

As usual, Madame du Bois was holding court among the other ladies at the event, despite the fact—or perhaps *because* of the fact—that she was not a wife but rather the fashionable mistress of the dashing General Jean-Luc Demonte. If the other ladies had any concerns about the propriety of socializing with a kept woman, those concerns vanished in light of the delicious gossip for which Madame du Bois had become famous—or rather, infamous.

"I hear he has been running all over town to prepare for the return of the king," said Madame Camille Gaspar, "although I thought His Majesty would not return for another month."

"It's happening sooner than anyone expected," confided Lady Millicent Fontaine, whose husband, Gerard, oversaw the king's itinerary and general travel. "I heard my husband tell the Minister of the Interior—in total confidence, of course—that His Majesty will be back in Paris in just a matter of days!"

"Surely it will take him longer than that to travel back to Paris," said Rose.

"Perhaps it would, if he were coming from Scotland or Russia," whispered Lady Millicent with a smug smile.

"But His Majesty is coming overland and is already in Belgium. He will be at Fontainebleau in a matter of days."

Lord Fontaine was not in attendance that evening, and he had severely underestimated how annoyed his wife would be when duty prevented him from escorting her to the evening's glittering soiree. In his absence, Lady Millicent felt perfectly justified in amusing herself by gossiping with the other ladies.

"Is it safe for him to return to Fontainebleau?" asked Rose. "It's been only a fortnight since Napoleon himself was there signing the act of abdication."

"It's the only place that has room to hold the entire royal entourage," said Lady Millicent.

As the ladies compared rumors and stories about Napoleon's abdication and subsequent banishment to Elba and the return of King Louis XVIII to Paris, two more gentlemen arrived.

The first man nodded briefly at the ladies, while his companion ignored them completely to leer at two ingénues across the room. The gentlemen eventually disappeared into the room where most of the men had had gathered to smoke and play cards.

"Who was that with Monsieur Chabot? He looks English and a tiny bit familiar," said Rose.

"I am not acquainted with him," observed Madame Gaspar. "But he certainly is handsome. And quite the physique, *non*? Perhaps it is because he is so tall."

"Or perhaps it is because he is with Monsieur Chabot who is…not," said Rose, causing the ladies to titter behind their fans.

Another, younger gentleman arrived and smiled when he saw the assemblage of ladies. Looking directly at Madame du Bois, he stopped and placed his hand over his heart, inclining his head briefly before joining the other gentlemen.

"Isn't that Monsieur Fabron?" asked Madame Nicolette Seville, wife of the Prussian Deputy Ambassador. She regarded Rose with a sly smile. "How kind of him to pay his respects."

"You mean to stop and worship at her feet?" said the beautiful and exceedingly clever Lady Antonia Maxton. Lady Maxton's husband, Viscount Maxton, had an unfortunate tendency to talk in his sleep, which kept his enterprising young wife supplied with the very best tidbits of gossip, especially after his chameleon-like change from Bonapartist to royalist only hours after Napoleon's defeat.

"Tell us, Rose, dear," said Lady Antonia, "are you ever going to take pity on that poor man and at least blow him…a kiss?"

"Antonia!" squeaked Madame Seville.

"What would be the harm in blowing him a kiss?" asked Mademoiselle Francesca, the only daughter of the powerful Minister of War.

"That's not what she meant, Francesca, dear," said Madame Seville, her eyes sparkling with excitement. She plied her fan frantically, as if to wave away Lady Antonia's risqué words. "I'll explain it to you later," she whispered to Francesca.

"Lady Maxton, I believe Madame du Bois has been a rather wicked influence on you," proclaimed Lady Barrymore, sniffing her disapproval.

"To the contrary," said Rose with a laugh. "I think Lady Maxton has been a wicked influence on *me*!"

"Don't you find Monsieur Fabron's adoration and

his worship of you romantic, Madame du Bois?" Mademoiselle Francesca had stars in her eyes."

Everyone, except possibly Mademoiselle Francesca, knew that the gentleman in question was a dandy and loved an audience. At a recent assembly, he had dramatically taken a public vow of celibacy, vowing to break it only when Madame du Bois and General Demonte parted ways.

"The general was much amused by the gentleman's declaration," said Rose. "He said it was rather short-sighted of Monsieur Fabron, however, to choose such an impossible happenstance since he would never part from me. I assured him that there was nothing to worry about, since Monsieur Fabron cares more for his new stockings than he does for me. The only worshiping he might be accused of would involve the gold trim on my new gown."

Lady Barrymore sniffed. "One would think finding his paramour in such a delicate condition would have dampened the general's ardor, making the happenstance all the more likely."

The lady's thinly veiled disapproval of Rose cut through the ambient conversations and immediately silenced the group. While it had recently been observed that General Demonte's beautiful mistress was, in fact, with child, none of the ladies had been bold enough to comment on that rather scandalous condition. A mistress was not supposed to become pregnant. Her whole livelihood centered around pleasing the gentleman who kept her and providing him with the kind of attention and services he was unlikely to procure from his wife. A mistress should know how to avoid this type of situation. And, while undoubtedly a sign of her lover's potency, a pregnancy could be inconvenient—even embarrassing—for her protector.

Rose took her time answering the older lady's remark, carefully putting down her cup of tea and pressing the linen napkin to her lips before turning to face Lady Barrymore with a smile that was entirely too sweet. "I must tell you that I have not noticed a lack of…enthusiasm on the part of the general—if anything, the man has become more voracious and even more attentive. I find myself quite in demand, as it were."

Lady Barrymore huffed and turned away from Rose as Lady Antonia and the other ladies in the circle immediately started to chatter amongst themselves.

Down the hall, just outside the doors to the gentlemen's smoking room, but well out of earshot of the ladies, the same topic of conversation was being discussed in rather more bawdy terms over fine cigars and even finer brandy.

"It must have been a shock to learn that Madame du Bois was *enceinte*," ventured Henri Gaspar, a man with whom the general had numerous dealings.

"Considering how she and I spend most of our time together, no, it was not a shock," the general replied, grinning at the men around him. Three of them he knew well, two he was on a nodding acquaintance with, but the two gentlemen beside Ambassador Seville were unknown to him. "I must admit I am not unhappy at the prospect of being a father. And," the general leaned in toward the others so that his words would not be overheard, "the fact that there are no monthly cessations of affection gives rise to definite benefits, if you take my meaning. In truth, the lady's delicate condition has made her rather more…indelicate."

There was hearty laughter all around the circle.

"Wouldn't mind being a little indelicate with the woman right now," commented the shorter of the unknown gentlemen. He was staring at Madame du Bois over the general's shoulder. "She's certainly showing a bounty of curves in all the right places."

The other men froze at the remark, and as one, their heads swiveled to regard General Demonte, who was no longer smiling.

"Monsieur," said the general, addressing the obviously inebriated man with words colder than any winter night. "Am I to understand that you are speaking of Madame du Bois, the lady who is under my protection?"

"Well, she's not actually a lady, now, is she, General? Not really. I was just saying what everyone else was…"

The smack of a glove across his face interrupted the man's feeble explanation as the general stepped forward and issued his challenge. "My seconds will call on you later today, sir. I suggest you leave immediately to prepare yourself, because if you do not stop looking at Madame du Bois this instant, I will kill you where you stand."

"I meant no offense…"

"And yet, you offended," replied the general, his clipped words leaving no room for apologies or second chances.

"I only meant…" started the man again.

"Let's go," said his companion, pushing his slow-witted friend in front of him. "We have other places to be."

The group of men watched them go. "Well done!"

said Monsieur Colbert, the general's good friend and colleague.

One of the other men chuckled and said, "Here! Here!"

Soon they were all laughing—even Jean-Luc, who had a rather sheepish look on his face. Feeling a hand on his arm, he turned to see Rose standing beside him. Her signature honeysuckle-and-rose scent wafted over the group and, to a man, the gentlemen acknowledged her presence with smiles and bows.

"Oh, my dear," said Rose loud enough for all the gentlemen and many of the ladies to hear. "Have you gone and defended my honor again?" She slipped her hand into the crook of the general's arm and gave him a dazzling smile. "You are *the* most delightful, most noble, and bravest man alive." She looked up at him from beneath long eyelashes. "Is it not time for us to depart?" She smiled at the other gentlemen. "My delicate condition, you know," she whispered to those standing closest to her as she tugged at the general's arm.

The general tucked her hand into his arm and, smiling broadly at his friends, escorted her out to his carriage.

Watching the couple leave, Ambassador Seville remarked, "I'll bet everything I own that right now, in addition to being the most delightful, most noble, and bravest man alive, the general is also the horniest."

"And *I* will bet that he won't be that way for long." Monsieur Gauthier grinned. Then he sighed. "I guess I should be off as well. I suppose he means for me to make the arrangements for his dawn appointment."

"No need to hurry," scoffed the ambassador. "My guess is that in an hour's time there will be no one for you to call on. Everyone knows of Jean-Luc's mastery with the sword and pistol. I'll wager that pig is halfway to Brussels by now."

****

As his carriage pulled into the traffic on the crowded avenue, Jean-Luc studied the woman across from him. "Do you really feel ill," he asked, "or were you just ready to leave?"

"The latter. I have accomplished both of my tasks—I passed along the false information by whispering it to Millicent Fontaine and swearing her to secrecy."

Jean-Luc laughed. "That's as good as having it printed in *Le Monde* or writing it on the walls of the Louvre. Would it surprise you if I said I was feeling quite proud of myself when I confessed to my friends that you were indeed in anticipation of a happy event?"

"They noticed?"

"Of course they noticed. They are trained to notice everything. And apart from your usual ephemeral beauty, you do seem to have a special glow that has not gone unappreciated. Gerard was the first to say something to me, and I didn't deny it. So, of course, by the time I reached the card room, everyone else knew as well."

Henrianna sighed. "I was hoping to have a little more time before announcing anything."

"There's no need to announce anything formally. That's usually reserved for official family births." A look of sadness flashed over Jean-Luc's face. "We'll just let the grapevine take care of letting everyone know. By the end of the evening, it will be common knowledge."

Henrianna smiled, but she too had a flash of sadness. How different things would have been if only Grey were…

No, she couldn't go there. Not even for a moment. It was too dangerous—for her, for Jean-Luc, for Louisa, and for Grey's son or daughter. She determinedly turned her mind back to the matter at hand. Reaching down between her breasts she retrieved a piece of folded paper. "Also, I received this from Lydia. I plan to visit your parents tomorrow, so I will send it on from there. Will you and Louisa be available to come along?"

"I cannot, but I'm sure Louisa would love the opportunity to get out of the city. I do think she enjoys talking with you more than she does with me."

Henrianna smiled. "That's because you only want to talk about dreary old military things. Or which side of the coin Monsieur Talleyrand is defending today. You never want to talk about the new patterns of brocade in the shops or the lovely new hats on the *Champs-Elysées* or Lady Barrymore's ghastly gown. And you never want to hear about the darling cakes that Lady Maxwell's chef made for tea on Thursday. It's really no wonder Louisa enjoys being with me more than you."

"Careful, my dear. That's not what I said. I said she may enjoy *talking* with you more than she does with me. She and I don't actually do that much talking when we're together."

Jean-Luc smiled to see the woman known as the "Scandal of Paris" blushing like a schoolgirl.

Chapter 30

Whit was only vaguely aware of the extra commotion at the door to his club. Concentrating on the latest reports from the field, he was hoping to find something in them that might identify the traitor in his network. He was also praying that he was looking for only one person. He didn't register the presence of anyone until the man standing in the doorway cleared his throat.

"My God! Edgewood!" Whit stood immediately to embrace his best friend and shake his hand. He was shocked at the physical changes in Edgewood. The man standing before him was not the strapping Scotsman he'd traded words with more than three months ago. Although still powerfully muscled, this man was thin, almost gaunt, and there was a haunted air about him that had never been part of Edgewood's persona.

"Sit down, man. You look like hell. Have you eaten?" Whit was already gesturing to one of the stewards. "Bring us a steak-and-kidney pie and anything else you can have ready in the next few minutes. And cognac. Bring us your finest—"

"Whiskey is fine for me," countermanded Edgewood, sitting in the proffered chair. He leaned back for a moment and then sat forward, his elbows propped on the arms of the chair as he looked across the table at the duke. "Where is she, Whit?"

"I beg your pardon?"

"My fiancée, Henrianna. Henrianna Barbour?"

"I'm not sure what—"

"Don't play dumb with me, Whit. I know you better than I know myself, and you've done something with her. I know it. I've been to her home and I've spoken to her ass of a stepfather. He told me that everyone knew she had been ruined and was good for only one thing now. When I threatened to separate his head from his body if he ever spoke of her like that again, his tone changed considerably."

"I should hope so."

"He proceeded to tell me that if I made it worth his while he could probably find her for me, and I could have her with his blessing. It was all I could do not to punch him in the face. I asked him when he'd last seen her, and he said she'd gone away with some fancy man. He wasn't sure of this toff's name, but he described you well enough. So I will ask you again, my friend. Where is Henrianna?"

"Edgewood, you were gone for three months. Until I received your message a fortnight ago, I didn't know if you were dead or alive, and neither did Henrianna."

"Well, as you can see, I am very much alive, and I would like to get married. Where are you keeping my fiancée?"

"I put her on a boat to France with train tickets to visit friends in Switzerland."

Edgewood swore under his breath.

"She was devastated, Edgewood. She was angry and scared, and so sad. She said she wanted to get past everything that had happened and make a new life. She wanted to move on. She knows how to get in touch with me if she needs anything, and I told her I would send word if I heard anything of you...which I will do, of course."

"My landlord says he gave you a packet of letters that came for me."

"Yes, I have them in my office. That's how I figured out who Henrianna was. You didn't tell me her name before you left...the last time we talked. As it turns out, she lives near Terra Bella. Avery and her brother, Hill, were best friends growing up. I'd even met her before—although it was many years ago. When I tracked her down from her direction on the letters, I told her you had gone missing and were most likely dead."

"Bloody hell, Whit!"

"It was the truth, and I thought she had a right to know. She didn't know what to do but thought she might go to Switzerland to stay with friends. She couldn't stay at her home—something about her stepfather forcing her to marry one of his sons—so I helped her with passage to Paris and then on to Switzerland."

"And you've heard nothing from Henrianna since then?"

"No."

Edgewood's face reflected his disbelief.

"I swear, Grey. I have received no messages or communications from Henrianna Barbour since she left. But to be clear, even if I had, I'm not sure I would tell you. I don't know how much I can trust you right now."

"The feeling is very mutual, my friend."

Scowling, Edgewood leaned back in his chair and watched the steward place a platter of tantalizing beefsteaks in the middle of the table. Whit served Edgewood and then took a steak for himself. "So what are your plans?"

"What do you mean?"

"I mean, are you going to go and try to find her in Switzerland?"

"I don't know. If she truly wants to move on, I don't want to stop her. Maybe I should just let you send word that I've returned. Then, if she wants to find me, she can. And if not…"

Edgewood abruptly turned all his attention to cutting his meat. Both men ate in silence until Whit spoke again.

"You know it will take a while for a message to get to Switzerland. Europe is a mess."

Edgewood said nothing.

"The allies are squabbling with each other, and nobody trusts Napoleon to stay on Elba. His spies are everywhere and bolder than ever."

Edgewood put another bite in his mouth and chewed in silence.

"Damn it, man! What I'm saying is that if you have no other immediate plans, I could use your help while you wait."

Edgewood refocused his attention on Whit. "I beg your pardon, your grace—I was thinking of something else. What did you say?"

"I said I could use your help while you wait to hear from Henrianna. There's a leak, and I don't know who I can trust."

"But you trust me?"

"I probably shouldn't, but on this, yes."

Whit would watch him, to be sure. It was standard operating procedure when any operative returned from being missing or captured. Generally, the person was given light duty until it was determined they had not been compromised. Guilty until proven innocent, as it were. And, of course, even as Whit's second-in-command, Edgewood would be subject to Whit's golden rule of dispersing information only on a "need to know" basis.

Edgewood continued his silence, watching Whit watching him. It would take some time before the two of them could return to the level of trust—of friendship—they'd shared before. He didn't really believe Whit had heard nothing from Henrianna. He did, however, believe that Whit was not going to tell him anything more—at least not right now.

He would have to bide his time and somehow figure out a way to take his mind off her, even though—ever since his memory returned—he could barely function for wanting her. Sometimes he wondered if it had all been a dream, but he knew it was not. For one thing, he no longer had his mother's ring—the ring he'd given to Henrianna before they parted. For another, he could not get the scent of her out of his head or the feel of her out of his mind. No dream was that real.

In their time together she had unselfishly given him everything he asked for—everything he could ever desire. He had taken her virginity and taught her everything she knew about physical passion, but in her innocence, she had taught him about making love.

On his mission, before he'd been attacked, he had relived their time together over and over. He'd decided then that in their next time together he wanted to teach her to be selfish and tell him what *she* wanted. And then he would proceed to give her everything she asked for, loving her the way she should be loved. The way she had loved him.

But now he was afraid. What if there was no next

time?

What if—even when Whit's message finally found her—too much time had passed? What if she had found someone else and no longer wanted him?

He thought his troubles were over when his memory returned, but now he realized they were just beginning. How would he ever bear the waiting? He needed something to distract him while he waited for Henrianna to respond to Whit's message.

Whit was still waiting for an answer.

"Very well," said Edgewood. "I'll help you."

Chapter 31

The days had taken on a kind of routine since Louis XVIII had returned to the throne. Paris was full of factions representing the full spectrum of politics—from the Revolutionaries to the Bonapartists to the Royalists—all vying for power. The volatile situation in the City of Lights changed almost daily. Getting timely information out to Britain's spymaster required constant diligence and a dedicated network of operatives.

Almost every day, Rose obtained information that might be useful to England from her own group of friends and their servants. Various drop locations allowed her to pass along her information with relatively little risk. Once every two weeks or so, under the guise of visiting the general's parents, she took her turn at transporting the collected messages to the spymaster's contacts outside the city so they could be delivered to London. The officials monitoring the roads and ferry crossings had come to recognize her and usually sent her through the checkpoints without searching her or her carriage, but just to be safe, Rose always took care to hide the messages. Lately, the most promising location to hide such contraband was between her chemise and her growing belly. That she occasionally appeared further along in her pregnancy than the calendar indicated was a detail few people noticed.

Rose was taking tea with Louisa on the morning

after her bi-weekly visit to Evreux when the general entered the room with a frown on his face and a bundle of papers in his hand.

"Jean-Luc, darling, whatever is the matter?" Louisa was alarmed at her husband's sudden appearance.

"One of Roberts' men was in an accident and badly injured on his way to the pick-up location and I have no way to get this information out of the city. I know there are maps and information in here that the Ice Duke is waiting for, but I do not have time to take them, and I cannot think of anyone else to send." The general dropped a bundle of papers on the desk in the corner. "I'm afraid it will have to wait until the next courier."

"How far outside Paris is the drop-off?" asked Louisa, standing up to give her husband a kiss on the cheek.

"It's just north of Argenteuil—in the village of Beauchamp. There's a coach stop there and an inn—I can't remember the name...something about a goose, I believe—and a few other shops and a bakery. The baker is our contact. It's not that far, but the problem is I must join Talleyrand this afternoon, and then we are going to a meeting at Versailles with His Majesty. I will be gone for at least two days."

"I could go," said Rose, setting down her cup and saucer.

"No," said the general, shaking his head. "Definitely not. You just returned yesterday. For you to travel again today might cause suspicion. Besides, I do not know the route. It may not be safe. It is not the same as driving on the well-traveled road to my parents' farm."

The general glanced at the clock on the mantel. "I have to go. I mustn't keep the great man waiting." He swept Louisa into an embrace and a passionate kiss. Rose turned away, busying herself with pouring more tea and hating the sharp pang of envy that pierced her heart.

With his arm still around Louisa, Jean-Luc turned to Rose, his eyes twinkling. "I will be back in time for the Seville's soiree on Friday. I believe Monsieur Fabron will be in attendance, so you should wear your lowest-cut gown."

Rose and Louisa laughed as they waved the general out of the room and then sat to finish their tea.

"What if it wasn't me?"

"What are you talking about?" asked Louisa.

Rose took a sip of the hot, fresh brew. "What if it wasn't me who took the messages?"

"Have you thought of someone else who could deliver them?"

"No. Well, maybe. I mean what if I took the messages, but no one knew it was me? What if I wore a disguise? I could dress up like a shopkeeper's wife. I could take the mail coach instead of taking my carriage. I could pretend I am on my way to visit my sister and stopped at the bakery. Once I deliver the messages, I could take the next coach back to Paris. No one would be the wiser, and the package could go out today."

"But Jean-Luc told you not to go," protested Louisa half-heartedly.

"Jean-Luc was concerned that people would be suspicious when I took my carriage again to Evreux. But I'm not going to Evreux, and I won't be in my carriage. I won't even be me!"

"You will still be pregnant. Don't you think people will notice?"

"Exactly! Of course they will notice. I'm counting

on that. They will notice that I have a big belly and that I take up extra room on the seat, but they won't remember *me*. It's one of the first lessons Jean-Luc taught me—make a scene. Draw people's attention away from what you don't want them to see. What do you think?"

Louisa studied Rose for a moment and then narrowed her eyes. "I think you are going to do it whether I agree or not, so I'd best help you."

Rose laughed as she hugged her friend and then hurried off to see if she could squeeze into one of the dresses she'd brought with her in anticipation of her happy event in Switzerland. And she purposely decided not to listen to the little voice in her head that warned of all the possible pitfalls in her plan.

Chapter 32

Edgewood lay motionless beneath a bed of straw listening to the driver of the wagon pass the time of day with one of two soldiers stationed at the border crossing from Spain into France. Crossing borders was never easy, but right now it was especially treacherous. The borders were constantly changing and there were almost no maps—mapmakers simply couldn't make them fast enough. And, even though Napoleon was on Elba, his supporters had not conceded his defeat. Whit thought—and Edgewood agreed—that anyone who believed the emperor would admit his loss and simply stay on that blessed island just hadn't been paying attention. Chaos and confusion reigned across the continent, and it was his job to make sure England's spymaster had the best information available. Which was why he was hiding in the back of this hay wagon.

Slashing sounds at the back of the wagon ripped his attention back to the situation at hand. The soldiers were searching the wagon by stabbing the hay with their bayonets!

"Oi! What you doing back there?" Edgewood heard the driver call out as the slashing noise came closer and closer.

"What do you care if we poke at it?" one of the soldiers replied. "Ye be carrying something asides hay?"

"I'm in a hurry," grumbled the driver. "I'm already

late because the bridge was washed out, and now you lot feel the need to look at every blessed straw? Why don't I just pull over and you can count out each piece and tie 'em into pretty bundles? Probably be faster'n what you're doing now."

He heard the driver pull the stopper out of a flask, and the noise on the other side of the wagon stopped.

"Fancy a swig?" offered the driver. "What they got you doing up here anyway? Don't they need fine soldiers over at the coast keeping up with that devil Napoleon? Ol' King Louie better watch his back or the emperor will come back and put his royal highness on an island."

Nearby, the slashing stopped just two stabs short of Edgewood's head. After a few more half-hearted pokes, the second solder moved on to the front of the wagon to answer the driver. Edgewood held his breath, not daring to make a sound.

"Napoleon's not going anywhere," said the second soldier. "He's on an island, for God's sake."

"What, you never hear of a boat?" said the driver. "How do you think he got on the island in the first place? He can get off the same way—and slip right back into Paris while all them foreign types are squabbling over who gets what. Nobody's watching him. I've had enough of 'em all. And ain't none of 'em cares about the likes of us. Here, have us a drink."

"Now, that's the god's truth," said the first soldier. "And I thank you." The man was so close Edgewood could hear him gulping from the flask. "You're right, they don't care about naught. We're stuck here at some crossroads, and they tell us to guard it against people who want to go into the city. And then they tell us to guard it against those what want to come out. Why don't they make up their minds? Want some, Hector?"

Evidently Hector declined, because the first man said, "Aw, go on. Take a swig. Ain't nobody cares." And then a moment later, "Suit yerself, then, and pull up the gate."

As the wagon started forward, Edgewood heard the driver say, "Keep it. At least I get to go somewheres with my job. You lot are stuck here until what, sunrise? You need it more than me, my friend."

Chapter 33

Jean-Luc strolled into the room where Rose was reading. "Louisa tells me you took a little trip," he said quietly.

Henrianna marked her place and closed her book. Jean-Luc's calm words were more ominous than any shouted accusations.

"Was it a pleasant journey?"

Henrianna stood to greet her faux paramour. "It was, as a matter of fact. It was a beautiful day, and the mail coach was amazingly comfortable. Plenty of fresh air and clean as a whistle. Delightful company, scintillating conversation. And I was home and in bed sooner than I would have been if you and I had gone out for the evening."

"I must say you have become an excellent purveyor of barefaced lies, my dear. If I weren't so relieved that you made it back safely, I would wring your neck. As it is, I'm strongly weighing the merits of locking you in your room and throwing away the key. If you were my wife…"

"What would you do if she were your wife?" Louisa had entered the room behind him.

Henrianna peered around the general and raised her eyebrows at her friend. "I thought we agreed *not* to tell him about my adventure, Louisa. You make a horrible spy."

"What was I supposed to do? When he returned home, the first thing he asked—" Louisa blushed scarlet. "Well, the *second*, or perhaps the third thing he asked was where the package of messages had gone. What was I supposed to say?"

"We agreed to keep this between ourselves."

"No, *you* said we should keep this between ourselves. I never agreed."

"You didn't *disagree*," muttered Henrianna.

"Enough!" Jean-Luc held up his hand. "It doesn't matter now, does it? What's done is done. Henrianna, Louisa said you dressed as a shopkeeper's wife and took the mail coach by yourself. Please tell me she exaggerates."

"It went like clockwork," said Henrianna with an innocent smile. "I wore one of my old dresses and a bonnet I found at the bottom of my trunk. I put my hair up in a braided coronet, and I hid the bundle of messages under my dress like I always do. I looked another whole month along. I had Thomas hail me a cab that took me to the inn where I bought a ticket to Beauchamp and boarded the mail coach. When we arrived in Beauchamp, I found the bakery and delivered the messages and maps to the baker in time for him to take them that very evening. His wife let me wait in their parlor until the next coach to Paris arrived. And, when I got back to the city, a kind gentleman hailed a cab for me. I had the driver drop me several doors down, and I walked back to find Louisa waiting up for me. There really was nothing to it."

"Tell him about the man who recognized you."

"*Mon Dieu!*" groaned the general.

"Louisa!" exclaimed Rose. "I told you that in

confidence!"

"And I didn't tell. I'm just telling *you* to tell him."

"Explain, please," said Jean-Luc, narrowing his eyes at his wife. "You and I will discuss this later," he muttered. "Rose?"

"It was nothing. Not really. But just as we were about to leave Beauchamp, they changed drivers. The new driver turned out to be the same man who ferries us across the river on the way to Evreux. He looked into the carriage to see if there were any seats left, and I knew him immediately. He gave me an odd look, and it seemed like he was getting ready to say something when someone outside called his name and he left. He never said anything—not even later when I disembarked in Paris. I hurried away while he was seeing to the horses. I really don't think he recognized me."

The room was silent as the general paced, processing all the information he'd just acquired and assessing its impact on his wife, his mistress, and his household. He was going to have to have a few words with Thomas. Running his fingers through his hair as he did when he was at a loss, he sighed deeply before turning back to Henrianna. "I've told you before that you should not be taking such chances. There are other ways to get the information out."

"Yes, and those ways take weeks. Everything is changing so quickly, Jean-Luc. London needs the information as soon as possible."

"That's always the case. Sometimes it's just too big a risk. I'm serious, Rose… Henrianna. We can't chance losing another agent."

"I'm always very careful, Jean-Luc," said Henrianna with a disarming smile. "You know that."

"What I know is that you think you can flirt or sweet-talk your way out of every situation, but that's not always the case. Do you think Jenny had a chance to sweet-talk the Frenchman before he slit her throat?"

For once, Henrianna had no clever response. Jean-Luc let the silence do his work before he finally spoke again. His tone was softer, but his words were firm. "You're being too reckless. Promise me you will be more careful. I know you think you have nothing to lose, but you do. If you won't be more careful for yourself, then do it for your baby. He or she is already without a father. They don't need to lose their mother as well."

Henrianna angrily brushed at a tear that insisted on running down her check. "Very well. I promise I will be more careful, but don't expect me to stop altogether. If I can't do something to help catch people like Jones, I know I'll go mad. But I promise I will be smarter about taking chances."

"That's all I can ask," sighed Jean-Luc.

A scant second later, Henrianna smiled up at the general with a disarming look of innocence. "My delicate condition *is* the perfect disguise. Men are immediately uncomfortable when they see me and they never want to prolong any interactions in case I might have the baby right then and there. So they just hustle me along. It's really quite amusing. I'm considering keeping the pregnancy even after the baby is born."

Jean-Luc laughed as he shook his head. "You're incorrigible, Rose. You're not wrong, but you're still incorrigible."

****

"Edgewood, a minute?"

"Is there something I can help you with, your

grace?"

"Yes, as a matter of fact, there is. Do sit down. Would you like anything? Tea? Perhaps something stronger?"

"If you could just get to the point, your grace?"

"Very well." Whit sat, but immediately stood up again. "What in bloody hell do you think you're doing? Are you *trying* to get yourself killed?"

"I'm not sure what you mean, your grace."

"And you can stop 'your gracing' me. We both know you're not using it as an honorific. Over the past month, I've had no fewer than eight reports from you. That's two missions a week. In all but one of them, you took chances that any sane man would describe as reckless and irresponsible."

"I know what I'm doing, Whit."

"Yes. I know what you're doing too. You're displaying a stunning lack of good sense because you think you have nothing to lose."

"Think what you like, *your grace*. I'm just doing my job."

"You're going to get yourself killed, and then you won't be able to do your job at all."

Edgewood shifted angrily in his seat. "Whit, the word is you've got a seventy-five-year-old man sending you reports from Scotland and a pregnant woman on the front lines in Paris. I don't know why you think what I'm doing is any more dangerous than what anyone else is doing. You are the one who asked for my help, did you not?"

"I did."

"And isn't it helpful for me to complete as many missions as I can?"

"It is, but within reason, man! If you get captured or hurt again or, God forbid, if you get yourself killed, then you're no help to me at all."

"I do beg your pardon, your grace. I admit I hadn't considered how my actions would affect the great and powerful Duke of Whitley. I will certainly take that into consideration the next time I see an opportunity to collect valuable information. I'll just stop and take a minute to think, 'What would Whit do?'"

"Edgewood…"

"And then I'll bloody well go ahead and do it! Just like you would if you were in my shoes. And don't say you wouldn't, because we both know you would!"

The two men stared at each other in silence. Finally, Whit sighed. "I'm concerned you're being reckless because of what happened with…"

Edgewood came to his feet before Whit could finish. "Why on earth would you think that? I'm sure by this time your message has reached Switzerland. Miss Barbour obviously doesn't want to pursue things any further, so that part of my life is over and done with. And now I'm embarking on the next phase of my life. Hell, I even have plans to go out later tonight."

" 'The lady doth protest too much, methinks.' "

"You're quoting Shakespeare to me? What's that supposed to mean?"

"It means you're trying to convince me of something even you don't believe. I know you, Edgewood. You never 'move on' from things. You never stop asking questions until you're absolutely, one hundred precent satisfied with the answers. And as for the people you love, there aren't many, but you never, *ever*, give up on them."

Edgewood was silent. He sat back down in his chair, scowling. He let his eyes wander to the shelves of books, to the window, to his hands—anywhere except to his friend's face. After a few more moments of silence, he stood up and headed for the door with a muttered curse.

Whit took a step toward him. "Edgewood, I didn't mean to—"

But his friend was already gone.

Chapter 34

On September 18, 1814, exactly at sunset, Eleanor Rose Barbour was born.

The birth had been quite difficult, partly due to the fact that the attending physician had no factual knowledge of the process and no sympathy for delivering the bastard child of a woman he referred to more than once as a prostitute. Once Louisa realized the doctor's incompetency and bias, she summarily dismissed the odious man and quickly dispatched her husband to fetch his mother, who, among other things, was a midwife in the little village of Evreux.

Louisa had not left Henrianna's side since the contractions started, and while she waited with her friend for her husband to return with his mother, she gave orders to boil water and have clean linens ready. She encouraged Henrianna to walk in the garden rather than take to her bed, and when the pains began in earnest, she helped Henrianna breathe through the contractions that were coming harder and closer together.

By the time Jean-Luc returned, Henrianna was in hard labor, but the birth was not progressing as it should. Marie Demonte needed only a cursory examination to determine that the baby was breech. Between contractions, she pushed on Henrianna's abdomen, trying to turn the baby to a head-first position while also trying to keep Henrianna from pushing too soon.

After almost twenty-four hours of intense labor, the baby was at last turned and ready to be born. Completely exhausted, Henrianna could barely manage the last efforts to push and deliver her daughter.

Eleanor Rose was perfect, with only a small "stork bite" high on her forehead where she'd scraped against her mother's spine. After taking her first breath, Ella let out a hearty cry, protesting her abrupt arrival into a cold new world.

Henrianna smiled weakly at the strong cries and marveled at the wisps of golden-red hair her daughter had evidently inherited from her father.

It was only after everyone left and Henrianna was alone with Ella that she let the tears roll down her cheeks. She cried for what Grey had missed. He would have been so delighted at the arrival of his "bonny wee bairn" with her tiny rosebud mouth and chubby cheeks. Together they would have watched her sleep, making promises and plans, and pledging their love to each other and to their child.

Henrianna finally fell asleep with the unmistakable feeling that Grey's arms were holding her and their daughter tight on this eventful night.

Chapter 35

"How *do* you do it, Madame du Bois?" said their hostess, leading the way to the conversation cluster of Empire chairs covered in soft blue velvets and rich green brocades and shaded by potted palms in enormous, hieroglyphic-covered planters that reflected the *beau monde*'s current obsession with anything Egyptian. "I cannot convince my husband to let me go anywhere these days."

"My dear countess," said Rose. "I would not presume to give advice to the woman who is the very heart and soul of Parisian society, but I *would* point out that you *were* able to convince your husband to let you completely redecorate, and it is stunning. The palm trees are delightful and your colors are inspired. I feel as if I were floating down the Nile on Cleopatra's very own barge."

"But Lady Rocheleau is correct, Madame du Bois," said Lady Helaine Cadieux, who was following closely behind so as not to miss any tidbits of the conversation. "You convince the general to take you everywhere. What is your secret? My husband listens to nothing I say." Lady Helaine's husband had provided Napoleon's army with munitions before the emperor was banished, and had then generously provided the same to the reinstated king. However, now that Napoleon had returned to France and Louis had fled the country again, Monsieur

Cadieux was trying to find a path between the emperor and the Allies. It was understandable that, under the circumstances, he had no patience with his wife and little time to indulge her. Unfortunately, that was a choice that would end up costing him a fortune.

"Yes, do tell us, Rose," said Lady Antonia. "General Demonte is putty in your hands. What wicked magic do you perform to convince him to do your bidding? We are all waiting to hear your secrets."

Rose chuckled at her friend as she settled herself on the sofa, flanked by two sphinxes. "I don't know what you're talking about, Antonia. All I did was remind the general how much I love Mozart, *et voilà!*—we had tickets to attend opening night."

"Surely it cannot be as simple as that," said Lady Pembroke, whose husband was well known for his excessive frugality. "When I asked Lord Pembroke if we might attend opening night, he was quite adamant in his refusal, even though I cried buckets of tears. Is there something you're not telling us?"

Rose thoughtfully considered the question. "Well, the city is quite dangerous right now. Perhaps your husband thinks only of your safety?" She picked up the delicate Limoges cup and saucer and took a dainty sip.

Lady Pembroke's raised eyebrow indicated she was not convinced by that explanation.

"Very well, then," said Rose, "perhaps the next time Lord Pembroke refuses to accompany you to an event, you might offer to find a lover who *would* have time to escort you around town."

"Madame du Bois," said Lady Helaine, smothering a giggle. "Are you suggesting we all abandon our husbands and take lovers instead?"

"Absolutely not!" replied Rose, indignantly. She set down her cup on the gilded palm leaf table and daintily reached for a tiny tart from the delectable assortment. "I never said anything about *abandoning* your husband, Lady Helaine. That would be most unkind. And quite possibly illegal. But I do find that, compared to a lover, husbands can be so dreadfully stuffy about so many things—except, of course, for my own husband, who has been most accommodating about my association with the general."

After a moment of perplexed silence, the young, new Lady Cecily Amelotte asked timidly, "But Madame du Bois, are you not a widow?"

"Just so…" said Rose, picking up her cup again. "So accommodating…"

Lady Amelotte furrowed her brow as the other ladies chuckled. Soon another gentleman—this one with a huge, drooping moustache—stopped in front of Rose and executed a formal bow, kissing her hand before continuing on to join the men on the terrace.

Antonia rolled her eyes. "That's the third one, Rose. Honestly, is *every* man in attendance tonight hoping to get into your knickers? I realize that after the baby you've become even more…voluptuous—if that's even possible—but this is ridiculous, and a little bit insulting."

Rose laughed. "Truly? Baron Sovay? Perhaps *you* would like to play Beauty to his Beast, Antonia, but for myself, I am not enamored of the way he wears his hair."

"What way is that, Madame du Bois?" asked Madame Désirée Fasquelle, wife of Napoleon's Minister of Foreign Relations. Madame Fasquelle had arrived without her husband this evening, explaining to Rose that he was traveling to northeastern France—actually to

Belgium, outside a little village called Waterloo—where he was trying to broker a peace by convincing Napoleon to negotiate rather than engage with the Prussian army and the British-led coalition army at the same time.

Madame Fasquelle craned her neck to see the gentleman in question. "I see nothing untoward about the style of his hair. Whatever do you mean, Rose?"

"I dislike the style where he wears his hair on his upper lip!" Madame du Bois opened her fan to hide a giggle. "How would he even know if I were to kiss him? I imagine it would be like kissing the tail of a squirrel!"

"Indeed," added Lady Marchand, "the man has little enough chin as it is. With that great droopy moustache, it's as if he has none at all." Madame Marchand's own husband was currently leading troops into Spain, but he had a habit of sending his wife passionate love notes that divulged more than they should.

"But, Madame du Bois, your General Demonte has a full beard," persisted Madame Fasquelle. "Surely that is akin to kissing not just the tail of the squirrel but the whole animal!"

Rose smiled and turned to Madame Fasquelle, tapping the lady lightly on the forearm with her fan as she whispered loudly enough for all to hear, "Luckily for me, the general's kissing leaves no room to imagine any animals—except him, of course. I adore running my fingers through all that lovely hair on his head, on his chin, and especially on his…" Madame du Bois paused to confirm that every wide eye was upon her—

"*Bon soir*, ladies." General Demonte appeared from nowhere at the side of his paramour.

The ladies heaved a collective sigh, plying their fans like so many frustrated butterflies.

"I beg your forgiveness for the interruption, my dear, but I find that I require a waltz. It has been too long since we have...partnered, *n'est-ce pas*?"

Madame du Bois blushed. "Of course, General. It would be my pleasure." She stood gracefully and took his arm as he escorted her into the ballroom where the opening strands of a waltz could be heard.

"What do you suppose he meant by that?" whispered Madame Fasquelle to Antonia, who was fanning herself briskly.

"I don't know, but it certainly means something more than a dance," her friend replied. "Did you see how she blushed?"

Madame Fasquelle sighed. "I *do* wish he had better timing. Just a moment or two later and we would know what else happens when Madame du Bois runs her fingers through his hair."

She and Antonia giggled behind their fluttering fans, the ballroom having become exceedingly warm.

****

"Jean-Luc, I have warned you not to make me blush like that!" Henrianna hissed in her partner's ear as he turned her around and around on the dance floor. "I am *supposed* to be your very talented and *very* sophisticated mistress—not some simpering miss."

The effect of her scold was lost by the smile on her face. She did so love to dance, and waltzing with Jean-Luc was heavenly. She almost felt guilty until she remembered how much Louisa detested dancing in public. "If you compromise our cover, sir, you will have only yourself to blame."

"I needed to tell you something and I was not in the mood to explain myself to that brood of hens you cultivate. You'll notice not one of them said a word when I implied that I was claiming you for my own pleasure."

"You're fortunate Lady Cecily didn't faint right then and there. She hangs on at the outskirts—literally—and you can almost see the battle of right and wrong raging inside her. She was brought up to believe that one did not socialize with fallen women, but she has since learned that we mistresses always have the best gossip. *Quel dilemme!*"

Jean-Luc chuckled as he skillfully guided Henrianna around the dance floor. "May I just say, *cherie*, that you dance remarkably well for a woman who made it through a rather terrifying and difficult childbirth less than a year ago."

"*Merci beaucoup.* But what was it you wanted to tell me?

Jean-Luc did not mince words as he swept Henrianna into yet another turn. "Napoleon is planning to mount an attack on the British and Prussian armies in Belgium. He wants to attack them separately before they can join forces. He's planning to return to the front and lead the charge himself—we just don't know where."

"Then you will be most pleased with the conversations I just had. Madame Fasquelle confided how much she will miss her husband, who is leaving at dawn to meet up with the emperor in northeastern France to travel to Belgium—outside a little village called Waterloo. Viscount Maxwell is also traveling tomorrow, but to Cologne to escort the king back to Paris once Napoleon abdicates, which he believes is imminent."

"Very good, *cherie*. The Ice Duke will be pleased. Everyone seems to think the emperor cannot hold out much longer and this could be the end. If Napoleon cannot win against the Allies at Waterloo, he will certainly abdicate."

"And if he does abdicate, will the Allies reinstate Louis XVIII?"

"That is the plan. Hopefully this time His Majesty will be able to hold on to his crown. We need to get this information to London as soon as possible."

"I have a trip planned to see Ella tomorrow. I can take a message to Roberts."

"I do not like your traveling outside the city, especially with things so volatile."

"Nonsense. I'll be in your carriage with your coat of arms on it. I'll take an extra footman. Everyone knows I go often to see our love child." She smiled up at Jean-Luc.

"See that you give her my love, then." The general smiled as the dance drew to a close. Bowing to his partner, he kissed her hand before escorting her home for the evening.

Chapter 36

"Is that news from the continent?"

Edgewood nodded at the paper he saw stashed behind the bar. He'd stopped at an inn near the docks in Port-Town hoping to find some dinner before boarding the fishing boat that would take him across the channel.

"It's from France," said the barman as he pulled a pint and set it in front of Edgewood. "But who can tell if it's news. Now that the Corsican's been banished—again—and his royal self is back on the throne—*again*—who knows what's going on with the Frenchies? One day it's Bonaparte and his generals, the next day it's the czar and *his* generals, and now it's King Louie and *his* generals. Even old Talleyrand left the country since he can't figure out who's on top."

"Mind if I take a look?"

"Help yourself." The barman pushed the newspaper across to Edgewood. "I've already seen it. This one's about some uppity-up's mistress who's been scandalizing the toffs in Paris. Good for her, I say!"

"I agree with you," said Edgewood, putting down his mug and reaching for the paper.

"Some say she's a traitor because she's English. Hell, I say as long as she ain't shooting at our boys, she can do whatever she wants and tell the rest of 'em to sod off. It'd serve all of them fancy French frogs right to have a smart English lass scuttle their lily pads. There's a right nice drawing of the lady at the bottom there. She's a looker, don't you think?"

Edgewood found the drawing at the bottom of the page. His first thought was that it didn't do Henrianna justice.

****

Edgewood kept the newspaper—he left the barkeep some extra coins—and put it in his saddle bag. If he made it back from this particular mission, he'd make a point to discuss semantics with Whit. Evidently, for Whit and Henrianna, being "devastated" meant running away to Paris and finding herself a rich man to keep her in style. According to the article that accompanied the drawing, Madame Rose du Bois was a widow "under the protection of" one of Napoleon's more ambitious advisors—a general who had also been the *charge d'affaires* for Talleyrand. The article was unclear as to the man's role after Napoleon's hundred days and second abdication. Perhaps it was to engineer the Corsican's escape from St. Helena, in which case Edgewood would be more than happy to volunteer to shoot the man for treason—even if it was on behalf of France.

Henrianna had certainly done well for herself. Her outrageous, unconventional behavior seemed to have made Madame du Bois a scandal in a city known for its scandals. Edgewood chided himself for being so naïve. No one falls in love over the course of a one-night—fine, a two-night—stand. He should have suspected something when she so eagerly let him take her to bed. She acted surprised when he confided that he was the Duke of Marsden, but more likely she'd already done her research and knew exactly what she was about.

While part of him reminded himself that she had

been a virgin before he bedded her, the new, cynical Edgewood saw that as just another type of semantics—a tool she employed to bind him to her and make him feel responsible for her. It wasn't love so much as it was being in the right place at the right time. If not him, then she probably would have used her wiles on one of the other titled gentlemen at Haversham House that evening. He'd certainly dodged a bullet there.

Edgewood told no one—especially not Whit—that he knew of Henrianna's life in Paris. He did, however, quietly stop all efforts to find her in Switzerland, and then he turned to his work with a new fervor. He worked nonstop, day and night. And those nights when he was not on a mission, or when he didn't drop from exhaustion and fall immediately asleep, he found the nearest pub or the closest bottle and drank himself to sleep with too much whiskey or ale—anything except cognac. Never cognac.

When spirits stopped relieving his pain, he decided to find another woman to replace the one he had lost. He paid a visit to his friend, Madame Iris LeClerc, whose establishment, the Secret Garden, was the most expensive and the most exclusive in all of London. The Garden also boasted the most beautiful women in the city, but tonight all he could see were women who were not Henrianna.

Sitting moodily at the Garden's well-appointed bar, Edgewood nodded at the bartender to pour him yet another shot and then stayed the man's hand to leave the bottle. He wasn't totally surprised when, just a few moments later, a cloud of gardenia scent announced the presence of Madame Iris herself. He felt a firm hand on his shoulder and stray curls tickling his ear as a sultry voice whispered, "Do us a favor, love, and go home. Don't waste your money or my girls' time. You're making yourself and everyone around you miserable."

Edgewood responded by downing the shot in front of him and pouring another. Iris signaled her employee behind the counter to give them a minute alone, and then perched on the padded stool beside Edgewood.

"You have it bad, my friend. Is she still alive?"

"Yes," said Edgewood, not even bothering to deny that his misery was caused by a woman.

"Do you love her?"

"No!"

Silence from the lady beside him.

"Yes… No! No, I don't…at least I don't want to."

"I'm so glad to see you're a man of conviction. Is she married?"

"No, but she may as well be. She's…involved."

"Does she love him?"

"I would certainly assume so."

Iris scoffed. "Never, *ever* assume anything, my friend. Especially when it comes to love. Didn't Whit teach you better than that?"

"Do *not* mention that pompous ass to me."

"Ahhh," said Iris. "So the lady is not the only source of your anger. Did she say she didn't love you?"

"No."

"Does she know how much you love her?"

Edgewood shrugged his shoulders and said nothing.

"You should tell her. Tell her you love her, and if you're lucky, you *might* be able to win her back."

"I've told her that and more. Many times…before."

"Before?"

"Before I asked her to marry me."

"And what did she say?"

"What?"

"When you told her you loved her and you asked her to marry you, what did she say?"

"She said, 'Yes.'"

"And *that* is what leads you to believe she doesn't love you anymore?"

"You're confusing me," said Edgewood, trying to catch the eye of the bartender.

"No, you're confusing yourself."

"She doesn't love me anymore. I don't know that she ever did."

"And she told you this when you talked with her?"

"Of course not. I haven't spoken to her since—it's been more than a year and a half."

"You haven't spoken to her since you returned from Spain?"

"No."

"Does she know you came back safely?"

"I don't know."

"You don't…?" Iris shook her head slowly. "You're an idiot!" she said to her friend.

Edgewood looked over at the beautiful madam in surprise.

"You're a bloody idiot!" she continued. "A woman has this much of a hold on you, and you don't even know if she knows you're alive?"

Iris motioned to the bartender for two more shots. She downed one of them and stood up.

"Let me give you some advice," she said, holding up her hand as Edgewood started to protest. "If you love this woman, go and find her. If you can, convince her that, even though you've behaved like an arse, you still love her. Let her know that you will not treat her like one of your possessions but instead will cherish her as no other man can. Beg her forgiveness and tell her you love only her. Promise to tell her that every day for the rest of your sorry life. And then do it."

Iris bent to kiss his cheek. "I must get back to my customers. But darling, if you insist on staying and throwing your money away, please do it at the tables and not with my girls. They're all worried about you, and it's starting to affect their work."

Only after the smell of gardenias faded did Edgewood drink his shot. He decided to take at least part of Iris's advice and wandered over to the gaming tables where he proceeded to lose several hundred pounds at *vingt-et-un,* since counting higher than twenty-one was simply more than he could manage at the moment.

Two hours later, he finally dragged himself back to his rooms, but even as intoxicated as he was, sleep eluded him and he found himself remembering a cold night under the stars of the new year. He remembered the warmth he shared so completely with her—his Hanna—and he wondered what had become of that man and that woman.

He also wondered if Whit had told Henrianna that he wasn't dead—and then he spent the rest of the night wishing he were.

Chapter 37

Haversham House, New Year's Eve, 1815

"Why am I here, Whit?

"I'll explain after breakfast. Then we can—"

"The hell you will! Damn it, Whit! You drag me
here, tell me you need me to go to Paris because
Henrianna is in danger, and now you refuse to explain
until *after breakfast*? I would truly hate to cause a scene
and spoil Avery's day by murdering his half-brother, but
if you don't tell me what I need to know immediately, I
swear on all that's holy I will do just that."

Whit paused for just the briefest of moments as if
considering the likelihood that Edgewood would make
good on his threat. Thinking better of it, he turned and
led the way into Lord Haversham's library, away from
the revelers.

Edgewood said nothing as he followed his
commanding officer down the empty halls, but his mind
was racing. Only when the heavy door to the library
closed behind them did he finally speak, his voice soft
and menacing with just a hint of the Scottish lilt that
foretold of nothing good.

"Talk, your grace. What do you know about
Henrianna, and why is she in danger?"

Instinctively, Whit assessed the possible means of
exiting the room in case he needed an escape. He

mentally inventoried the weapons at hand, and then he gestured at the chair closest to the fire.

"You're aware of the situation in France and outside Paris?"

Edgewood took the proffered seat as he replied, "I take it you mean the new White Terror? They seem to be randomly executing anyone that offends them for no discernable reason. What has that to do with Henrianna?"

"They call themselves ultra-royalists, but they are anarchists, as far as I can tell. They have no loyalty except to chaos. Right now, they are targeting everyone who had anything at all to do with Napoleon. They're not waiting for trials—not even biased ones. They've already ravaged the countryside in the south of France and now they are proceeding to Paris. In light of this information, I need the Duke of Marsden to do an extraction of an operative in Paris."

"Again. What has that to do with Henrianna?"

"Henrianna is the operative."

The silence was heavy. Edgewood could hear his heart beating and the blood pulsing through his body before crashing into his brain. Slowly, he said, "Are you telling me that Henrianna Barbour is working as one of your spies?"

Whit nodded his head.

"And she has been in Paris this whole time?"

"Yes."

"Working for you."

"Yes."

Again, silence. The fire popped and crackled, but no other sound was heard until Edgewood finally spoke again, his voice tight. "So you lied to me. When you said you hadn't had any word from Henrianna, you lied right to my face?"

"Not exactly."

"Don't toy with me, Whit," he warned. "What do you mean, 'Not exactly'?"

"I mean that I never received any messages from *Henrianna*. I did, however, receive messages from Madame Rose du Bois, the name Henrianna uses as her cover."

"That general's mistress."

"Yes. Henrianna and General Demonte are both working for the British Crown."

"And you didn't think it necessary to tell me this?"

"No. Not until now. You didn't need to know."

"You *bastard!* Why are you bothering to tell me now? And I warn you, leave nothing out, for I am longing to smash my fist into something, and your face is most convenient."

"As I said, the White Terror is getting closer to Paris. The general, his wife, and his household are leaving in two days, but I need someone to bring Henrianna back to London."

"What the hell makes you think she'll want to leave?"

"I don't bloody care what she wants!" snapped Whit. He stood up, towering over Edgewood. He was tired of defending himself to everyone.

"Henrianna works for me, and she'll obey my goddamn orders! And my orders are for the Duke of Marsden to go to Paris, take charge of General Demonte's mistress, and bring her back to England. Immediately and by whatever means necessary! Is that understood?"

"Yes, your grace." Edgewood was quiet for a minute and then he stood as well. "Might I inquire as to whether you have any suggestions about how to make this happen?"

"You may," sniffed the duke, resuming his seat. "But I don't. Which is one reason I called on you. Oh, and just so you have all the information you need, you should also know that our latest intelligence confirms that Jones has left England again. He may be going to Vienna to team up with other Bonapartists, but his plans are unclear. I don't need to tell you that he would very much enjoy taking his revenge on you—on all of us, actually, including Henrianna, were he to learn of her connection to me and especially her connection to you."

"*Now* you're giving me information?" muttered Edgewood.

Whit shrugged. "You need to know. Enter," he said, in response to the soft knock at the library door.

"Lord Edgewood's horse is ready, your grace," said the footman smartly dressed in Haversham livery.

"Very good," said Whit. He turned to his friend. "Actually there is one more thing, Edgewood.

"Yes?"

"You need to leave now."

Chapter 38

Paris was not his city. He never felt comfortable here, and tonight was no exception. There were too many perils associated with this mission—too many questions and too few answers—just too much he didn't know. His mind fairly screamed of the danger as he calculated all the risks in play.

Whit's brief explanation of why he had neglected to mention that Henrianna was working for the Crown left much to be desired, but there had simply not been enough time to learn more. There were so many things he wanted—needed—to know and didn't. At best, Whit's actions were arrogant. At worst they were a betrayal of their long-time friendship. However, no matter what the circumstances that brought them all to this point in time, Edgewood was here on a mission—one that he intended to do as quickly, as efficiently, and with as little drama as possible.

What could possibly go wrong?

According to Roberts, Edgewood's contact in Paris, pretty much everything.

Just that morning, Roberts had twice covered Edgewood's missteps—mistakes that could have cost both men their lives.

"Pull yourself together, man," his fellow Scot warned him as he helped Edgewood dress for the evening.

"I'm not used to taking orders from my valet," retorted Edgewood, though he knew Roberts was right.

"I'm not your valet, you bloody *nyaff*," grumbled Roberts as he tied Edgewood's cravat in a complicated knot. "There's not enough money in the world would make me take that position. But if you don' start pullin' your head outta yer arse, you'll be gettin' us all killed."

As his carriage approached the Prussian embassy, the agreed-upon location for his meeting with General Demonte and...and his mistress, Edgewood made a determined effort to clear his mind so he could fully adopt the arrogant, all-knowing, and condescending persona he had created for the Duke of Marsden. The duke would not be cowed, impressed, or even bothered by most of the people he was about to meet. He would dispassionately yet elegantly go about the business of publicly taking possession of the general's mistress. In truth, Edgewood wasn't even certain that he would see the lady in question tonight. His meeting might be with just the general. Under normal circumstances, were he any other candidate vying to take over as her protector, *she* would be interviewing *him*. But these were far from normal circumstances, and for better or worse, this mistress had no choice in the matter.

Edgewood had no idea how Henrianna would react to learning that her new protector was the same man who had once asked for her hand in marriage, but he tended to believe she would not be amused.

He took another deep breath, and with it, he *became* the Duke of Marsden. Holding his head high and acknowledging no one as he passed, the duke walked assuredly up the steps, under the archway, and into the ballroom to find General Demonte.

****

"Whit's emissary has already arrived, *cherie*." Jean-Luc could feel the tension in Henrianna's body as she stood beside him at the top of the stairway leading down to the glittering ballroom. At his request, she had worn his favorite gown.

As she descended the stairs on the general's arm, her silk skirt flashed shades of both emerald and a darker green with each step. A deep border of tiny emerald beads weighted the gown's hem and had it swirling around her matching slippers. The only other decorations she wore were a net of pearls in her dark-brown hair, chandelier pearl earrings, and, on her right hand, a plain, rather masculine signet ring with a small, square-cut emerald.

Though simple, the cut of her gown was obviously *haute couture*—nothing like the gauzy, high-waisted, empire silhouettes that so many of the other ladies wore. The austere lines of the gown showcased her figure as no amount of ornamentation ever could. The curves that motherhood had enhanced after the birth of her daughter were on bounteous display, framed by the square cut of an outrageously low neckline. This was a gown made to be seen, made to be noticed, made for dancing.

It was their last night together, and Jean-Luc had promised he would dance as many waltzes as she wished. It was his way of saying goodbye. She looked, he reflected with a mixture of pride and sadness, as if she was on the hunt for a new protector—as indeed she was.

Rose, Louisa, and Jean-Luc had started the rumors exactly two weeks ago—as soon as the general received word from Whit that they should be ready to leave Paris soon. Not wanting to expose their covers, Whit had instructed Jean-Luc and Henrianna to create a touching scene wherein the general sadly told his mistress that his wife, now in the family way, would no longer countenance their relationship. He would—so the plan went—find her another worthy gentleman, and indeed he had. Whit had sent the Duke of Marsden to take the general's place, and tonight Jean-Luc was to publicly introduce his mistress to her new protector. The duke would then insist that she accompany him to London to take up residence there, and Paris society would be none the wiser.

"I still don't understand why we can't just come with you and Louisa."

"I will be honest with you, *cherie*. I don't know either. All I know is that I am to introduce you to your new protector tonight, and he will be responsible for keeping you safe until you are back in London. Perhaps it is safer if we do not travel together."

"But Louisa may not be feeling well in these early months. I could help." One of the happy coincidences of this plan was that Louisa, was, in fact, in the family way, and, of course, she and the general were delighted.

Jean-Luc turned to Henrianna and looked her squarely in the face. "Hush, *cherie*. I know you could help. And I know Louisa will dearly miss having you to see her through her confinement, but it is not to be. We have our orders. Now, dry your tears."

He gently touched a handkerchief to her cheek. "This is not the end. It is just for now. And for now, I want to know that you and Ella are safe. Please do not look so sad. Think of the time when we will all see each other again and our children will play together. Think of this as the beginning of that happy time."

Henrianna threw her arms around his neck and hugged him as he gathered her in his arms and held her close. After a few moments, he whispered, "It's time to go in, *cherie*."

****

When Edgewood saw her approaching the top of the stairs, his mouth went dry and he felt his body harden with desire. He narrowed his eyes as he watched his one-time fiancée put her arms around another man for what was obviously much more than a casual farewell embrace. He saw her tears, and he saw the tender actions of the general toward her. And even with those obvious displays of her affection for another man, he still wanted her.

It seemed impossible, but she had grown even more beautiful since their time together, and now it took every bit of control he had to maintain his composure. The gown she wore showed her lush figure more clearly than if she had worn nothing at all, and, in a flash, he remembered another time when she had worn the emerald green of his clan.

Edgewood knew both Henrianna and the general were working for Whit, but he also knew there was nothing false about the way she clung to her escort. The emotions she tried to hide told Edgewood everything he needed to know—that the two had shared much more than a cover story to hide their covert activities.

By the time Henrianna and General Demonte reached the entrance to the ballroom, Edgewood's desire had turned to icy fury, and he deliberately turned away. He couldn't stand to see the man touching her, knowing what she had been to him. Damn Whit anyway! He should have told the great Ice Duke to go to hell. Whit

226

could have sent someone else—anyone else. Hell, the great man could have come and "fetched" Henrianna himself, for all he cared.

"Your grace?"

Edgewood turned toward the man who had usurped him. "Ah, General Demonte. What an honor to meet you at last. Thank you for your kind invitation." He purposely ignored looking at Henrianna.

"The honor is mine, your grace. May I present my very good friend, Madame Rose du Bois?"

Henrianna sank into a perfect curtsy in front of him like a proper underling. He had steeled himself for this moment and thought to approach it with as little emotion as possible, but when all color disappeared from the face of the woman in front of him, he lunged forward to steady her. When his eyes finally met hers, he did not know what he saw. Was it shock? Anger? Or did they reflect the desire that filled his own?

****

When Jean-Luc presented Henrianna to her dead fiancé, she automatically sank into a curtsy as the blood drained from her face. The general was saying something, but the buzzing in her ears was so loud that she was only slightly aware of Edgewood taking her arm to steady her before raising her from her bow and pressing her fingertips to his lips.

A thousand questions raced through her mind. Was he well? Was he injured? How had he returned? *When* had he returned? What had happened to him? Why had he not come for her? Why had Whit not told her?

When he took her hand, she couldn't help trembling, and when she finally met his eyes, she could not discern what she saw.

"*Ravissant!*" said the Duke of Marsden as he employed his quizzing glass and examined her like a rare painting or some other *objet d'art* he had set his sights on acquiring. He looked her up and down, pausing for more than a moment at her *décolletage*. "She is just as you described her, General. A vision, a temptress. A rare jewel of the highest quality."

Henrianna cast her eyes downward as her thoughts and emotions did battle in her head. Did Grey and Whit think this some kind of *joke*? She had been mourning this man for two years while he was...what? Laughing behind her back? She nearly died having his child and every day grieved that he would never know his daughter, and all that time he was hale and hearty and playing spy games with his best friend?

And Whit. If she ever *did* return to England and if she *ever* saw the Duke of Whitley again, she would personally strangle him with her bare hands.

And then she would strangle Edgewood.

Finally he spoke directly to her. She tried to make out his words over the deafening beat of her heart.

"It is a great pleasure to meet you at last, Madame du Bois. I have heard so very much about you. The reports of your beauty do not do you justice. You are quite exquisite, and I am eagerly looking forward to knowing you more." He smiled like the amorist he was, clearly appreciating the picture she made.

Her color had returned, and she knew very well how the green of her dress complemented the red tones in her dark-brown hair and how the neckline of her tight bodice showcased her plump breasts.

"How lovely for you, your grace," she said, smiling her most brilliant smile. "I regret to say I have heard nothing at all about you."

Those watching the spectacle—which included just about everyone in the ballroom—gasped as one. Surely even the flamboyant Madame du Bois was aware that her very livelihood would soon be dependent upon this man.

After a second or two of stunned silence, General Demonte chuckled into the silence. "Did I not promise she would keep you amused, your grace?"

Never taking his eyes off Henrianna, the duke replied coolly, "I am not so easily amused, General, but many say I *am* easily annoyed. Nevertheless, I look forward to getting to know Madame du Bois in a more intimate setting, *n'est-ce pas*? May I have the honor of calling on you tomorrow, my dear?"

Plying her fan to hide the tell-tale flush creeping up her throat. Henrianna batted eyes that now flashed in anger.

"I'm sure you have more important things to do than to call on me, your grace, and I am afraid I will be too busy to receive callers tomorrow. Perhaps another time." She sank into another curtsy, making sure Edgewood had an excellent view of her full breasts and large expanse of creamy skin. When she rose, she murmured an excuse to Jean-Luc, and, turning on her heel, walked quickly toward the ladies' retiring room.

Stunned by a courtesan's public dismissal of a duke, the crowd soon found its voice and broke off into smaller groups to further adjudicate the scene they had just witnessed. Edgewood and the general were left alone. At first, neither spoke, but when the general turned to plead Henrianna's case, he was startled to hear the duke chuckle. Jean-Luc started again to explain, but the duke waved him to stop.

"No explanation is necessary," said Edgewood in a low voice so only the man beside him could hear. "In fact, it is quite reassuring to see that my fiancée has not changed. Perhaps we might find a snifter of cognac to enjoy, General?"

Chapter 39

How *dare* he speak to her that way in front of everyone! He acted as if she were a piece of horseflesh or a prize milk cow. She was surprised he didn't haggle with Jean-Luc right there on the floor of the ballroom or demand cash payment for taking her off his hands.

It was good that she did truly have so many things to do. Holding in so much anger couldn't possibly be good for one's wellbeing—much better to beat rugs or take linens off beds. Last night, on the ride home, she had established to her satisfaction that the general was blameless in this whole debacle. As he reiterated before he and Louisa and their entourage left earlier that morning, his orders had been simple: start the rumor, publicly introduce the duke to Madame du Bois, and then take his household—except for Henrianna—and leave Paris. He'd had no idea the duke was Henrianna's lost fiancé, but he also didn't have too much sympathy for her unbridled anger.

"I'm sure Marsden is also following orders," he pointed out to Henrianna. "I don't know that you can blame him for that."

Louisa, on the other hand, wanted everyone to be as happy as she and Jean-Luc were and, in her current condition, saw romance at every corner. "It's fate," she said, placing her hand protectively on her still-flat belly. "You never know how these things will play out."

"It's not fate so much as it is the devil in the form of a duke who likes to manipulate people," grumbled Henrianna.

"No matter what your feelings, Henrianna," cautioned Jean-Luc, "the fact remains that you must go with him. You need to get out of Paris, and he is your way home. Wait until you reach England's shores before you totally alienate him."

Henrianna said nothing, but she narrowed her eyes at her friend.

"I mean it, Henrianna," said Jean-Luc sternly. "I want your promise that you will go with Marsden. I don't care what happens or what he says to you. I'll have your word on the life of your daughter, for that is what is at stake."

"Very well," said Henrianna. "I promise. I will go with him. I know I need to get Ella and myself out of France. I'll wait until we're safe in London. And then I'll kill him *and* his friend."

"That I will leave up to you," said Jean-Luc, giving her a final hug and a kiss on both cheeks before joining Louisa in the carriage.

Henrianna waved her handkerchief until the carriage turned the corner and her friends were out of sight. She brushed at the tears. There was no time for sadness. She put on an old gown—it was a sturdy cotton print in the empire style, but like all her old clothes it didn't fit and pulled tightly across her breasts, exposing more than it should. Henrianna pulled an apron on over it and started gathering items to pack.

Most of the servants had left with Louisa and Jean-Luc. The few who would be staying in Paris had already left for their homes. Ella's things were at the farm and would take up much of the space in the second carriage that would also carry a second footman and Rose's maid, Katy, who had agreed to be Ella's nursemaid for the time being. Roberts had cautioned her to take only a single case, promising to have her trunks sent later.

"Rose? Rose, where are you?" Henrianna could hear Roberts' voice echoing through the empty house.

"I'm in the upstairs parlor," she called back. Soon she heard footsteps in the hallway. "Are you sure I can't take more than one case? There's hardly room for—" She stopped short, almost colliding with the Duke of Marsden. "I beg your pardon! Oh, it's you."

Edgewood laughed. "Yes, it's me. Who did you expect? Are there other protectors on their way for you to insult?"

"I don't know what you're talking about. I didn't insult you."

"You're right. You embarrassed me—and you did it quite well. Not that it matters, of course. I could care less what that crowd thinks of me. I'm here on a mission, not on holiday."

"Yes, you have made it exceedingly clear that you are here only to complete your mission, so let us not have any illusions about there being anything else between us. You may not care what those people think, but I do. They are—at least some of them are—were—my friends. You embarrassed me in front of them by treating me as though I were some prostitute you'd found on the street."

"I beg your pardon, Madame du Bois. Have I mistaken the particulars of this mission? You are here, posing as the general's mistress, to gather information from your so-called friends, are you not? I hardly think treating you like a prostitute is too far off the mark—

233

unless there is something more I should know about your association with the general. Does your affection for your paramour go beyond the charade?"

"As I understand it, you are here to escort me back to London, your grace. Nothing more. And since you have made it crystal clear that you are here only to complete that assignment, my relationship with the general is none of your business."

"I beg to differ, madam," said Edgewood, drawing upon his most arrogant Duke of Marsden persona. "If there is any aspect of this mission that I am not privy to, it could very well endanger lives and jeopardize assets. You and I are both under orders from the Crown, and I am the officer in charge. So I will ask you again. Is there something more about your relationship with the general that I should know?"

Henrianna glared at the man in front of her. How could she ever have thought herself in love with him? He was an arrogant, insufferable, pompous bully. The sooner she was back in London, the sooner she would be rid of him. He raised his eyebrow, waiting for her to reply.

"The general and I were colleagues, your grace. And I have become friends with both him and his wife— something you don't seem to set much store by."

"To the contrary, madam, I place a great deal of value on the bonds of friendship. And on honoring one's commitments. What I don't have much time for are those who break those bonds and conveniently forget about their commitments."

"Finally something we agree on, your grace."

"Excellent. Hopefully that will make things easier." He looked around the room with a disdainful eye. "How soon will you be ready to leave?"

"Perhaps you should just tell me when you plan to leave so we can dispense with the fairy tale that you care what I think."

"By all means. I would like to get an early start tomorrow, so we will leave at sunrise."

"If that's when you order me to be ready, then that's when I'll be ready. Your grace." She should have curtsied, but instead she just looked at him, daring him to remark upon her breach of etiquette. When he bowed, she felt a little childish at her small rebellion.

"Very good. I will expect to see you ready to go when I arrive tomorrow morning."

He was almost at the door when Henrianna called out after him, "I do have one stop that I need to make near Evreux," she said. "It won't take but a—"

"Absolutely not." He paused for a moment before turning back to her. "We are on a strict schedule, and I cannot have you stopping hither and yon to shop for trinkets we don't have room to carry."

"I'm not talking about shopping," snapped Henrianna.

She had spent most of the previous night trying to figure out the best way to tell Edgewood about Ella. She truly had no idea how he would react. They had talked about children during their short time together—he had even cautioned her that she might be pregnant—but that was when she was under the illusion he cared for her. And this was now. So much had changed—*he* had changed, and truthfully, she had no idea how he felt about anything. Perhaps it would be best not to antagonize him just now. Perhaps she should adopt a less confrontational demeanor.

"This is not about shopping, your grace. I need to—
"

"No," said Edgewood, interrupting in his most imperious tone. "Once we leave, we will not be stopping except to change the horses. Tell Roberts about any errands you have and he can take care of them after we have left the country."

"No, you don't understand. I—"

"I don't need to understand. This is not a game, madam. There are very bad people on their way here. Right now. If they take it into their heads to burn down this house because the previous owner was friendly with Napoleon, what do you think they will do to his mistress?"

"But—"

"Enough, Henrianna!" exploded Edgewood. "I will not continue to listen to your petty attempts to manipulate me simply because you are annoyed. Whit sent me to fetch you. It wasn't your call then and it's not your call now. I, and I alone, am responsible for getting you back to England. You will be ready tomorrow morning at sunrise, and we will be on our way. We will stop for nothing except to change and water the horses until we get to Le Havre. Is that understood?"

Henrianna looked murderously at Edgewood.

"Henrianna, I asked if that was clear?"

"Crystal clear, your grace."

Henrianna's eyes were huge as she looked at him with something akin to hatred. Bloody hell! He hadn't meant to be such a sodding bastard about things. She looked exhausted, and she was probably scared to death. Not to mention that she would be traveling tomorrow with a man she had thought dead for almost two years. A man who, when she saw him last, had requested and received her hand in marriage. A man who proceeded to take her virginity and make love to her as if it was his last day on earth. A man who introduced her to the heights of pleasure and then vanished into thin air.

No wonder she was conflicted and a little testy. He certainly could have been more accommodating, more understanding, and maybe a bit less arrogant.

He took a deep breath and started again in a gentler tone. "Henrianna…Hanna, I didn't mean to be—"

"I must finish my packing, your grace. Was there anything else?" Her tone would have made the Ice Duke proud.

He searched her face for some sign of truce, but she refused to let her eyes meet his. Fine. If that's the way she wanted it, then so be it. "Very well, madam. Please see that you're ready when I call for you in the morning. I don't care to be kept waiting."

Out of habit, Henrianna dropped a perfunctory curtsy and hurried from the room.

Edgewood felt like a worm.

Chapter 40

"Are you certain you don't need any help? I'm more than happy to stay, if you do."

Roberts stopped at the front door to wait for Henrianna's response. He was on his way out. He still needed to find another footman to accompany them on the trip north, and time was growing short.

"I'm quite sure," called Henrianna. "There's not room for me to pack much anyway."

Clutching her favorite shawl, she walked into the front hall and smiled at Roberts. "Better go find your footman. We leave in just a few hours." She sighed. "And as obnoxious as the duke is, he's also right. We have to get out of Paris as soon as possible."

"I'll be back before sunrise then. Lock the door behind me."

It was strange being in the house alone. Henrianna went from room to room on a last-minute sweep to check for anything she couldn't bear to leave behind, but her mind was somewhere elsewhere entirely. She *had* to tell Edgewood about Ella as soon as he arrived in the morning. Maybe he wouldn't be so unreasonable once he knew why she had to stop. If he had just let her explain earlier…

"Or if you had been a little more receptive when he tried to make amends," she told her reflection in the gilded mirror in the empty entry hall.

It was a side of her former fiancé she'd never seen before—although, to be fair, there was really only one side of Edgewood she *had* seen. All other facets of the man had been only hinted at in the relatively few hours they spent together. This particular side of him had not been in evidence at all.

Did he still love her? Had he *ever* loved her? Surely she had not mistaken his affection, but it was such a long time ago. He had changed. *She* had changed. Did *she* still love him?

Henrianna couldn't help noticing earlier that Edgewood walked with a slight limp. What had happened to him when he was away on that ill-fated mission? He was obviously injured. Was he still hurt?

She had plenty of questions, but there was definitely a dearth of answers. "I suppose we'll figure some of this out on our way to Le Havre," she mused aloud to herself. Then she laughed. "There's nothing like spending hours trapped in a carriage with your estranged lover to learn how you feel about each other."

Being cooped up together had certainly worked for them before. Except that then—on that snowy New Year's Eve—they had been anything but estranged.

A shiver went down her spine. From anticipation or dread she truly couldn't say.

For the first time since the shock of seeing Edgewood alive, Henrianna let her mind travel back to that blissful time—before Grey didn't come home, before Whit arrived to tell her that he was missing and most likely dead, before she became Rose du Bois. For so long she'd been living with grief that she couldn't bear to face—mourning a man she had known for only an instant but who had stolen her heart for eternity. She still found it hard to believe he was alive. She allowed herself a small smile. Grey was alive!

But her smile faded quickly. It seemed that one nightmare had simply been replaced by another.

Grey might be alive, but he despised her. When she'd first seen him tonight, the anger in him was almost palpable—and she had no idea why. They weren't married, so he couldn't complain that she'd tricked him into the parson's noose. Perhaps he was angry about being Whit's errand boy—although that wasn't really her fault either. Whit was the one who'd ordered him to bring her back to England.

Henrianna sighed. If Grey was angry with her now, how much more furious would he be when he learned about Ella?

Entering the general's library, she spied a bottle of cognac that had been left behind. Ever since that New Year's Eve with Grey, she had always chosen sherry or wine as a nightcap—never cognac. But now? She picked up the bottle and studied the label before tucking it under her arm. Perhaps it would soften the space between them. God knows it couldn't make things worse.

A knock at the door interrupted her thoughts. Roberts must have forgotten something. Or maybe he'd had good fortune and found a footman right away

"Are you back already?" she called as she unlocked and opened the front door.

On the stoop, just inside the circle of lantern light, stood Grey.

"You shouldn't have opened that without asking who it was," he said, entering the foyer and closing the heavy door behind him.

"You should be glad I didn't," she retorted before

she could stop herself. "If I'd asked who it was, I wouldn't have opened it at all."

Grey looked at her in silence for a moment and then took a step toward her. She stiffened, bracing herself for his anger.

"I don't want us to fight, Henrianna," he whispered, taking her by the shoulders and pulling her close to him. Before she could say anything, he placed his cheek against her hair and gathered her into his arms. "Please, Hanna."

Henrianna tried to swallow the lump in her throat as tears filled her eyes. It felt so good to be held like this. By this man. Without thinking, she slipped her arms around his waist. Maybe they could just stay like this forever. She would be happy to live all of her days just in this embrace. The weeks and months since he'd last held her slipped away, and it was as if they were back in the guest cottage at Haversham House on New Year's Eve again.

After a few minutes, he bent down and brushed his lips against hers. He was tentative, asking her permission and breaking down the barriers that had been so angrily erected in the ballroom. She answered his question by kissing him back—a thousand kisses in the space of a few seconds as he moved from her lips to her throat and down her bare neck as she answered his words.

"Oh, my love, neither do I. Neither do I. But Grey—"

He came back to her lips then, interrupting her words with his kisses. "Hush. Don't say anything. It only seems to get us in trouble—the talking."

"And you don't think this could also get us in trouble?" She stepped back and raised her eyebrows, smiling up at him. Even in the dark candlelight she could see his beautiful gray-blue eyes, alight with passion.

"I'm willing to risk it," he growled, pulling her back into his arms and finding her lips again. This time he pressed harder, seeking the perfect angle, until they were both gasping for air. With his tongue, he traced the line of her throat down to where it met her bare shoulder and placed a kiss at the juncture. She shivered, and he brushed his fingers over her breast, stopping to find the places where her nipple strained at the snug fabric.

She threw her arms around his neck, determined not to lose him again. She stood on tiptoe, pressing herself against every part of him and reveling in his hardness and how her body remembered and fit perfectly to his. His kisses left her breathless, but still she traced his lips with her fingertips over and over, trying to convince herself he was truly there with her.

He pulled her against him, his kisses and his hardening body promising that he was very real and would accept no hesitation from her. After the first few seconds she offered none. Feelings from almost two years ago—feelings she'd kept hidden for so long and tried so hard to forget—returned with an intensity she'd not known was possible. Her breasts ached for his touch, for his mouth. And at her center she ached to feel him inside her once again.

His lips traveled over her—her face, her hair, her throat, and back to her lips. She finally let herself respond to his insistence with demands of her own. She caught his lips with hers, nipping and punishing their absence while tangling her tongue with his and pulling him even closer.

When Grey finally broke their embrace, it was to

reach behind him and lock the front door. He took her hand in his and led her toward the stairs. "Where is your room?"

"It's the one—"

He put a finger over her lips. "No words, remember? Just take me there."

He stood aside so she could lead, but one step up, she hesitated and turned to face him, her mouth even with his. "Grey, there's something I need to tell you—"

He stopped her words with a kiss, long and full of desire. A kiss that stole her words and made her knees weak. "No, my darling," he murmured between kisses. "Not now. Right now, there is nothing more important than this—than us. Everything else can wait."

In her room, a single candle beside her bed was the only illumination as Grey slowly and gently undressed her. He paused to kiss each section of pink-flushed skin, reacquainting himself with her curves and learning new places. He sighed as he took down her bodice and released her breasts, letting her gown fall to the floor. "Hold them up for me," he growled and then took one of her aroused nipples into his hot mouth, his hands covering hers as she offered herself to him. He licked and suckled first one breast and then the other. A few minutes later, his fingers stole down to the soft curls at the apex of her thighs. With one finger he stroked inside her, groaning at the dampness he found there.

"You want me," he whispered in her ear as he caressed her again.

"Always," she whispered back. "I never stopped."

He pushed her gently back onto the bed while he pulled off his coat and neckcloth and let his waistcoat and shirt fall to the floor. Kneeling in front of her, he spread her legs apart and with his fingers separated the soft folds to find the aroused, tender bud at her center. He bent his head and touched the tip of his tongue to the tip of her sex, licking and sucking her there. He found her hand and held it in his until he felt her entire body tense and spasm with desire.

Writhing beneath his ministrations, Henrianna was overwhelmed by how right it felt to be with him. They had been together for only a short time, but he acted as if he knew her body as well as he knew his own. She watched him undo the falls of his trousers and release his straining erection. He watched her watching him as he guided himself to her wet center, stroking her with the tip of his hard length. His eyes, dark with passion, watched her frustration and pleasure build.

"I have missed you so, my love," he said, teasing her, teasing himself. He slowly, slowly pushed himself all the way into her as his fingers stroked the swollen nub at her sensitive center and he watched her face as he took her higher and higher. She pushed back against him, taking all of him inside, and when she finally cried out his name, he felt her contract all around him. Unable to contain his own need, he pushed deeper inside, thrusting over and over and over again until at last, buried inside her, he found his own release.

Though without words, their joining was a complete melding of heart, mind, body, and soul. He was spent. He lay down beside Henrianna and pulled her close to his chest, adjusting a quilt to cover them both and wrapping his arms around her as he vowed never to let her go again.

****

When she finally came back down to earth,

Henrietta was cuddled up against Grey, her back to his front and his arms wound tightly around her. She fell asleep feeling safe for the first time in years.

She woke in the dark to find him bending over her, fully dressed. She reached up to touch his cheek. "Grey," she began sleepily, "there's something I—"

But before she could say anything, he put a finger over her lips. "I'll be back soon. We can talk about everything once we're on our way." He replaced his finger with a kiss and was gone.

Chapter 41

Edgewood hadn't felt this good since…well, since New Year's Eve 1813, when he'd first chased a snowflake out into the cold winter night. He had found her again, his Hanna—against all odds, against fate, and against everything else that contrived to stand in their way, Edgewood had found his love.

When he arrived back at the general's home, he was happy to see all but one case had been loaded. With any luck they would be on their way before sunrise—none too soon, if the message he'd received that morning was accurate. Jones had been sighted near the Belgian border, and Edgewood didn't want to take any more chances. He needed to get Henrianna back to the safety of England— and the sooner the better.

"Roberts, whose case is that? Why is it not in the carriage?"

"It belongs to Madame Rose, your grace. She said to leave it out until you arrived."

"Well, I'm here now. Load it up."

Roberts raised an eyebrow at him. "I believe she wanted to talk to you before we loaded it, your grace."

Edgewood took the stairs two at a time—calling up to Henrianna as he did.

"In here, your grace."

Edgewood followed the sound of her voice to the parlor where she waited for him in her travel clothes.

"*Bon jour, cherie*," he said, crossing the room and pulling her into a quick kiss. He stepped back, admiring how beautiful she was, even after only a few hours of sleep—a fact he knew from personal experience. "Why is your case not in the carriage?"

"I asked Roberts to wait until I could talk with you. I just wanted to make sure you understood that I *must* stop in Evreux on our way to Le Havre so I can—"

"Henrianna, please don't start this again. We don't have time for detours, no matter how important you might think they are."

"You don't understand. I—"

"I refuse to put you in any more danger, my love, so please, come along with me. We'll get everything loaded and be off."

Henrianna pulled away from Edgewood. "What I'm trying to tell you is that I must pick up—"

"Henrianna, I insist you stop all of this nonsense and get into the carriage. Now!" Precious time was ticking by, and Edgewood was losing patience. "You are endangering the lives of others, as well as yourself, with your silly demands."

"My *silly demands*? If you would just listen to me for one minute—"

"We don't have a minute. We need to leave *now*. Stop being so damned difficult!"

"Very well. Go. But you leave without me."

"Henrianna…"

"I am not going with you until you agree that we will stop at Evreux." Henrianna crossed her arms over her chest.

"Enough!" roared the duke. "If I have to throw you over my shoulder and carry you down to the carriage, then I will do so." He stepped closer as if to make good on his threat, but Henrianna glared up at him and stood her ground. He was so much taller. She had to tilt her head up to keep looking into his eyes.

In the calmest voice she could muster, she said clearly, "I will not go anywhere until you promise that we will stop in Evreux. I have something very important to pick up there and I will not leave France without it."

Edgewood looked up at the ceiling for a moment. Then he closed his eyes and sighed. "And we can't have this very important item sent later?"

"No." Henrianna hadn't moved since delivering her ultimatum.

Roberts appeared in the doorway, looking uncomfortable as he took in the silence of the two figures in the room. "Ah…your grace? The horses are ready. They shouldn't stand long in this cold."

Edgewood narrowed his eyes as he looked at Henrianna, mentally calculating what it would take to carry her down the stairs kicking and screaming.

"Very well. Roberts, tell the drivers that we will be making a very quick stop at…" he looked at Henrianna.

"The Demonte farm just on the other side of Evreux. You know the way, Roberts."

"If Roberts already knows the way, couldn't we just have him go there and—"

"You promised…"

"Yes, I suppose I did. And now, if you would be so kind, get yourself down those stairs and into the carriage. We'll need to make up time if we're to stop in Evreux and still make the ferry."

"I will. Let me gather a few more things and—"

"Henrianna!" roared the duke.

"Yes, your grace?"

"Now."

****

They had traveled for several hours before Henrianna finally got up enough nerve to ask one of her many questions. Edgewood was reading papers from a satchel he'd brought with him, and she had dozed for a bit with her head on his shoulder. Awake now, she said, "Why didn't you come for me when you returned to England?"

"What did you say?" Grey bent his head to hear her better.

Henrianna sat up straight in the plush seat and turned to face him. "When you returned to England from your mission, why didn't you come for me?"

Grey removed his spectacles and looked into her eyes. "I did. It was the very first thing I did. Before I even went home or talked to Whit, I went to Brockway House to find you. The man I spoke to wouldn't let me talk to your mother, but he told me you'd run away with the man who ruined you. He described the man and then told me to leave his property."

"It's not *his* property," mumbled Henrianna under her breath.

"That wasn't exactly the part I was focused on. Since I knew his claim to be false, I went to talk to Whit. Who was he, Henrianna? Who was the man you ran away with only a month after we were supposed to be wed?"

Henrianna rolled her eyes. "Oh, for goodness' sake. You know it was Whit. He came to see me because of the letters I wrote to you. He told me there was a good possibility you were dead. My imbecile stepfather must have made up the other story. I told my mother only that I was going to visit school friends out of the country. She doesn't know anything about—"

She stopped abruptly and looked down at her hands. Then her head snapped up. "Wait. Whit knew you were back? And he's known since—when did you get back?"

"At the beginning of June. 1814."

"Whit knew you were alive and well a year and a half ago?"

"Yes."

"When did he tell you I was working for him in Paris?"

"Three days ago."

"New Year's Eve."

"Yes. At Haversham House. I expect Whit thought he was being ironic. He was there playing host at the wedding of Avery, his half-brother, the Duke of Easton."

"Avery is married? And a duke?"

"Oh, that's right. You and your brother knew Avery growing up, didn't you? Whit and his wife—"

"Whit is *married*?"

"Yes, just this past summer. His wife's cousin is Avery's bride. Anyway, Whit summoned me in that way he does and told me he needed the Duke of Marsden to 'perform an extraction.' I told him to go to hell—or something like that—and then he told me it was you. I knew you were in Paris. I just didn't know you were working for Whit."

"You *knew* I was in Paris? Since when? Why didn't you come and find me?"

Edgewood slowly closed the ledger book he'd been studying. "It was last summer. I had been looking everywhere and discreetly trying to find you since I returned. Whit said he would send a message to Switzerland to inform you that I was alive, and since I'd heard nothing back from you, I assumed you didn't want to see me. But I was still determined to find you. To see you and talk to you."

"Whit may have sent a message to Switzerland, but he never sent anything to me."

"I was at a bar in Port-Town, about to cross the channel. There was a French newspaper there and I started reading a story about how one of Napoleon's advisors had a mistress who was scandalizing Paris. The story said the man was one of Napoleon's generals and that he was infatuated with the woman, barely leaving enough time for Napoleon. It said he never allowed her far from his side, so he gave her a house next to his own. I remember laughing with the bartender that only in France could a man have his mistress living next door to his wife. There was even a rumor that he fought a duel over her. And then I saw a drawing of her. It was a picture of you surrounded by a roomful of men who were all fawning over you. I was furious. I felt betrayed. I didn't know what to think. Maybe you *had* run away with a lover. It wasn't hard to go from there to believing that you had chosen to become someone's mistress." Edgewood paused, drawing a deep breath before continuing.

"After I saw the picture, I stopped looking for you. At some point later, I told Whit I was no longer interested in finding you, so he never mentioned you again. Until New Year's Eve."

"Three days ago."

"Yes. That's when he told me that being the general's mistress was your cover, and I thought...I thought maybe I had a chance to get you back. So I came to Paris, but when I saw you in the general's arms just before the two of you entered the ballroom, it was obvious to me that you were more than two people working together."

Henrianna said nothing, waiting for him to finish. Waiting for him to ask her directly.

"But then, after last night…well, after last night, I realized I didn't care what had happened between you and General Demonte, because finally, you were mine again."

Henrianna smiled and picked up his hand, rubbing the backs of his fingers against her cheek. Oh, how she loved this man. As much as he wanted to know whether she and Jean-Luc had been lovers, it was clear he wasn't going to ask her. It was naughty of her to string him along, but she needed to be very certain of him before she showed all her cards.

Chapter 42

They were getting close to the Demonte farm, and suddenly Henrianna was nervous. She fiddled with her purse strings as the coach made its way down the shaded lane that led to the farmhouse.

"Edgewood," she finally blurted out, "there is something I must tell you—"

"I believe that is the first time you have ever called me Edgewood."

"Please. Stop interrupting me and just listen. There is something you need to know. I have a daughter. She lives out here with the general's parents and has lived here ever since she was six months old because it wasn't safe for her in the city."

Edgewood's face froze. The change in the man before her was at once imperceptible and complete. The temperature in the coach seemed to plummet as he carefully disentangled his arm from hers. His voice was hard. "And you were going to tell me this…when?"

"I tried to tell you," began Henrianna, and then, "It's not what you're thinking."

"I would rather you didn't presume to know what I'm thinking." He had lapsed into the same arrogant tone he'd used with her two nights ago in the ballroom. "You have no idea what I'm thinking at the moment."

He sat back in the corner as far away from her as he could manage. "What an idiot I've been. I saw it with my own eyes, and yet I foolishly allowed myself to believe that you loved *me*. I could tell your relationship with him was more than just a cover—it was clear from the moment I first saw the two of you together." He laughed bitterly. "That certainly explains the mystery of your figure. I had not remembered you being so voluptuous, but I have to admit I have enjoyed the change a great deal, as I'm sure the general has. Thank him for me, and thank you for apprising me of the situation before I made an even bigger fool of myself—although I would have appreciated knowing about it before I repeated the mistake I made on that New Year's Eve."

"What the devil does *that* mean?" demanded Henrianna, her eyes flashing.

"New Year's Eve, 1813—although by then it was the first day of 1814, wasn't it? You remember, darling…the frigid night? The cognac? The protestations of love? Surely you remember losing your virginity?"

"Of course, I remember. I was there too, and I remember every minute…every second. In fact, as I recall, you asked, no, *insisted,* that I marry you. You did not seem to think it such a mistake then."

"That? That was simply a gentleman's duty and all that. Of course, a gentleman's responsibility is absolved when the injured party becomes another man's mistress. Everything else can be attributed to…the holiday spirit. Simply a moment of weakness, I assure you. As was last night. I shall endeavor to make sure it never happens again."

The carriage rolled to a stop, and the footman pulled open the door before Henrianna could reply.

"A moment," Edgewood snapped at the man, who quickly shut the door. "Madame du Bois, I assume the general knows of his daughter? Or did you also forget to mention her to him? I would not have thought you to be such a careless mother."

"Of course the general knows I have a child. This farm belongs to his parents. Did you think I would leave her with total strangers?"

"I have to admit I'm not sure what to think. How old is the child now?"

Henrianna hesitated. "She will be two in September."

"Well, you certainly didn't waste any time, did you, my dear?"

"You *ass!*"

Edgewood caught Henrianna's hand before it made contact with his face.

Jerking her arm away, she hissed, "I told you the arrangement between Jean-Luc and me was a cover. He and I were *never* intimate."

"You forget that I saw the two of you together, my dear. No one is that good an actress."

"Oh? I was good enough to convince *you* that I loved you, wasn't I?"

The hurt on Edgewood's face stabbed her heart, but she could not afford to be weak now. Her daughter's life depended on it. She opened the carriage door and took the hand of the footman who waited just outside. The instant her feet touched the ground, she walked quickly toward the front door of the cozy farmhouse, her heart in pieces.

The man in the carriage was not the man she had fallen in love with. This man was cruel and cynical and cold—the polar opposite of the man who had rescued her from that frozen rosebush on New Year's Eve so very long ago. Any hope that she could be reunited with *that* man had been dashed by Edgewood's callous words.

All that was left for her now was to get her daughter to safety. Once she and Ella were back in England, she would figure out how to start her life over again.

Chapter 43

When Henrianna knocked on the door, a curtain was pulled aside and the face behind it broke into a smile. An older woman opened the door and kissed Henrianna in greeting.

"Rose! *Bienvenue*, welcome! I wanted to be certain it was you. I didn't recognize the carriage, and Jean-Luc sent word that he and Louisa were followed to the border."

"Did they get to Switzerland, then?"

"Yes, and as soon as they crossed the border, the men following them turned around. Hopefully they realized any further pursuit was futile."

"That is a relief. When do you and Jean-Pierre leave?"

"We are all packed. We were only waiting for you." Marie leaned forward and whispered as if conveying an important secret, "We tried to keep her awake—your journey will be much easier if she sleeps—but I think she is cutting another tooth. She is usually such a sweet baby, but today she has been so fussy. She only dozed off a few minutes ago. I had just tucked her in her bed when we heard your coach."

A man holding a sleeping child on his shoulder came into the room. "Welcome, my dear," said the general's father in a low voice. "Your sleeping beauty has only just closed her eyes. We rocked in my chair, but I had to sing all six verses of the sleeping song before she would close her eyes. Of course, now that you're here, she is sound asleep."

Marie gestured to a basket beside the door. "We knew you would be in a hurry, so I have already packed her things. I also packed cooked carrots and oatmeal, along with some goat's milk and some hard biscuits for her gums." Madame Demonte's voice began to quiver as the moment of farewell approached. "You must promise me, Rose…" Her voice broke. "You must promise that you will bring her to see us as soon as you are able."

"Jean-Luc and I are already planning reunions in Switzerland," said Henrianna, her eyes brimming with tears. "And soon you will have another baby to cherish."

A big smile broke out on Marie's face. "We were so happy when Jean-Luc told us the news. I told Jean-Pierre that it made giving up Ella a tiny bit easier, knowing we would soon have a grandchild of our own."

"Ella is not your grandchild?" Edgewood had come into the house behind Henrianna, and now took a step forward.

"Your grace! Please, please come in!" Madame Demonte bobbed a curtsy and smiled as she gestured for Edgewood to join them. "Jean-Luc said you would be bringing Rose to come for Ella. She has told us so much about you. Your whirlwind courtship is *très romantique!* Almost like my own story with my dear Jean-Pierre."

"I do beg your pardon," said Henrianna, "Your grace, may I present Madame and Monsieur Demonte. They are the general's parents. Madame and Monsieur Demonte, his grace, the Duke of Marsden."

Edgewood bowed his head at Marie, but froze when he saw the child asleep on Jean-Pierre's shoulder.

"It is time to go, little one," crooned Jean-Pierre, "but we will see you again." He kissed the cheek of the sleeping child as he shifted her weight and slipped her into her mother's arms, Ella stirred and opened one eye. Seeing Henrianna, she popped her head up and crowed, putting chubby hands on each side of her mother's face.

"Mama!" she said approvingly, gently patting her mother's cheeks. Her golden-red curls were flattened on one side.

Edgewood stared at the tiny child who looked exactly like his youngest brother as a baby. When Ella turned her eyes on him, it was as if he was looking into the past.

Why hadn't Henrianna told him? Why hadn't she told him about their child? Why hadn't Whit said anything?

Edgewood stood there, time suspended, as he played back in his mind all the things Henrianna had said to him. He heard her tell him again that her relationship with the general was simply a cover story and a friendship, and instead of believing her, he had called her a liar and a whore. Given what he knew now, he couldn't believe he had missed all her attempts to tell him about Ella, along with all her attempts to ascertain how he would feel about discovering he had a daughter.

"Hello, my darling Ella," whispered Henrianna. "Are you ready to go for a carriage ride with me?"

Ella took her finger out of her mouth and pointed it at Edgewood.

"Ella, my love," whispered Henrianna, kissing her daughter's ear as she turned slightly toward Edgewood, "this is your papa."

Ella looked at Edgewood suspiciously and then

looked at her mother, who nodded with a smile. Ella turned her head the other way to look at her honorary grandparents, who both smiled and nodded. Turning back, she studied the stranger for a moment longer.

The footman appeared in the doorway. "Your grace?"

I'm sorry," said Edgewood, "but we must go." At his words, Ella reached out her arms to him. Instinctively, Edgewood took the child in his arms, cuddling her to his shoulder. Ella popped her finger back into her mouth, put her head on his shoulder, and closed her eyes.

"She's the spitting image of her papa," said Marie with a smile. "Two peas in a pod. I know it eases Rose's mind to have you back, your grace. She told us you had been lost in the war, but she always said she would find you again someday. And now that day is here." She smiled again as she watched Ella snuggle into Edgewood's shoulder as if it were an everyday occurrence.

"I will never be able to thank you enough for taking such good care of my baby." Henrianna's voice was hoarse.

"Just be safe and keep Ella safe. And someday bring her to play with our grandchildren."

"I will," promised Henrianna, trying to hold back the tears as she hugged each of her dear friends.

"Thank you for your kindness and for your care of…my daughter," said the duke. "If there is ever anything I can do for you, please let me know. I am in your debt."

He took Henrianna's elbow, gently guiding her out to the carriage. When she was settled, he handed up the sleeping child and went to speak to the driver about the circuitous route they were to take to Le Havre. Once settled back inside the carriage beside Henrianna, he reached out his arms to take Ella back to hold on his shoulder. Ten minutes later, the carriage was rolling down the lane, headed for Le Havre and a ship bound for English soil.

Chapter 44

Ella shifted in her sleep.

"You can put her in her basket, you know," said Henrianna. "You don't have to hold her all the time."

"I have a lot of time to make up for. She seems to be sleeping well."

"Certainly she's sleeping well. She's safe in her father's arms. There's no better place to be. I'm not worried about *her*. I'm worried about you and your shoulder."

"I like holding her."

"I know what you mean. Some nights I just watch her sleep. She will undoubtedly be the most spoiled child in the history of the world, but I don't care."

Ella stirred again in her sleep, and Henrianna smiled as she watched Edgewood gently stroking his daughter's back to soothe her.

"You do that quite naturally. Holding a baby."

"I had a lot of practice with my youngest brother. Ella looks very much like he did as a baby. The woman who saved me in Portugal had a baby daughter. Isabela. When I was recovering, I would sometimes mind the baby while her mother worked in the garden. I could always get Isabela to go to sleep. I seem to have that effect on women."

"You were in Portugal? We haven't had a chance to talk about it, but I have so many questions. You were missing for months, and you were obviously hurt." Henrianna touched his knee. "What happened?"

"I had completed my mission and was on my way back to England and you. I probably wasn't paying as much attention as I should have been because I was in 'friendly' territory, but my contact betrayed me. He gave the soldiers my location and told them I had valuable information. Actually, that probably saved my life because they didn't kill me immediately but instead took me captive. They knew I was an English spy, and for days they tried every way they could to beat the information out of me. The physical torture was one thing—I'll spare you the details—but they were also very proud of their torture of the soul."

Edgewood paused before continuing. "Somehow, my captors knew I was planning to marry. They told me they had kidnapped my fiancée and would let you go only if I gave them information. The problem was I had nothing to give them—at least not about the mission. Whit has always been extremely careful about compartmentalizing. He never tells anyone more than what's needed. I assume that explains why he never told me you were in Paris working for him. I'll try to remember to ask him that before I kill him." Edgewood shifted Ella to his other shoulder.

"Anyway, I gave my captors some old information and made up a few other things and they said they were going to take me to Napoleon. A few days later, we were attacked by guerilla soldiers fighting for Portugal. I didn't relish the thought of getting caught in the crossfire, so I managed to escape. Unfortunately, the way out was down some very steep cliffs with big, jagged rocks at the bottom. I had just started my climb down when they saw me. I had no cover—for them, it was like shooting ducks in a very small pond—and I lost my grip and fell.

"When I woke up, I was in a bed in a tiny room bound up in so many bandages I could hardly move. The little boy who had been set to keep watch on me ran to tell his grandmother I was awake. Her name was Maris. She told me I was in her daughter Sofia's house near Azurara, Portugal. The boy, Sebastian, was her grandson, and was the one who found me at the bottom of the cliffs. Somehow they got me back to Sofia's house—presumably to die. They called in the doctor, who agreed I would most likely succumb to my injuries. But he told them if I did wake up there was a good chance I'd live. I had bullet wounds in my chest—all but one of the bullets had gone through and through, which was good—a badly broken leg, a broken arm, and broken ribs. I also had a head wound from hitting the ground. The worst thing was I couldn't remember anything—I had absolutely no memory of who I was or why I was there."

Henrianna listened in horror as Edgewood told his story. Tears filled her eyes as she thought of him alone and so injured. She sent up a silent prayer of thanks for the woman in Portugal who had saved him.

Edgewood shifted in his seat so he could straighten out his leg, and then he continued. "Sofia found papers in English saying my name was John Marsden."

"Your brother's name?"

"Yes. That was the name Whit and I had agreed on for my cover, but I had no memory of it. Those two women brought me back from death's door—they even had the doctor try to reset my leg, but it never did heal properly." He patted the straightened knee.

"I still had no memory of my life before my fall, although every once in a while I would get a flash of something that was vaguely familiar."

Ella stirred in her sleep and Edgewood again gently soothed her. Henrianna watched his movements with a smile in her heart. "You seem to have a special touch with the very young ladies," she whispered.

Edgewood grinned at her and took her hand. "That's what Sofia said too. I could always get Isabela to stop fussing."

"So when did your memory return?"

"A few weeks later. I happened to overhear Sofia tell Maris about some gossip she'd heard in the village. Her husband had been killed by soldiers, and now tongues were wagging about the man who was living at her house. I walked in on their conversation and told Sofia I would leave in the morning. She knew I wasn't recovered yet and she begged me to stay. I owed her my life and she had been nothing but kind, so I did as she asked and stayed. But I knew the gossip hurt her, and I knew she worried about how it would affect Sebastian. I think that's when I decided to marry her."

Henrianna gasped as she pulled her hand away and sat up on the seat. Her heart dropped into her stomach. He was married? How could she have been so naïve? Was last night simply part of his work for Whit—a way to get her to come back to London, no matter what he had to do to accomplish the mission? And now she had introduced him into Ella's life.

"Wait." Edgewood grabbed her hand back. "Please, Hanna. Please listen to the rest. The next day we took Sebastian down to the beach for a picnic. He was playing on the little beach at the base of the cliffs when a huge rock started to fall. With my bad leg, I barely managed to reach him before the boulder crashed to the ground. Sofia saw it all. I think she was in shock. She sent Sebastian to sit with his sister and kept thanking me over and over for saving her son. She kissed me and I kissed her back, and that's when my memory came back—all of a sudden I was kissing you.

"Sofia knew immediately something had happened. I told her that I remembered, and then I told her everything about you and me. It was as if a door finally opened and let my past back in. Even though I owed Sofia my life, I didn't belong there and we both knew it. She's the one who insisted I leave at once to find you. She said she knew you would be waiting for me."

Chapter 45

The carriage had gone several more miles before Edgewood broke the silence with a soft question of his own. "Would you have told me? If Whit had sent someone else to bring you back from Paris, would you have told me about Ella?"

Henrianna drew a deep breath. "I think you're forgetting that until two days ago I thought you were dead. If I'd known you were alive, of course I would have. When Whit came to see me at Brockway House, I had only just realized I was pregnant. I was trying to figure out what to do, and he offered me a way to get away from my stepfather and the threat of marrying his sons by posing as a widow traveling to France with her maid."

"All Whit told me was that he put you on a boat to France with a ticket to Switzerland. He said nothing about your working for him. Did he know about Ella?"

"Yes. I blurted it out when he came to tell me about you. I didn't want to accept his offer of help, but I was desperate and he said 'Please.' "

Edgewood raised an eyebrow, but Henrianna continued. "The woman who acted as my maid was supposed to be Whit's new operative in Paris. Jenny was her name. But right when we docked, she was killed. Roberts said it was a man named Jones who killed her. The odd thing is that this Jones had been talking to me just minutes before he killed Jenny. I don't think he knew who I was, but I had the oddest feeling we had met before. His voice sounded so familiar, but I couldn't place it."

"Did you tell all of this to Whit?"

"I never communicate with Whit directly—only through Roberts or through the general. Another example of his compartmentalization, I presume. The only time I ever contacted him directly was when I told him I was taking Jenny's place."

"So working for him wasn't his idea?"

"No, it was mine. I wanted to do something to help. To avenge your death…and Jenny's. I wrote Whit that I was going to pose as the general's mistress, and I signed my name as Madame Rose du Bois."

"What was his response to that?"

"As I said, we never communicated directly with each other. I know that he did send a response, but Jean-Luc never let me see it. He burned it and said it was not something a lady should see, but I got the idea Whit was not pleased with my decision. I really didn't care. They had taken you, and then they took Jenny right in front of me. I had to do something." She could feel Edgewood tense beside her.

"And you never thought about how dangerous it could be for you and for our daughter?"

"Well, she wasn't born yet, so I didn't know she was a girl, but I felt I was protecting her as much as I could by defeating Napoleon. And, in a way, she was protecting me. No one ever suspected a pregnant woman to be a spy. It was perfect."

Chapter 46

They were close enough to the coast to smell the sea air, and for the first time in days, Edgewood took a cautious breath of optimism. He felt certain the White Terror would not have made its way this far north, and there had been no more sightings of Jones, who by now was most likely making his way to Paris.

The two coaches had made good time, even with several stops. After the last stop, Ella went with Katy into the second coach with Roberts while Edgewood and Henrianna rode in the first coach. Everyone was travel weary, but in just a few short hours, they would be boarding the ferry that would take them back to England.

Henrianna dozed, resting her head on Edgewood's shoulder, until all of a sudden they heard gunshots. Bolting upright, she looked at Edgewood in terror. "Ella!"

Edgewood opened the trapdoor to speak to the driver. "What's going on?" he shouted over the noise of the horses.

"Riders approaching from the east, your grace!"

"Pull up, man," shouted Edgewood, already opening the carriage door. Praying that his injured leg would hold him, he jumped to the ground right in front of the second coach. Roberts, carrying a pistol, had the door to the second coach already open.

Motioning for Roberts to get up on the box with the

driver, Edgewood called up to him, "Proceed to the ferry! Get Ella and Katy on board and go with them. Don't stop for anything and don't wait for us! If we don't make it in time, leave without us and contact the ice man when you get to England. Do you understand?"

Out of the corner of his eye, Edgewood saw Henrianna step down from their coach. She heard his instructions to Roberts and her eyes met his with approval. She nodded at Roberts. The coachman whipped up the horses, urging them down the road at breakneck speed.

Once the other coach was on its way, Edgewood called up to their driver. "We need to give them a head start. Bring your pistol and come down. We'll pretend there's something wrong with the wheel. Just follow my lead. Henrianna, come over here behind me." Edgewood drew his own pistol and handed it to her. "Do you have your knife?"

"Yes, of course."

In just a few short minutes, three mounted gunmen surrounded the coach.

"*Bon jour*," said the man at the front. His hat was pulled down to cover his face, and a scarf wrapped around his neck added to his disguise. He wore rough clothes, but when he spoke it was with a distinctly upper-class British accent. Two other men, both wearing half masks, rode up behind him. One had a huge droopy moustache that hid the bottom of his face.

"I am the Duke of Marsden," said Edgewood. "Who are you, and what is your business with us? If you are looking for money or jewels, you should know I travel with only a small amount of both."

"I am not looking for money, Duke," said the man,

"although I'll not turn it away. Who is that with you?"

"No one. Just a servant girl."

"Oh, I doubt that. Come out of the shadows, madam. I should like to see you."

Henrianna came out from behind Edgewood, the pistol hidden in her skirts. She dropped a deep curtsy to the man on the horse.

"Why, you were right, Sovay. It *is* Madame du Bois, the lady who has taken Paris by storm. Allow me to introduce myself, madam. I am Monsieur Jones. Our paths have crossed before, do you remember?"

Henrianna said nothing and the man continued.

"No? It was on the ferry coming into Le Havre a few years ago. I believe you had just lost your husband, and you were traveling to the beautiful City of Lights with your maid. I do hope you were able to manage without her services. I also saw you at the Rocheleau ball with General Demonte. It took me a moment to remember where I'd seen you before, but now we meet again. It is a pleasure to make your acquaintance at last. You are indeed most attractive—just as they say. But, alas, I hear you are no longer with your general. I hear he has fled like a coward to Switzerland. One wonders why he did not take his mistress with him when he…"

"His wife is with child," interrupted Henrianna, trying to sound annoyed instead of frightened. "She threatened to leave him if he didn't stop seeing me."

"Ah, yes. Now I recall. One hears so many rumors, you know. And you believe that this…this Duke of Marsden will be a satisfactory replacement?" The man's eyes darted over to Edgewood and then back to Henrianna.

"He is not nearly as distinguished as the general, is

he? I do hate seeing you coming down in the world, Madame du Bois. What do you know of this man? Has he told you that he lives as a recluse? No? Well, he does. No glittering society balls in your future, my dear—in fact, no social life at all. It seems the duke hasn't appeared in society since he came into the title after the untimely death of his brother. I'm surprised he did not mention that to you. Such an unfortunate accident—at least that was the coroner's finding. Good man, Dixon. Longtime friend of the family, you know. He did tell me there were some that suspected foul play, but I told him to ignore all that. No need to bother the authorities with a little gossip."

Jones urged his mount closer so that Edgewood had to look up at him. "Now that I think on it, however, I believe that gossip pointed to the heir. That would be you, would it not, *your grace*? Wanted the title for yourself, did you? Is that why you've not gone out in society?"

Jones laughed and wheeled his horse in a tight circle. "It would be most unfortunate, would it not, Madame du Bois, to find yourself saddled with a murderer as your protector?"

Henrianna could feel Edgewood tensing beside her. She stepped forward. "I am not 'saddled,' as you put it, with anyone, monsieur. I make my own decisions about who I entertain in my boudoir."

"I'm sure you do. Perhaps the next time you are in the market for a protector, you might allow me an evening to plead my case."

"Perhaps," said Henrianna, looking bored. "And where would I apply to pursue that option should this particular situation prove untenable?"

Jones chuckled. "You are a brave woman, madam. Don't worry about finding me, *cherie*. When I am ready to quench my desire, I will find *you*. In the meantime, I need you to take a message to the Ice Duke for me. Tell him that I *will* have my revenge, and I will start by eliminating all those he holds most dear. First his beloved codemaker and then his lieutenants—we almost had one of them in Portugal, you know. Last, but not least, I will have my revenge on the great man himself. They all worked together to thwart me in what should have been the greatest moment of my life."

Jones was practically shouting now, unaware of the glances his men exchanged as they listened to their leader's deranged ranting.

"Because of them, the most brilliant man in history has been exiled on an island in the middle of the Atlantic. I *will* avenge my emperor and secure his place in history!"

Jones looked down at Henrianna. "Tell that to your friend the Ice Duke, Madame du Bois, and then heed my advice and find a place far, far away from them all. *Au revoir.*"

Edgewood and Henrianna stared in stunned silence as Jones and his minions rode out of sight.

"He is truly mad," said Edgewood. "Why can't I remember where I have seen him before? It's infuriating. He is so familiar and yet I still cannot figure out where I know him from. It's clear he changes his disguise. I got a good look at him when we rescued Vivian—she's the codemaker he hates so much—but today he looked like a totally different person. Did you recognize him?"

Henrianna shook her head. "From the boat, yes, but there's something else. He reminds me of someone I met before I came to Paris. Something about his speech or what he said was familiar—I just can't place him."

"Well, he obviously knew you. And he at least knows you have access to Whit. Do you think he knows you're one of Whit's spies?"

"I don't know. He's been watching me—he said he saw me with the general at the Rocheleau party, and that was last summer. Maybe he thinks because Jenny was with me that I have a connection to Whit, but maybe he doesn't know Rose is a spy."

"What I don't understand is why he didn't recognize *me*? He must have gotten a good look at me with Whit and Vivian in Selby, but he only seemed to know me as the duke—as John's younger brother. And what was all of that about my brother's death? He's right. Dixon was the name of the coroner who said that John's death was an accident."

Edgewood helped Henrianna back into the carriage. "For some reason, he doesn't connect the Earl of Edgewood with the Duke of Marsden, which is lucky for us. If he did, we'd both be dead."

Once they were settled, Edgewood rapped on the ceiling and they started down the road to Le Havre.
****

They reached the ferry only minutes before the captain ordered the gangplank to be raised. Katy had taken Ella down below out of the wind, and Roberts was helping the dockhands cast off.

Henrianna and Edgewood stood at the rail, catching their breath and watching the French shoreline fade into the distance. Ahead of them, the sun sank into the horizon, leaving them in the pink glow of the twilight's Belt of Venus.

Henrianna sighed as Edgewood put his arm around her and pulled her close. "It's so peaceful. At least for the moment. Once we land, everything changes and life becomes complicated again. Is it wrong of me to want to stay in this moment forever?"

Edgewood chuckled. "It's not wrong, and it's certainly understandable. Here, I have everything I need—everything I've ever desired."

"What's that?" asked Henrianna tentatively.

"You."

The twilight deepened into darkness. The night was cold, and the stars were bright above them. Henrianna scouted a spot out of the wind and called to Edgewood to join her.

"I see Orion's belt," he said squeezing into the space beside her.

"I can always count on it," said Henrianna. "Oh, look! A falling star. Did you make a wish?"

"I don't know what else I would wish for," said Edgewood, hugging her tightly against him.

"I wished we could be married. Soon."

"Well, the Earl of Edgewood could get a special license in about a week, and we can be married then."

"Oh, that would be lovely!"

"Or, the Duke of Marsden could get a special license two hours after we dock."

"Even better." Henrianna smiled. "I think I might learn to like the Duke of Marsden after all."

Edgewood found her hand and brought her fingers to his lips. At the sound of footsteps, they looked up to see Katy carrying their daughter.

Ella reached out her arms to her mother. "Mama!"

"I'm so sorry, Madame du Bois," said Katy. "She

wouldn't stop crying until I promised to come up here and find you."

Henrianna took Ella into her arms. "It's not your fault, Katy. She's just not used to sharing me with anyone." She cuddled Ella and turned toward Edgewood. "You'll have to give her some time to—"

She stopped as Ella reached out her arms to Edgewood. "Well, I take it all back. She seems to have become quite comfortable with her papa after all."

"Up!" commanded Ella, determined to be the center of the conversation.

Henrianna shook her head as Edgewood took his daughter and tossed her into the air.

Ella shrieked and laughed and demanded another toss. Then she put her arms around Edgewood's neck and cuddled into his shoulder, resting her head on his chest. "Mine, Mama," she said before popping her finger in her mouth.

"She's a shameless baggage," said Henrianna, watching Ella's eyelids flutter and close, "but she *does* know what she wants."

"Just like her mother."

"You're going to spoil her rotten, aren't you?" Henrianna sighed and leaned against Edgewood's other shoulder, looking up at the man she had loved from the very first time she saw him.

"You know...there's really only one way to avoid that," said Edgewood.

"So now you're an expert on raising unspoiled children?"

"In a way," he said, brushing her lips with his.

"And in what way is that, my love?"

"I'm an expert at creating brothers and sisters," said

Edgewood, kissing her again with the promise of tonight, tomorrow, and so very much more.

Continue the Dukes in Danger series with Hill's story …

The Duke's Denial

by

Carolina Prescott

Dukes in Danger:
A Haversham House Romance
Book 4

Chapter 1

"*Must* you stand so close?"

"I was here first. If you don't want to be so close to me, then I suggest you move."

When Lady Genevieve Richards first met Hill Barbour, the Duke of Camberton, he was writhing on the ground—a victim of her well-placed knee to his groin. It was a clear misunderstanding for which Eve, as she was known to everyone who mattered, was almost certain she had apologized.

At the time, she had been playing matchmaker for her friend Avery, the new Duke of Easton, and his beloved Linney. Unbeknownst to her, Camberton was playing the same role, which explained why they now stood as witnesses to their friends' high-society wedding.

What it did not explain was the animosity between the two.

"I am standing precisely where I am supposed to be," hissed Eve. "I am the maid of honor. I'm to assist the bride with her bouquet and veil. *You* are the one out of place. And must you always tower over people so?"

"I cannot help that your lack of stature is made more evident by my height, but may I remind you that *I* am the best man, and I have the rings—without which, I might add, this entire ceremony is moot." Disregarding the narrowed eyes of the lady at his side, Hill continued,

"And, as best man, I have a right—no, a *duty*—to ensure that the bride finds her way to her future husband unimpeded."

"It's a fairly straight shot. I feel quite certain she won't get lost," said Eve, jabbing an elbow into the duke's side as the more than two hundred invited guests rose in support of Miss Linea Braddock, who, on her father's arm, had started down the path that would end with her becoming the new Duchess of Easton.

"Ow!" whispered Hill, catching the offending elbow before it retreated from whence it came. "That hurt!"

"Let go of me!" hissed Eve, pulling away.

Avery, unwilling to take his eyes off his lovely bride for even a moment, turned his head a small fraction. "If the two of you don't shut it right now, I swear I will put you in Haversham's dungeon for a month…together!" His low, menacing voice booked no doubt that he was serious about his threat.

As the bride drew closer, her smile was evident even under her veil. Eve glanced over at Avery and saw his face, filled with wonder as he feasted his eyes on Linney in her wedding finery. Eve knew from confidences that Avery had already seen a great deal more of his bride than was proper, but the look on his face was something she would remember forever. Awe, pride, and disbelief, along with something akin to possessiveness and unbridled lust, combined to create a love that shone like the sun.

"*That*," thought Eve to herself, "that is what *I* want."

In her mind's eye, Eve saw herself in a lacy white gown standing beside the man of her dreams, a gentle, tender, refined man with tousled, golden locks and pale blue eyes that looked deep into her soul. A man who wrote sonnets to her eyes and odes to her lips and who knew her every thought and all of her dreams. Not just a husband, but a colleague, who respected her intelligence and supported her work in cartography and her passion for mapping the world. In return, she would treasure her beloved's every word, basking in his wisdom and goodness. Together they would live in perfect harmony with never an angry word or raised voice as they—"Hill, stop it!"

Trying to improve his viewing position to better witness the solemn occasion, Avery's best man had inadvertently pushed against Eve's shoulder, interrupting her from her reverie and throwing her off balance. Eve grabbed for Hill's arm and ground her heel into the toe of his boot, smiling at his muffled yelp. At the sound of the archbishop clearing his throat, she looked over to see Linney and Avery staring at her. Meekly, she took Linney's bouquet of Christmas roses and trailing ivy and then turned to follow her friends to the altar, obediently taking Hill's arm and standing woodenly beside him as Avery and Linney exchanged their vows.

When the archbishop asked for the rings, Hill stepped forward with two plain gold bands. The cleric blessed the rings and then offered the first one to Avery to give to his bride. As Eve listened to Avery repeat the age-old promises, her eyes misted. What would it feel like, she wondered, to be so in love with someone— someone who was so in love with her?

"With this ring, I thee wed, with my body I thee worship…"

As Linney put the ring on Avery's finger and recited her promises to him, Eve felt rather than heard Hill clear his throat. When she glanced up, he was looking at her with an odd tenderness that tugged at her heart. She cocked her head and glanced again, but this time he saw her looking and quickly changed his expression, leering at her as he waggled his eyebrows. She must have mistaken his earlier glance. Rolling her eyes at him, Eve looked away. He was *such* a rogue.

There was a time, after she was properly introduced to Camberton, when she had felt a strong attraction. Besides being devastatingly handsome, Hill exhibited none of the arrogance and conceit that Eve had come to expect from most of the aristocracy—especially those who were young, unmarried, handsome, and male. To the contrary, Hill had been charming, gallant, and attentive, and the four of them had spent a great deal of time together in the waning days of summer, helping Avery settle into his new role as Duke of Easton.

Giving Avery and Linney privacy meant that she and Hill also spent a great deal of time alone together. And although Eve was anything but an expert in the matters of love, it certainly seemed that Camberton wanted more than just a friendship. No one kissed a friend the way Hill had kissed her. At the end of the summer, before they parted, Hill asked for permission to write to her. Her heart was beating wildly when she said, "Yes," and she couldn't stop smiling as he tenderly brought her fingers to his lips. She waved her handkerchief as he galloped away. And never heard from him again.

Until today.

A word about the author…

Carolina Prescott writes historical romances, but she enjoys reading them just as much. The first "real" romance novel she read? Victoria Holt's Mistress of Mellyn. One spunky governess and one brooding hero later, she was hooked. Carolina Prescott's penchant for history coupled with her love of happy endings makes writing historicals a wonderfully logical career choice.

Carolina Prescott divides her time between an apartment in the trees (and a block from Starbucks) in Northern California and her native North Carolina where she has a home with lots of room for family, visitors, and a very understanding Brittany spaniel.

Visit her at:

carolinaprescott.com

Thank you for purchasing
this publication of The Wild Rose Press, Inc.

For questions or more information
contact us at
info@thewildrosepress.com.

The Wild Rose Press, Inc.
www.thewildrosepress.com

www.ingramcontent.com/pod-product-compliance
Lightning Source LLC
Chambersburg PA
CBHW070059030726
47506CB00002B/515